W9-CYV-550

FRIDAY

CONTENTS

FRIDAY

SATURDAY

CONTENTS

SUNDAY

MONDAY

TUESDAY

TODAY   269

CHAPTER I

Lookout

IT'S TEN TO TWO in the afternoon and I've been waiting for my little sister, Vivi, since one-thirty. She's finally coming home, at sixty-seven years old, after an absence of almost fifty years.

I'm standing at a first-floor window, an arched stone one like you'd find in a church, my face close up to the diamond-shaped leaded panes, keeping lookout. For a moment I focus on the glass and catch the faint, honest reflection of my eye staring back at me, a lock of gray straggly hair in its way. I don't often look at my reflection and to peer at this moment directly into my eye feels more disconcerting than it should, as if I can sense I'm about to be judged.

I pull my wool cardy—an old one of my father's—more tightly around me, tucking the loose end under my arm. It's dropped a degree today, the wind must have changed easterly during the night, and later we'll get fog in the valley. I don't need a barograph or a hygrometer these days, I can sense it—pressure changes, a shift in humidity—but, to tell the truth, I also think about the weather to help me take my mind off things. If I didn't have it to ponder right now, I'd already be getting slightly anxious. She's late.

My smoky breath turns to liquid as it hits the window and, if I rub the mist into heavy droplets, I can make it trickle down the glass. From here I can see half the length of the grassy drive as it winds through the tall skeletal limes on either side, until it disappears right, curving downhill towards East Lodge and the lane and the outside world. If I move my head a fraction to the left the drive elongates and the tops of the limes veer suddenly to the side, distorted by the imperfections of handmade glass. Moving it a little to the right splits the beech hedge in two on either side of a bubble. I know every vagary of every pane. I've lived here all my life and, before me, my mother lived here all her life and, before her, her father and grandfather.

Did I tell you that Vivien said in her letter she was returning *for good*? For some final peace, she said, because now, she said, we ought to be keeping each other company for the rest of our lives, rather than dying lonely and alone. Well, I'll tell you now, I don't feel lonely and I certainly don't feel as if I'm dying, but even so I'm glad she's coming home. Glad, and a little nervous—a surge of apprehension is swelling in my stomach. I can't help wondering what we'll talk about after all these years and, I suppose, if I'll even recognize her.

I'm not, as a rule, an emotional person. I'm far too—how shall I put it?—levelheaded. I was always *the sensible sister* and Vivi was the adventurer, but my excitement at her impending arrival even surprises me.

She is late, however. I look at my wristwatch—the digital one on my left wrist. Her letter most specifically read one-thirty and, believe me, it's not my timekeeping that's gone awry. I keep a number of clocks just so I can be sure that, even if one or two let me down, I can always find the correct time. When you live by yourself in a house that you very rarely leave and is even more rarely visited, it's essential that you don't lose track of the time. Every minute lost—if left uncorrected—would soon accumulate to an hour, and then hours, until—as you can imagine—you could easily end up living in a completely erroneous time frame.

Our mother, Maud, and I were always waiting for Vivi: in the hall before we went to church or shouting for her from the landing to hurry up for school. And it's now, as I wait for her again, that I find snippets of our childhood jumping into my head, slices of conversation, things I've not thought about since they happened: our first pair of boots, which Vivi had chosen for us, long black ones that laced to the top; long afternoons in the summer holidays spent damming up the brook to create our own tributaries and islands; sneaking into the loggia at harvest time to drink cider before taking it to the men in the fields; giggling with Maud at Clive's rare excitement when he created a Six-spot Burnet with five spots; our first trip to boarding school, holding each other's clammy hands with shared anticipation, squeezed among the chemical bottles in the back of Clive's car.

It was a childhood in perfect balance, so I'm wondering what it was that came along and changed everything. It wasn't just one thing. There's rarely a sole cause for the separation of lives. It's a sequence of events, an inexorable chain reaction where each small link is fundamental, like a snake of upended dominoes. And I've been thinking that the very first one, the one you push to start it all off, must have been when Vivi slipped off our bell tower and nearly died, fifty-nine years ago.

CHAPTER 2

The Bell Tower

WHEN MAUD GAVE BIRTH to Vivien, on 19 October 1940, I thought she'd borne twelve other children of varying ages at the same time. I was almost three and I remember they all came home from hospital in a minibus. When I asked Maud why she'd had so many she said that we had the largest house in the district and could fit them all in, and two maids and a housekeeper to help her look after them. My father, Clive, told me later they were called evacuees. They had come from Bristol to play with us and to double the attendance at Saxby village school. I always thought Vivi was one of them and when, three years later, the worst of the blitz was over and the evacuees all went home, I couldn't understand why baby Vivi had stayed.

"She's your little sister, Ginny. *This* is her home," Maud had said, hugging us both to her in the hallway.

I took a good look at Vivi then, in her little red woolen jumper, her fluffy hair sticking up and her big round eyes gazing at me. From that moment on, I worshipped her. Two more war years passed, and V-J Day brought weeks of celebrations. Then, while everyone else was adjusting to life in a country on its knees, Vivi and I were just getting on with our childhood together, sharing our secrets and our sugar ration.

Not only is Bulburrow Court the largest house in the district, it's also the most striking. Tucked away in the soft folds of the West Dorset countryside and buttressed against the slope of its own hill, it overwhelms the village of low-lying houses below. A vast Victorian folly.

There are four stories and four wings. In the reception rooms marble fireplaces stand squarely under ornately corniced ceilings. In the paneled hall, a large oak staircase pours majestically from the vaulted ceiling onto the parquet floor, while behind the pantries at the back of the house—the north side—winds a much smaller, secret staircase designed to shuttle domestic staff discreetly up and down. By the time we were born, Bulburrow Court's glory days were buried well within the previous century, when the house and gardens would not have run smoothly on less than twenty staff, more if you counted the surrounding tenant farmers and farm laborers, all originally part of the estate.

As we grew up, the Red House, as it was often called on account of the Virginia creeper that turns the south side a deep red each autumn, became better known as a local landmark than for its splendor. It was a reference for directions, a passing spectacle for West Country holidaymakers—iced in Gothic extravaganza and topped with castellated turrets, an observatory, the bell tower and mock-Elizabethan chimney stacks that rise above the peaks and valleys within the immense landscape of the roof, all arrogance and late-Victorian grandeur.

Outside, at the back of the house, the cobbled courtyard is enclosed by stables and apple stores, an old parlor and a butchery, still stained with slaughtering devices hanging grimly from the rafters. Behind them the loggia and then, at one time, Maud's kitchen garden and cold frames, a former vegetable patch and a spinney lead up to the north water garden. To the south, meadows run down from the terraced gardens to the brook, the peach houses and the riveted tail section of a Halifax bomber that landed in our fields. Then there are the things that only Vivi and I knew about, like the holm oak that looks solid from the outside but is completely hollow in the middle. If you climbed up its branches it was possible to lower yourself into the guts of the tree, where we'd agreed to hide when the Germans came.

BULBURROW COURT has been in my family since 1861 and since then, Maud told us, each generation couldn't resist stamping its mark on it so that the house has become a conspicuous register of its own history.

"Either Victorians were vulgar or we were very vulgar Victorians," our mother would say. "Each of us put his crest here, initials there and a turret or two everywhere," and it was true that if you wandered around the house you were reminded of the relative self-importance, or vulgarity, of each of them. The first, Samuel Kendal, who made his fortune illegally importing agricultural fertilizers from South America (which Maud was *not* proud of), commissioned an enormous stained-glass window as a backdrop to the hall stairs, spanning the height of two floors. It depicts four completely fabricated—Maud said—family crests along with pompous Latin mottoes as if he had in fact been the progeny of the coming together of four great families. Samuel's son, Anthony—Maud's grandfather—had too much time and all his father's money on his hands, so he added a star-gazing tower on the east side, which, since I've been alive, has had a far better purpose housing a rare colony of greater horseshoe bats. He also embossed his initials wherever he could around the house, which Maud said was a dreadful mistake because he has been remembered only as ANK.

Since then nothing has been added and lots has fallen off. Like-wise, Samuel's fortune hasn't been added to but, rather, has slowly dwindled, as those who came after him pursued a far less lucrative profession—the study of butterflies and moths. So it is that Vivien and I are direct descendants of an eminent line of lepidopterists—including our own father, Clive. The vast attic rooms and the expansive cellarage of Bulburrow Court, along with many of the north-wing rooms and most of the outhouses, have for more than a century been reserved solely for the study of lepidoptera, with net and tank rooms, laboratories, winter rooms, caterpillar houses, pupation troughs, display cabinets and an internationally renowned entomological reference library.

While life for the other village children revolved around cattle and sheep rearing, or the harvest, our yearly calendar centered around the life cycle of a moth. For us it was endless hours of pupae digging in the autumn, moss gathering in the winter, spring evenings spent dusking and sallowing, and long summer nights light-trapping and sugaring in secret glades and forgotten wastelands. But spring was the busiest time, the time of emergence, as Clive called it, when our captive breeders would emerge from their winter cocoons in our attic rooms and the mating season would start.

BULBURROW COURT was saturated with the belongings of four generations. Furniture, pictures, books and also *things*—artifacts, possessions, mementos, letters, papers and countless other bits and pieces—so that the moment you stepped inside, you were aware of the historic progression of the house. The walls leached the desires and fears of those who had peopled it. The style of the furniture, the pictures on the walls, the quality of the rugs and carpets, the toys we played with in our nursery, all spoke of the wealth, tastes and virtue of its past owners. The silverware, crockery, tapestries, even the linen for the beds, monogrammed for posterity, the stains on a tablecloth, the marks in the woodwork, the wear of the stairs, the wistfulness of an ancestor inadvertently revealed in the eyes of his portrait. They all told part of the same story, so that the house and its contents became a museum to the Kendals, a claustrophobic tribute to one dynasty.

Visitors were left in no doubt as to the family profession or their eminence in the field. The oak paneling in the hall was barely visible behind framed photographs, letters and commendations, honorary entomology memberships, framed newspaper clippings (" 'Largest Moth in Asia' Found by Dorset Expert") and supercilious photos of one or other of them meeting royalty or receiving yet another accolade.

The centerpiece in the drawing-room cabinet was a black-and-white photo of a fresh-faced ANK in a dense jungle, looking dapper with a clean flat cap angled to one side, surrounded by mud-soaked local porters. He's holding up a board pinned with around two hundred moths that we assumed were the Blue Sapphires he had recorded collecting from Peru in 1898. Next to it, as if in perpetual competition, was the one of my grandfather Geoffrey solemnly shaking hands with the king of Mustang on an internationally acclaimed butterfly expedition to the Himalayas during the first part of the last century, his young assistant behind him, beaming into the camera while holding aloft a setting board and a huge bottle of killing fluid as if they were trophies.

Above this, framed specimens were arranged on the walls; *Incatua molleen* from Brazil, the size of a child's hand, faded and worn and lifeless; a completed box-framed plate of all the known Brazilian Underwings, unidentifiable without the tabulated index beneath, set and pinned in the days before they knew how to fix the colors with ammonia. In the next display cabinet, caterpillar skins were laid out and labeled, the name of the famous nineteenth-century case makers, White and Sons, stamped across its mahogany top. The skins had been carefully pricked and blown, then dried papery and rigid over a Bunsen burner. Other, larger insects from across the world had their places lining the walls or in glass-topped mahogany cabinets: a bird-eating tarantula, a giant Australian cockroach, an Atacama scorpion, labeled as gifts from other eminences in the field of Victorian entomology, all of which led to the impression that rather than my family having been fond of the natural world, they had scoured the earth in a bid to kill and pin every poor insect that crossed their path. Maud thought the displays repulsive and Clive thought them unnecessary, but neither took them down.

. . .

MAUD HAD ADDED her own small exhibit to the museum. Half a dozen framed photos of our family stood together on an occasional table alongside the back of the sofa in the drawing room. One was of a young Maud and Clive embracing on a balcony in a foreign city, Paris perhaps, with the evening light behind them, eyes only for each other. It must have been taken before the war, before I was born. Maud is wearing a pretty peacock-print dress. She's lifting her chin and arching backwards with happiness, Clive's arms looped round the small of her back, supporting her preciously. Then there was the one of me as a baby, wrapped up so you can't actually see any of me at all, Maud and Clive holding up the package between them next to the sundial on the top terrace. Snow hid the ground and lay, heavy and precarious, on the fir-tree limbs above us, and the image was blurred in a couple of places where snowflakes had caught the lens.

Most visitors would remember the house, foremost, as cold. It was built in the days when the vast rooms with their high ceilings and box bay windows could be kept warm only if constantly stoked by a staff that outnumbered the family. But after the war Maud said we couldn't afford more than one help in the house and two in the garden so our maids, Anna Maria and Martha Jane (two of nine sisters from Little Broadwindsor) were sent home, and we were left with Vera. Vera was our housekeeper.

Vera said she didn't work in the house but she was part of it, like the hall stairs or the potting shed. She didn't talk very much but she was most interesting to study. She had wiry gray hair, and she'd been alive so long that her whole body was slowly shrinking, except for her nose, which grew instead and became slightly redder and more bulbous as time went by. Vivi said that Vera's nose was sucking the life out of the rest of her body for its own independent growth. Sometimes another little lump would appear, or an aberrant gray hair an inch or so long as if it had arrived overnight already at full length. Maud would laugh when Vivi pointed out these things—Vivi was always making Maud laugh—although she said that she'd be Very

Cross Indeed if either of us mentioned it in front of Vera as it was "a condition." It was as if Vera's face was in a constant state of flux, perhaps weather dependent or in response to what she'd eaten the day before.

The way we got around a diminishing staff was an evolving fluidity in the volume of the house throughout the year, a constant expansion and contraction, like a lung. In the most bitter winter weeks, we'd lock up the extremities and retreat to the inner sanctum, huddling in the heart of the building—the kitchen, the study and the library—where the fires could be kept continuous.

When we were children, Vivi and I were inseparable. When she went to play in the stream, scour the ridge for mushrooms, collect acorns for the farmers' pigs, turn the apples for cider or go scrumping in the next-door village, whatever the pursuit, I'd go too. Our parents liked us to stay together. Sometimes Maud would check when she saw one of us setting out. "Have you got Ginny?" or "Are you with Vivi?" she'd shout, often out of a window from a higher level of the house. And if she ever saw Vivi set out without me she'd call her back, even the times I didn't want to go: "Will you take Ginny, please?" and I'd feel I ought to go along for Maud's sake. Vivi was always the leader, even though she was younger: She'd have a plan, a contingency plan and an emergency strategy. But I'd be right there, next to her, following her every move.

So, the day we went up the bell tower for the last time, of course it had been all Vivi's idea. She was eight and I had just turned eleven. We'd crept up there after breakfast with a piece of toast each that we'd been saving, luxuriously spread with our mother's famous loganberry jam. It was Vivi's favorite place.

"We're going to ask Vera if she's seen a stray cat we fed yesterday," Vivi told Maud at the table.

"With your toast?" Maud had asked.

"No, we'll eat it before we get there," Vivi said, as we rushed out of the kitchen.

"See? Told you it would work," my little sister gloated when we reached the second pantry unrecalled. The second pantry, where

Maud stored her cheeses, hung her meat and dried her gourds, was also the start of the secret set of back stairs. Halfway up the stairs was a little oak door, one where even I, at eleven years old, had to stoop slightly to get through. It had a hole you put your index finger through to lift the latch on the other side. From there was a steep oak staircase, unlit except for a shaft of natural light that coursed down from the top, tumbling the dust in its path. It was a magnet for a child like Vivi—any normal, imaginative child, in fact—and at the top was a little wooden platform open to the air and a small turret, surrounded by a low stone parapet.

The turret had a peaked wooden hat held up by wooden posts, all painted a kind of limey green, and hanging from its apex was a beautiful, dainty, blackened brass bell. A thick, furry, red-and-white striped rope, like an enormous piece of the sweets the American soldiers used to give us (they called it candy), hung from a brass hoop on top. It was just too thick for either of us to connect our thumb and fingers when we gripped it, and it disappeared through a hole in the wooden platform, ending up in the back passage on the ground floor beyond the pantries. It was on this platform, under this bell, in our own little turret, that we found just enough space for two small children to dream. Truth be told, it was Vivi who dreamed and I who listened, enraptured, for I was very aware that it was a gift that she'd been given and I had not. We'd go there when Vivi wanted to plot her next adventure or scheme her next scheme. Just sometimes I'd offer her a little idea, and just sometimes, not often, she'd latch upon it to help her see through the puzzles in her head. And I'd feel ever so slightly triumphant.

Vivien was from a fantastic world, definitely not the same one as mine. I thought when God made Vivi he was giving me a window to see the world in a different way. She lived out her dreams and fantasies in our house or in the woods behind it, or in the eleven acres of meadow that stretched out down to the brook. She spent hours meticulously planning her life—and mine.

"Ginny," she'd start, "you promise, cross your heart hope to die, not to tell anyone?"

"Promise," I'd say. I'd cross my heart with my right hand and I'd mean it.

I never tired of Vivi's company, and I always took her side, even against Maud. Vivi might have been able to make our mother laugh, but she knew how to infuriate her too. (I never argued with Maud, but I rarely laughed with her either.) After they'd had a row Vivi would storm off in an uncontrollable temper and Maud would send me to try to comfort her. Often I'd find her sobbing with such abandon that I truly believed that even the little things sent her mood spiraling downwards, that they really affected her. When she was young she couldn't control her emotions, swinging easily from good temper to bad.

So, if I hadn't been there, squatting in the bell tower with her, I might have thought she'd jumped. But I saw how she'd slotted herself into a huge crescent-shaped stone, which made up part of the low parapet round the platform. For Vivi, it was an irresistible place to perch. She was making herself comfortable while holding her toast level in her left hand. I remember saying that I didn't think she should be there, that it looked too dangerous, and just as she said, "Ginny, don't be so bor-ing" a pair of martins, scouring the eaves for a nest site, startled out from underneath her little ledge. My heart leapt but Vivi must have lost her balance. I watched her trying to regain control of the toast that danced about, evading her grip like a bar of soap in the bath. For those slow seconds it seemed as if repossessing the toast was of utmost importance to her and that she was losing her balance didn't register. I've never forgotten the terror in her eyes, staring at me, replayed a thousand times since in my nightmares, as she realized she was falling. I didn't see her grabbing the bell, but she must have stretched out for it as she went, because it rang and the echo of that strike gave to me a resounding significance, a lifetime of noise. As I looked over the edge I saw her lying, not on the ground, three long stories below, as I'd imagined, but hanging motionless over the battlements that run above the porch. Later, they said the algae, recently proliferated because of the first few warm days of spring, had made the ledge more slippery than usual.

Peculiarly, she didn't die. Or, rather, she died and came back again. Two ambulance men in red and black jackets carried her limp little eight-year-old body, full of plans for our future, on to a stretcher and down a wooden ladder from the top of the porch. But I was watching her all the time and I remember the moment she died; while she was on that stretcher I actually *saw* her Entire Future give up the struggle to survive and leave her, and at the same time I felt my own future reduced to a dead and eventless vacuum, a mere biological process.

It seemed longer but later Maud said that really it was just a minute before they got her back again. She was resuscitated in front of the porch by the ambulance men. I was in the driveway, watching, when Maud rushed up to me, red-faced and frantic, tugging at my arm in a frenzy. Her usual calm and poise had been shattered, giving way to raw terror. She was leaning slightly forward, as if she were about to vomit, her hair angry, eyes acute and desperate.

"Tell me what happened," she pleaded. I said nothing. I stared at the hydrangea crawling up the side of the porch, its branches woody, split and peeling. If it weren't for the fresh buds appearing at the tips, you could have been forgiven for thinking it was dead. I had already told her how Vivi had slipped off the tower, how she'd tried to catch her dancing toast.

"Ginny, darling," she sobbed, folding her arm round my waist, pulling me gently to her, squeezing her cheek to mine, her mouth near my ear. "I love you," she whispered slowly, and I knew it was true. "I love you and I don't blame you. I just need to know the *truth.*" I could feel her whole body trembling, her tears gluing our cheeks together. My mother wasn't this wretched person; she was usually the source of all strength. I stood rigid, thinking of the wetness on my cheek, feeling her shaking and trying to understand, trying to fathom what she wasn't blaming me for.

The next minute Clive was striding towards us from where he'd been helping to lift Vivi into the ambulance. He looked at me as he approached, searching my eyes and finding my confusion as Maud clung to me. He leaned over and kissed my forehead firmly while unclasping Maud's hands from my waist.

"Come on. We're going," he said, pulling Maud towards him, fastening her arms round him and leading her off to the ambulance.

When they were sent home from the hospital that afternoon they had no news yet of Vivi's prospects. Clive showed Maud into the library to get her a drink, which was what she needed at times of crisis. I helped to pour it. "Open the cabinet, get a glass, no not that one, the little one. Can you see the bottle that says Garvey's?" I found it and put my finger on it. "That's the one, finest old amontillado. Mother's sherry." I stayed out of my parents' way after that but later in the day, as I passed their bedroom on the landing, I heard them arguing, my mother sobbing.

"It's all my fault. I thought we could be a normal family." She was hysterical.

"We *are* a normal family. Stop jumping to conclusions," I heard Clive say softly.

"Her sister's dying. . . . She's not even crying. . . . She stood there staring at the shrubs." Maud's voice was scathing. "There must be something—"

"Pull yourself together," Clive interrupted in a tone I'd never heard him use before, not unkind, but firm and authoritative. "Save your hysterics until you have the facts."

I knew they were talking about me and guessed Maud was angry about something to do with me, but I had no idea what.

Half an hour later I was in the kitchen, huddled next to the wood stove with Basil, our elderly Great Dane, when I heard the front door's brass goat's-head door knocker being rattled. I went to open the door, and Dr. Moyse, our family doctor from Crewkerne, greeted me effusively.

In our household, Dr. Moyse was the most trusted member of the outside world. He had cured three of our evacuees of diphtheria, nursed Vivi and me through whooping cough and devised a potion for Clive's gout. But everyone seemed to forget that he had consistently failed to rid me of the four warts that cursed the underside of my fingers, which I'd developed the habit of chewing when I was eight. In the end Clive froze them off with pure liquid nitrogen.

The doctor was a favorite of the village children, giving them rides in his white convertible and telling them gory stories between puffs on his pipe. He was in his mid-thirties, incredibly tall and lanky, stooping through most of the doorways even in our house, staying hunched when he was standing. He'd get to his knees to talk to children. He had curly blond hair, wore round rimless spectacles and carried a doctor's case over his shoulders with straps like a sports bag. When he walked he put a little bound in his step as if he'd just got a piece of good news. But Dr. Moyse had always made me feel uneasy. He singled me out for little or long conversations, losing his casual manner and becoming more serious, as if allowing me the intimacy of confiding in him, making sure I was aware he was on my side. Maud wouldn't have heard a bad word against him, and I suppose he was nice enough. He was patient and kind perhaps, but he got on my nerves. He'd come and find me, then ask me daft questions right when I was in the middle of something. That day, as usual, I didn't feel much like talking to him.

"Ginny," he said, "I came as quickly as I could." I said nothing. I hadn't known he was coming at all. I opened the door so he could get past me. I was still battling with why Maud was angry with me. "Your mother wanted to see me," he said to clarify his presence. "Any news from the hospital?"

I shook my head. "Maud's upstairs," I said.

I left him in the hall and went into the library. A fire crackled and hissed in the grate. Wasps, butterflies and crickets, painted daintily on the tiled surround, were brought to life by the flickering amber flames. I sat on the smooth oak window seat looking out at the valley in the distance, reddened by the low sun, and the pretty terraces just outside, trapped in the shadow of the house. Two low box hedges with last summer's topiary efforts were still vaguely evident, the stone steps disappearing into rough pastureland, which, in a couple of months' time, would be waving with the rare meadow grasses Maud had sown there. Basil followed me in, his uncut claws tapping on the parquet floor as he walked. He rested his chin on my lap, his jowls cold and wet from lapping at his water bowl. From this position his eyes, atop his head like an alligator's, gazed at me, blinking and steady, imploring me, I imagined, just to be happy. I stroked his head and his tail started to bash the window seat in appreciation, steady like a metronome.

Maud had told me that when I was born we were snowed in for a month. For six days and six nights the snow had fallen, until it had reached the height of the ground-floor sills. Maud said that when you sat right here on this window seat and looked out onto the Bulburrow valley you had the impression the house had sunk. The tops of the hedges on the south terrace looked like hedge trimmings scattered on the ground, and the stone goose that topped our fountain, stretching his neck and bill high into the air to spurt out the water, looked as if he were just managing to keep his head above the ground in a desperate bid to breathe. It was this weather at my birth that had apparently swayed the balance of my personality. Maud told me it had made me the stay-at-home type.

"Can I come in?" Dr. Moyse was at the library door. Basil padded over to sniff him, friendly, bottom low and wiggling in submission, looking for an alliance with all factions.

"No," I said, because it was what I meant, even though I knew it wasn't a polite answer. I turned back to the window, mainly to avoid my own insolence or the trouble it might get me in. The doctor ignored me and wandered in silently, pretending to look from one book spine to the next, musing among the shelves and the gallery of pictures that hung between them, mostly framed satirical sketches from Victorian periodicals—men in top hats, black trench coats and waders prancing about the countryside, bounding after insects in a bog or leaning precariously out of fast-moving trains, an enormous net in one hand and a bottle of poison in the other— reminders of a time when the pastime was at its most popular, when trainloads of Londoners would flock to the country for a weekend's mothing.

"Pretty, isn't it?" Dr. Moyse was beside me at the window, sharing my view as if that would allow him to share intimacies too. He appeared to arrive inadvertently, abreast of me, peering out of the window with casual indifference.

"Don't you worry. I'm sure she'll be fine, Ginny," he said, seizing the moment and laying a hand awkwardly on my shoulder. I turned to the fire, and was instantly mesmerized by the bright flames dancing between the logs, squeaking and hissing because, yet again, Vera had taken from this year's wood pile rather than last.

"Who?" I said, thinking of Maud seething upstairs.

"Who?" he said, astonished, pulling away his hand as if I were hot and bending his knees to be at my level. He looked directly at me, fixing my gaze. "Do you realize Vivien's in hospital in a critical condition?" he said patronizingly. As if I were an idiot.

"Yes, I know," I said, slightly irritated. "I just thought . . . Oh, it doesn't matter." I wouldn't have been able to explain it suitably for him. I find that once people think you mean one thing you're never able to change their opinion. But how could he be "sure she'll be fine"? He hadn't seen her or spoken to the hospital.

Dr. Moyse gazed at me with a most troubled expression. "No, go on, you can tell me. You and I are friends, Ginny." He was always saying that—"You and I are friends." I wasn't his friend and I didn't want to talk to him. It seemed far too complicated to explain.

"I just forgot," I lied.

"We're all on your side you know, Ginny, but sometimes you have to help us a little," he said. I didn't know what he was talking about. Then he asked if I was angry about what had happened, how I felt about it, if I was cross with Vivien or with my parents. He went on and on with the most peculiar questions, and really I just wanted to tell him that the only person who was making me angry was him, couldn't he leave me alone. I know Dr. Moyse was a good man and he was always trying for the best, but sometimes it felt like he was interviewing me—what I felt about this and that and stupid things; if I ever wanted revenge. He never did it to Vivi. In the end, I told him I didn't feel anything. I'd come to realize this was the best way to end his diatribe. He never knew how to continue when I said that.

Later that evening the telephone rang through the silence of the house. Clive answered it.

"Crewkerne two five one," he said, pushing out his chin as he did habitually and stroking the thick-cropped beard that spread down his neck and merged with the hair rising up out of his shirt. He rubbed it with the back of his fingers, upwards against the growth. A moment later, "Thank you, Operator, put the hospital through."

My heart beat away the time as Maud and I watched him, searching in vain for answers in his firmly set features as he listened. But his face, much of it hidden under the cropped beard, gave nothing away and the rhythm of his hand strokes up his neck were slow and even, unaltered by the news he was hearing.

"The good news is that Vivien is okay. She'll be fine," Clive informed us matter-of-factly after the call. "They're watching her closely, but the doctor is confident she'll pull through."

My world regrew, not least because whatever the reason for Maud being upset with me soon dissolved into the many layers of a family's misunderstood memories. Later, when we'd come back from visiting Vivi in hospital, it was as if she'd never even thought it. She hugged me and told me how lucky Vivien was to have such a loving older sister. Maud was right about that. I've always loved Vivi, even all the years she's been away. And I always will, no matter what.

WHAT VIVI LOST that spring when she fell from the bell tower was not, luckily (as everyone kept telling her), her life, but the ability to have children. She'd been impaled on an iron stake, part of the balustrade that had run round the top of the porch. Maud said it used to be a balcony leading from the first-floor landing and my lookout window had been the door that led on to it. For the war effort everyone had to hand over any iron to the munitions factories, Maud said, to be melted down into guns and bullets, so the balcony—along with the house's main gates—had to go.

Vivien had ruptured her womb and the infection quickly inflamed her ovaries so that a week after her fall she had an operation to take away her entire reproductive system. She lost it to save her life. It didn't bother her, mind. She liked to tell people she had died once already, or give them the weeks, months or years since the accident that she "could have been dead for." In the village, Mrs. Jefferson assured her that she must have been spared for a reason, that there would be a "calling" later in her life, and Mrs. Axtell questioned her persistently about what she had seen, trying to get a preview of eternity. Later, at school, she impressed her friends with stories of what it had felt like to die. None of them had known anyone who had died before. And once, when she'd found out that all a woman's eggs are already in her ovaries when she's born, she told Maud's lunch guests that she'd lost all her children.

But Vivi herself was still a child. She hadn't yet developed the womanly urge to hold her newborn, to feel and need its dependence and to understand that that was what life was about and nothing else mattered. Nor had I, so at the time neither of us realized the true significance of her accident. Only that she'd been so incredibly lucky.

CHAPTER 3

Vivien, a Small Dog and the Missing Furniture

THIS FULL-LENGTH arched window at the end of the first-floor landing, where I'm still waiting for Vivi, is my lookout. I know it might sound funny but sometimes I think of the house as my ship, myself as its captain, and here I'm at the helm, in charge of its course and direction. I can see who's coming up to the house, who's walking their dogs on the footpath running up to the ridge and what's about to come down the lane from the top of the hill. For instance, I can tell you that every day, at eight in the morning, the woman from East Lodge—I don't know her name—takes her collie up to the ridge. Sometimes, not often, she'll glance this way when she gets to the bit that curves into view of the house, but she doesn't know I'm watching her—I make sure I've pulled back against the pillar in time. I feel in control in this captain's post: I see what I want to see and nobody sees me.

I have two other strategic lookouts. From my bedroom window I can see the church, the postbox in the wall on the other side, the lane leading up to the rectory and Peverill's bustling farmyard. From the bathroom I can see directly south to the brook and beyond to the peach houses, and to the Stables where Michael lives, the other gate houses and the lane that leads to them.

I don't venture out much anymore. It's unnecessary. Michael, who used to garden for us with his father, buys my groceries and does the odd job, like putting out the rubbish at the end of the drive. I don't employ him anymore so I don't know if he does it out of kindness or duty, but he's the only person I see close up these days, even though I spend hours watching the daily turns of the village from a distance. Bulburrow's houses are clustered in a valley bowl and from my three vantage points I can see them all, except a couple of new bungalows built halfway up the lane to the north. If I'm at the helm of a ship, then Bulburrow Court is at the helm of the village, the central control tower from which the rest can be monitored and directed.

When Vivi and I were growing up, we knew every single person in every single house, but I don't know any of them now. The ones we knew have died and their children moved away. It's one of the problems with getting old: the more people you outlive, the more your life reads like a catalog of other people's deaths.

Poor Vera, our housekeeper, was the first person I can remember dying. It took her four months. Maud said that, really, she blew up slowly and eventually burst. Vivi and I weren't allowed to visit her in her north-wing room, as Maud said it might give us nightmares, but I'm certain we had much worse ones just imagining what Vera's death looked like. But it was Maud's death that had the biggest impact on our lives. It was pain-free, although probably not as dignified as she'd have liked. She tripped down the cellar steps. But afterwards our lives changed direction forever. That was when Vivi left this house for the last time and she hasn't been back since. It's quite a thing, you know; she was twenty-one when I last saw her, not much more than a child. I was twenty-four.

My reverie is disturbed by the even hum of a modern car slowing down the hill and fading, then rising again in this direction, and I can tell it's cruising up the drive. It must be her. Not many people come up the drive these days. Mostly it's strangers who've taken a wrong turning and quickly reverse or turn round again at the top. Then there are the sort who have recently been coming more and more, in their tall, smart cars. They bang the door knocker, and when I don't respond, they go away and come back later with a letter asking if I'll sell up. Why on earth do they think I'll want to start moving house now? Once a month the woman in the stripy bobble hat walks up the drive. She's from Social Services, and when she gets no answer to her knock, she leaves her calling card and a pile of leaflets. I like to flick through them—it keeps me in touch with at least some of what's going on in the world—and all the junk advertising that comes through the door: offers on credit cards, holidays to win, how to switch my fuel supplier, or the free *Diamond Advertiser*, which they don't always bother to bring up the drive. I used to have a radio but it never worked very well so I got rid of it.

It's the leaflets from the bobble-hat woman that I find the most interesting, and relevant. It's how I know, for instance, that my gnarled joints and blotchy fingers, my loss of appetite, low energy, dry eyes and mouth are all part of my rheumatoid arthritis and that I should be eating a lot of green-lipped mussels. It's how I know that, because I have "flares" followed by "remissions," my case is fairly mild at the moment but will get a lot worse when it becomes chronic. Then it will be permanently painful and I'll have to have the joints "popped" to let out some of the excess synovial fluid and I don't like the sound of that at all.

A silver car rounds into view. It is broad and long and low, and purrs with an air of quality and arrogance. Vivien had told me *when* she would arrive, but not *how*. The car makes a wide sweep of the drive's circular frontage and comes to a standstill alongside the front door, as horse-drawn carriages would have done when Maud was a girl. My heart is beating so hard that when the engine cuts, the sound of hollow thudding fills the silence, and I've just realized I never *truly* believed until right now that she was going to come at all. At the same time I wonder—for a fleeting moment—if I really want her to. But then the thought is gone. She's coming back because she needs me now. After all, I'm her older sister.

The driver's door opens. Why is everything happening so slowly? Perhaps it's true that time is slowed by a quicker heartbeat, like the mayfly, with one hundred wing beats per second, which can fulfill a lifetime in a day. I imagine a young Vivi getting out, the girl I remember her as, quite forgetting I should be expecting someone I won't recognize. Instead, out steps a young man, no more than twenty-five, with thick dark hair and a smart blue suit. I'm stunned. Where's Vivi? Perhaps he has nothing to do with Vivi at all. My wave of excitement crashes around me. Has he the wrong house? Another person come to offer to buy it from me, leaving an obsequious letter when there's no answer? But instead of coming towards the porch, the man walks round the car and opens its back door, the one nearest the house. Now I know *she's here.*

A decorative walking stick is thrust out of the car onto the muddy gravel, the man holds out his arm and, leaning on the stick with one hand and taking the young man's arm with the other, Vivien emerges, guided like royalty. My face is pressed to the window but she is too close to the house for me to see her clearly. All I can see is the top of her head, gray like mine, but while my hair is long and lies flat against my head, hers is cropped short and obviously shaped. She walks to the back of the car, stops and faces the house. She plants the stick firmly on the ground in front of her, both hands resting on the pommel at the top, one over the other, her feet slightly apart for balance, and surveys Bulburrow Court. All the while the young man is collecting bags and boxes and hangers of clothes wrapped in plastic, and piling them outside the car. Vivien takes in the house slowly, looking crossways from one side to the other. I can imagine what she is seeing: the windows, a few cracked, others smashed with boards replacing the glass; gargoyles, exact copies of those from Carlisle's twelfth-century cathedral, whose farcical grimaces scared us as children; the corbels that hold up the porch; escutcheons carved under the mullioned windows, the battlements above. It is easy to imagine what she can see, but what memories does every window of each room stir in her? What emotions do the dark gray haunting stones bring, or the enormous quoins at the base of the house, each made from a solid piece of granite, the almighty foundation stones of our lives, holding up for generations the framework of our ancestry?

As she is gripped in her consideration of the house, so I am gripped by watching her from above, all at once desperate to know what is going through her mind.

Her head lifts as she studies each section slowly, methodically even, and I am about to make out more of her features when her eyes begin to run diagonally, crosswise, towards the top of the porch, and up, to the arch of my window. . . . I pull back into the shadows before she spots me, but as I do, it strikes me that I have seen a ghost. Maud. I hadn't expected that. I hadn't even tried to imagine what Vivien would look like but I'd never considered she'd be so like Maud. I feel like a little girl again. I don't dare look out of the window now for fear that I will meet Maud's all-knowing eyes. I'm numbed with indecision, for a moment paralyzed. I can't tell you how many minutes go by before I am slowly aware that the goat's-head knocker is being rattled from side to side (rather than banged as a stranger would do).

I glance at my clothes. I've been so busy wondering what Vivien would look like that I haven't considered the impression she'll have of me. I'm thinking now of how I might appear to her, but because I never check myself in the mirror these days, I can't really decide. My hair, I know, must be pretty unruly, like a vagabond's I should think, and whereas I can tell she's made an effort with makeup, I don't have any. Quickly I undo my ponytail, run my fingers through my hair in an effort to comb it and refix the elastic band. I check the front of my navy cardy and pick off a couple of specks of something white and crusty, toothpaste, perhaps, then go down to answer the door. I'm brimming with that sick, nervous apprehension, the sort that churns your stomach. When I get to the heavy oak front door I stop. I have to gather myself for our meeting. I begin to fiddle with the black plastic watch strap on my left wrist, a habit I find consoling. I run my finger back and forth along the inside next to my skin and rub the smooth Perspex face firmly with my thumb, until I know I am ready.

When I open the door Vivien is standing back a couple of paces in the porch, as if to give me a fuller view of her. She's discarded her stick, as if it was a mere affectation. I am impressed. She must look at least ten years younger than me, not three. She's smart in a pair of rust-colored cords and a thin gray jumper with a speckled furry collar.

A thickly beaded belt with an enameled clasp is draped loosely round her hips and she smells strongly of scent. She wears a simple twisted gold bangle on one wrist and a heavy bejeweled spider crawls up her left breast, rather reminiscent of the brooches Maud collected. She has dangling, brightly colored earrings, on each of which, at further inspection, a cockerel is painted. A small dog, I wouldn't know which sort, a wiry white one, is tucked casually under her arm. Although the resemblance to Maud is still a surprise, thankfully, up close like this, Vivien is less like our mother than she was from the landing window. She has Maud's intelligent face, shaped by wise, reflective lines at her brow and mouth, but her eyes are not Maud's at all.

"Hello, Vivien," I say coolly, though I'll admit I'm a little in awe of her immaculate appearance. I remember how Vivi, like Maud, always liked to make an impression, to strive for a reaction, and it used to rile her that I was impassive and imperturbable—or, rather, that I was able to hide my true feelings. My emotions weren't played out on my face, like hers. I'd always thought it was the price she paid for having a pretty, highly defined face, with delicate, precise features—a hard straight nose, distinctly curved lips, visible cheekbones. Such refinement was not well equipped to shield a disturbance rising beneath it, and every one of Vivi's emotions would surface and give itself away. None of my features were so elegant or clear-cut, but a thousand thoughts and feelings could be buried unnoticed beneath my broader cheeks and softer, rounded nose. My lips were too wide and full for my face, the bottom one too heavy, curving down a little to reveal a glimpse of the inside. While Vivi had worked on disguising her true feelings as she grew up, I had worked on finding a little muscle to lift my bottom lip so that it might meet its opposite.

"Ginny . . . ," she says warmly.

"Vivi . . . ," I reply, finding myself mimicking her tone.

"Is the east wing vacant?" she inquires, mockingly serious, as if she's addressing a hotel receptionist.

"The east, the west, and the north are *all* vacant," I say, more as an accurate answer than to affect her game.

"Well then, I'll take all three." She smiles, seeking my eyes. There is a brief, awkward pause as she stands watching me, and I her, openly studying each other like the meeting of two cats on one territory. When we were young I'd instinctively wait, even a split second, to judge her mood. She'd make the first comment, suggest the first move, and I'm irritated to find myself once again waiting to divine her reaction, as if the intervening years have just slipped away.

"Ginny . . . ," she says again, this time in a low questioning voice. Then all of a sudden her face relaxes and she breaks out into a loud irrepressible giggle, throwing her head back wildly, abandoning herself to laughter.

"What's so funny?" I ask, a little offended.

"Oh, Ginny," she manages, between hiccuped giggling. "Look at us, Ginny. Just *look* at us. We're *old* people!" she says, and then another uninhibited wave attacks her. It's a laugh I recognize instantly, that I'm surprised to have almost forgotten, the whooping little-girl giggle that carried me through my childhood, that I could recognize from the other side of a field, a laugh so catching it could infect even the iciest disposition.

And I'm off. I don't think I've laughed like this, bursting out uncontrollably, since we were children. It's the kind that makes you bend over double with a knot in your tummy and, at every lull, the frenzied embers of your hilarity are still so hot that you need only the smallest spark of absurdity to set it off again, burning through your stomach.

It's surprisingly liberating to laugh after a long time having not. Soon we are in unstoppable and unsteady hysterics and the dog under Vivien's arm is being thrown about, unfazed, as if this were a regular occurrence. Vivien's dog doesn't seem to comply with the most basic description of Dog, like barking or wagging a tail. I can't even see a tail. It seems less of a companion and more of a protuberance, most of the time forgotten like any other body part. Uncharacteristically giddy, I look past Vivien and find her driver inspecting the higher reaches of the turrets and battlements of the house, ignoring us, akin to a manservant not noticing the torrid affair of his master even though he keeps watch at the door. Vivien catches my eye and we set each other off again, laughing until I see tears chasing the makeup down her face. I can tell this is going to be fun.

Vivien sits down to rest on the stone bench that lines the porch and puts the dog on her lap. We're utterly exhausted. I allow a wave of nostalgia to sweep through me like a revelation. It was Maud and Vivi who used to fill this house with laughter. Sometimes, as I listened distantly to their late-night conversations, I envied how they could make each other laugh, and now, sitting here in the porch with Vivien, I'm aware for the first time that part of me went missing a long time ago, that without her I'd become a different person and I've just had a taste of who I used to be or even what I might have become, had she been there.

The dog on Vivien's lap gnaws the top of its paws, cleaning them, scrunching its upper lip in a concentrated effort to get into the gaps between its claws. I'm watching him and wondering if his paws have ever been dirty, if he's ever been allowed to walk, or if cleaning them is something dogs are programmed to do, whatever their state. To tell you the truth, I'm usually most wary of dog owners. In general I find them loud, meddlesome people, who invariably love their dogs in an unhygienic sort of way.

"This is Simon, by the way," Vivien says, following my gaze. "You won't even notice him. He's very old and I'm sure he won't last long," she adds.

I don't know whether to thank her for the reassurance that he will die soon or to say I'm sorry about it. Or to admit I'd almost stopped noticing him already. Instead I look at the creature and try to screw up my nose in a way that is supposed to indicate that it looks like a very sweet dog, like the faces people make at babies. By Vivien's reaction—or lack of one—my expression doesn't look remotely genuine or, worse, she doesn't register that it has any meaning at all. She looks away as if she's just witnessed me picking my nose.

I am, and always have been, hopeless at social expression. Our mother, Maud, was a master. She'd say all the right things and make all the right faces at exactly the right times. For it to come so naturally, I think you need to start believing you're earnest even if you aren't. I can't dupe myself like that; I'm too straightforward. If I don't believe it, I can't say it. It's partly why people don't feel comfortable around me, why I've always found it difficult to fit in. I can't work out if it was something I was never born with or something I've never learned.

Clive wasn't socially skillful either, but that was because he never made an effort rather than through lack of understanding. Clive preferred silence to small talk, but Maud could do both. She was instantly able to judge the person she was with and adapt herself to suit them.

Once, when I was twelve and Maud and I were buying me stockings in the ladies' wear department at Denings in Chard (for a barn dance that she was making me go to with Vivi), she rushed up to a fat, exhausted-looking woman with a pram and bent down over her new saggy-looking baby. Then she looked up and said "Oh, isn't she *g-o-r-geous*" (in the only way she would—really loudly), so that everyone in the shop turned and stared at us. Her insincerity was so blaringly obvious that I thought they were staring because she'd made a fool of herself. Later, while I was hiding alone in a dark corner of the dance, I resolved to let her know, kindly, so that it didn't happen again. When I did, she stroked my hair and thanked me lovingly. Years later, I realized I'd been wrong about the other shoppers: The ladies' wear shoppers hadn't questioned Maud's feigned delight for a second. Maud had thought to give the tired new mother a little gift of encouragement, a ticket to confidence. The mother had pulled herself up and smiled and, while I was tugging at Maud's trousers to encourage her to leave, that woman had felt warm and wonderful and worthwhile inside. What I want you to know is the part that baffles me isn't that Maud lied for someone else's benefit, or that she didn't let herself admit it, but that none of the other shoppers questioned it. They understood instinctively why she was complimenting that baby, as if they all belonged to the same club, born knowing club rules.

Vivien stands up and walks past me into the house and up the stairs, instructing the driver to follow with her bags. I'm still in the porch and I'm starting to wonder so many things at the same time, like a small child beginning to question the world. I wonder if she's as immaculately dressed every day; I wonder why she wants the east wing; I wonder if she too is plagued by arthritis; I wonder if she'll remember to miss the second from last stair, which squeaks (Vera had once told us it was groaning in complaint after a century of being trodden on, and we'd made a pact to let it rest for a generation); I wonder what Vivien's left behind in London; I wonder if this is the start of another special bond, like the one we had many years ago. Most of all I wonder why she's decided, finally, to come home.

From the doorstep, I look up at the east windows on the first floor. Vivien appears and stares out disconsolately, without seeing me. Beautiful, warm, fun-loving Vivi. Finally she's back at Bulburrow.

I'M STILL OUTSIDE when Vivien comes downstairs, followed by her obedient driver. "Darling, what happened to the house?" she asks reproachfully.

"Oh, it's beginning to fall down," I say, feeling wonderfully at ease with my sister.

"I mean all the furniture. Were you robbed?"

I'd forgotten she hadn't seen it like this. Selling the furniture has been such a gradual process. Bobby came once every few months and took another load in his transit van. I met him first when he worked for the water board and had been sent to fix a series of leaking pipes on our land. Three days later, when he'd finished the work (and all my biscuits), he told me he owned an antiques shop in Chard and suggested he sell some furniture for me. When he'd got rid of it he came back with an assistant and loaded some more, the heavier oak pieces, and then, a few months later he took more, until his visits became fairly regular over the last ten years or so. Each time he paid cash for the items he'd sold. It was an excellent system and it suited me. I converted assets into grocery money without having to use a bank or go to town. I lived amid my own cash pot! I laugh out loud at the thought, still giddy with exuberance from our doorstep hysterics, as if I've become tipsy on a single sip of wine.

"It's become my pension," I quip, readying myself to laugh again.

But Vivien isn't laughing. "You sold the lot?" she gasps, her darkly rimmed eyes widening in disbelief. The change in her throws me. Alongside the makeup, I find it impossible to judge if she's being serious. I look at Simon, who blinks, incapable of offering any clues.

"Well, I've kept all the clocks and barometers that work, and Jake's head," I say, motioning to the stuffed pig's head on the wall as we walk in. (To tell you the truth, Bobby had said he didn't want it, but now I'm glad. Jake was Vivi's pet pig when she was about six, and she was so upset when he died [of unnatural causes] that Clive had his head mounted for her so she could see that he was smiling happily when he died.)

I smile myself at the long lost thought of Jake, but Vivien can't hide her disappointment. "But Virginia, do you realize"—she says this like Maud would have done, slowly and emphatically, Do . . . You . . . Realize—"you needed only to sell the Charles the Second chest in the hall for your pension? Or the settle, or the sideboard, an Aubusson tapestry, a few caquetoire chairs . . ." Her voice rises until it cracks. She sits heavily on the porch seat, as if the very idea has whipped her legs from under her. "Or a fucking painting," she half shouts, half cries. "But *everything*?! The house was crammed with furniture, Ginny. Furniture," she says again, waving her arms in front of her, as if painting it back in its place. "Furniture, rock-crystal chandeliers, dressers," she rants, in a senseless naming game of anything that springs to mind, "carpets, canteens, silver, vases, mirrors"—she pauses for breath—"porcelain, that, that oyster mirror just there"—she points at the bare wall in front of her—"the William and Mary . . ." She puts up both hands to cover her face. "*Priceless* furniture, Ginny."

I assure you I am now in no doubt of her seriousness. I understand that it's been a shock, and one she had never expected, but I'd never have guessed it would affect her so deeply. Why is it that as people grow old they cling to possessions and let go of knowledge? After all, it's only furniture. Each generation has spliced down Samuel Kendal's original estate, first the land, then the estate houses and the outbuildings. Surely the unnecessary hordes of contents are a natural progression? Besides—and this is just between you and me—I don't think Vivien's thought it through. She thinks there's a legacy to continue, poor woman, but it's all over now. Vivien and I are the end of the line, there is no *future generation*. It would have been split up and sold off after our deaths, free money for the government, if it hadn't been sold already. Perhaps she's slightly doo-lally—our own father went demented much younger than this. I try to reassure her, as I used to when we were little. I always enjoyed comforting her.

"But it's completely, absolutely, entirely empty," she complains, as if there are recognizable degrees of emptiness. "No pictures, no clothes, no photos. I mean, you've wiped out every reference to our past. Our family might not have happened. There was no point in its existing for the last two hundred years if it's got nothing to show for itself."

It is an interesting view but not one I share. Is it really necessary to record your life in order to make it worthwhile or commendable? Is it worthless to die without reference? Surely those testimonials last another generation or two at most, and even then they don't offer much meaning. We all know we're a mere fleck in the tremendous universal cycle of energy, but no one can abide the thought of their life, lived so intensively and exhaustively, being lost when they die, as swiftly and as meaningless as an unspoken idea.

"I don't mind, Vivien, really I don't. I never used all those things and I don't want the clutter. I feel far better off without it," I say softly, sitting next to her. And I mean it. I found the furniture stressful. I didn't want to look at it for fear it needed cleaning or I'd discover a scratch that I'd not noticed before. Since it's gone so too has the constant tightness in my stomach, and I find the house and the space much more manageable. Vivien drags her hands down her face, smudging her eyes some more, and pushes her lower cheeks up with her fingers, making her mouth a duckbill. She seems to come to some sort of resolution.

"Oh, darling, Ginny." She sighs, more relaxed now. "That was our family's . . . our ancestors' entire collection of furniture, of belongings, of everything. It's taken nearly two hundred years to accumulate."

"I haven't sold any of the moth books. Or any of the specimens, or the equipment," I say quickly, a little too defensive. "The museum and the lab and the other attic rooms haven't been touched."

Vivien nods slowly.

"I forgot. You've always been hopeless with money, haven't you?" she vituperates. "You should have phoned me about it, you really should," she says wearily. She speaks as much to the flagstones on the porch floor, smoothed deliciously wavy with wear, as to me. I don't reply, not because I agree—I don't even have a telephone—but because it seems a good place to end the conversation. And, believe me, I desperately want it to end. I want to salvage our laughter, the excitement and euphoria I felt all too briefly. It's irrelevant, anyway. The furniture has gone because I wanted it to, and I needed the money. It was my choice, and that's that.

Now I'm irritated with myself for becoming defensive. After all, *she* left all those years ago and *she* invited herself back, and now she's disappointed with a decision I made and says I should have phoned her for advice. I remember now how Vivi sometimes patronized me, but I used not to mind. I always accepted that she was worldlier than I and, actually, I quite liked it, as if she was looking out for me. It was part of her color, part of her quality. Now that I'm self-sufficient, now that I've achieved my own goals in life, I find her criticisms more difficult to stomach. I force myself to stop thinking about it. I don't want to ruin our reunion.

I tell her I'm going to make us a cup of tea, then go inside to put the kettle on the Rayburn to boil. We are going to forget about the furniture. We are going to drink tea and talk, reminisce and laugh, and she will tell me funny stories about her life in London. I will sit, listen and relax, live them all through her and we'll laugh again. We are going to catch up, and what a lot of time we have to catch up on! Vivien was right. She was always right. The kettle starts its whistle, faint and hesitant at first. It was her idea for us to live together again and it feels natural that she is back as we near the end of our lives, companions and soul mates, devoted and inseparable. The kettle is now screaming at full steam, shrill and desperate. I slide it off the hot plate.

CHAPTER 4

Belinda's Pot

VIVIEN AND I haven't spoken to each other since our dispute about the furniture. I'm focusing intently on the tea-making process so that I do not have to look up and see her walking back and forth past the open kitchen door talking on her mobile phone, or her driver carrying her boxes and bags from the car into the house and up the stairs. I'm impressed that Vivien has such a phone, that she's kept up with the times like that. I pour until the teapot is a quarter full.

Out of the corner of my eye I see Simon, the small dog, trotting presumptuously into the kitchen. He stops next to me and wrinkles his eyes, ingratiating himself. I ignore him frostily and, accepting that he lacks the skills required to change my opinion of him, he takes himself off to lie by the Rayburn, first circling over his chosen resting place, then flopping to the ground.

Holding the handle in my left hand and moving it in a small circular motion, I swish the water inside the teapot while my right hand cups the outside, high up, waiting to feel the water's heat through the bone china. I study the pattern of small, prettily entwined wildflowers that ramble up from the base to the lid, while willing the swirling water to gain enough momentum to reach up the sides in its circuit inside the pot. To be honest, I have no idea why the china must be warmed or whether the tea really does taste better for it, but it's those little tenets your mother teaches you from an early age, which her mother instilled in her at a similar age, that become the most difficult to let go of in old age.

The teapot is an elegant one, tall rather than fat. Although it was Maud's, we've always called it Belinda's teapot. I don't know the details—I never knew the old woman—but the story went that Belinda had left it to Maud in her will as a way of thanking her for whatever help, advice or listening time Maud had given her, as my mother was naturally predisposed to do. During her lifetime, Maud came to fulfill the role of village consultant and appeaser. It was she who wrote, for instance, requesting more prisoners of war to help bring in the harvest at Peverill's farm and later, she who quelled the uproar when Charlotte Davis's horse was found trampling the graves in St. Bart's churchyard and later still, she who deflected the bloodshed when Michael gave the Axtells' youngest daughter a cannabis cigarette. Maud would counsel, correct and court-martial. She'd offer coffee at Bulburrow after church on Sundays, give a twice-yearly drinks party and open her garden for a week in the summer. Maud loved people. She understood them and liked to surround herself with them, whether to entertain or to help them. Vivi always joked that our mother wouldn't survive without doing things for other people.

All in all, I'd say Maud was a near-faultless woman. She had just the right amount of wisdom and wit and charity. Taller than her husband, she was also the sort of woman who looked elegant in whatever she wore, from her gardening clothes to her dressing gown. She had rows of mid-length floral dresses in her wardrobe, full-length sequined evening wear, long and short boots and hats and gloves for every occasion. Maud loved occasions.

Clive, on the other hand, was neither sociable nor well groomed, but he was not allowed to hide himself away. He trailed along to all the local events and gatherings and would smile wryly when Maud introduced them playfully as "the lady and the tramp." As I said, Maud would be dressed immaculately, while Clive would walk out in one of his two lifelong gray suits, which hung off him from the days when he ate more and were frayed at the collar and cuffs. Sometimes it seemed as if he dressed shabbily on purpose. Once—and I can swear to this—he wore his slippers to a luncheon in the neighboring village. He said there were fewer holes in them than in his shoes, but Maud teased him all afternoon as if she was enjoying his deviance from the social etiquettes she observed so stringently herself. After a few drinks, Maud became the soul of the party, and sometimes I'd see Clive watching her adoringly from afar, entranced by his wife's charm and vitality. But Clive himself—who never drank because he said it gave him gout—was also surprisingly popular, especially with the ladies who mistook his inadvertent nonconformity to be furtive anti-establishment, which excited them in 1950s Dorset society.

I PUT TWO of the new pyramid-style tea bags into Belinda's pot. Michael bought them for me instead of leaves two weeks ago, explaining that the extra effort required in dealing with the loose stuff was unnecessary, these days. My immediate instinct—as you can imagine—was to resist the novelty, but I tried it and found the bags so much easier to handle with the poor grip control I have in my fingers. I used to have such trouble, especially on those mornings when my fingers curl up with pain, in keeping the leaves on the spoon rather than shaking off and skidding all over the counter. Then, when I'd maneuvered as many as I could into the infuser, the trap that stops them free-roaming the pot, I'd fiddle about for several exasperating minutes trying to close the catch to shut the little devils in, only to be given yet more trouble hooking the tiny link over the pot's rim. In the end the strength of the tea was more dependent on my deftness for delivering the leaves into the tea trap, rather than consistent with my own preferences to taste, and often I'd have to start all over again. Now that I've tried the bags I'll never go back to the loose. Michael is trying now to convince me that teapots aren't necessary. I've been pretending I agree with him, to avoid having to discuss it, but between you and me, Michael knows nothing of the satisfaction in the ritual of making tea.

I fill Belinda's pot with boiling water and put on the lid to let it brew. Perhaps today it would have been better to deal with the leaves. I'd have had a longer task to concentrate on, to take my mind off what Vivien is doing and thinking. She's now upstairs making shuffling noises and wandering between the room directly above me and the one over the pantry that used to be her childhood bedroom. Her driver is carrying up the last of her belongings.

I take down two cups and saucers from the dresser and fetch the milk from the fridge, arrange them by the steaming pot and wait. I won't pour the tea until she comes down, or it might get cold.

I'll tell you a strange old thing that I'd never have predicted. I can feel the start of Vivien's and my relationship re-forming again, but—and this is what is odd—it's *exactly* the same as it was half a century ago, as if we've not matured at all, as if our childhood is flooding in and scrabbling to catch up with our old age. Here I am again, leaving the decision with her, waiting for her to judge whether our little altercation is over and to resume our reunion. Vivien sets the rules and the boundaries, she takes the risks, and I'm there waiting for her when she needs me. I'd almost forgotten that that was my role.

Those sisterly boundaries shifted when, two years after Vivi's accident, we were sent to Lady Mary Winsham's School for Girls. Maud gave us a little talk the night before we left for our first term. "I want you to look after each other so that if either of you gets into any sort of difficulty," she said, looking at us sternly, one after the other, "you know that you can go and find your sister and talk about it." As I was the eldest, I was sure she was asking me, especially, to look after Vivi.

Our parents thought that if we started at the same time we'd be a support to each other, but as it turned out, Vivi didn't need my support. While she started at ten in the lower fourth and found herself instantly popular with the forty other new girls, I was the new girl at thirteen, looking for a niche in a long-assembled year group where friendships and alliances had been brokered for three years already.

The school was an hour's journey away, and at the start of each new term, Vivi and I were squashed up with our trunks in Clive's light blue Chester, which he'd converted into a mobile moth-setting station. He'd ripped out the backseats to make way for a setting table that he'd bolted to the floor, so Vivi and I squeezed in on either side of it and worried that our heads might bump if the road got rough. Bottles of bromide, cyanide, ammonia, sodium nitrate and other noxious potions rattled casually in the back, loosely tied into a rack, while nets, traps, pins, scalpels, water baths, corkboards and other essential mothing equipment were arranged neatly in boxes and strapped down elsewhere. By today's standards, Clive would be vilified for carrying such vast quantities of poisons alongside his children on bumpy country roads, but in 1950, Clive's mobile setting station was the envy of his colleagues. It had everything required for killing, anesthetizing, relaxing, color fixing and setting moths when they were fresh from the field so he was able to prepare them before the common problems of wing damage, color change and rigor mortis had time to set in.

Lady Mary's was where well-brought-up girls might "acquire manners, posture and conversation" and a little bit of education. Each week our MPCs (manners, posture and conversation) were graded and suitable punishments set if they were found to have a low average. Even so, during my time there, I never found any evidence of manners in that school. Instead, I was severely subjected to the underhand taunting of an all-girl environment.

The first small incident took place during my second week, when I challenged Alice Hayward who was squishing flies for fun, flies that were desperately vying for freedom through the 5B windows, and I appealed to her to let me open one for them. Within seconds she'd managed to get the whole class laughing at me. The incident instantly marked her out as a leader and sealed my fate, stamping out any hope I might have held of making friends—all because I wouldn't hurt a fly.

I wasn't quick-witted or confident enough to play them at their cruel games. I'd feel the heat rush to my face as I fumbled for a rebuff, and I'd become highly aware of my heavy bottom lip, the position of my hands, of my entire body, and I'd end up looking silly and uneasy. I'd walk away hearing the other girls snigger, and it hurt. I didn't cry, but each time it changed something in me, deep down, shaping who I was and who I would become: each time less confident yet stronger; more insular yet more self-contained.

During the holidays I confided in Maud, who held Clive fully responsible for my not being able to cope with the gibes of other teenage girls. "I'm afraid you've got a bit of your father in you somewhere, darling," she'd say remorsefully. "He's not a fighter either."

Although I loved my father dearly, I didn't see it as a great compliment to be told I'd acquired any of his characteristics. On first impressions, Clive might seem no more than a small, dull man, but once you knew him, he was an interesting sort of dull. He was a uniquely two-dimensional person, either uncommonly interested in things or uncommonly uninterested. For instance, he wasn't interested in food so he wouldn't waste much time on it. He'd eat once a day at most, usually in the evenings, and even then he would often get up halfway through, distracted by a matter of greater importance that had come into his head, such as bleeding the library radiator or planning the order in which the vegetables were to be planted. He was punctilious about those things that interested him, yet completely chaotic with everything else, such as the mess in their bedroom, or a broken window which he'd Sellotape up as a long-term solution.

Maud tried her best to help me overcome the difficulties I had fitting in at school. First, she invested much time and energy persuading me to be proud of myself, giving me the confidence to see my best sides and not worry about what other people might think. She'd hold my face and make me look directly into her eyes, as if to hypnotize me. "Don't you ever forget," she'd threaten, "you're a beautiful, intelligent and kind girl. They're just jealous because it's so rare to be all three." She'd often end with something like "Now you go back out there and show 'em," as if I was acting a part in a play.

Second, she'd do all my fighting for me. She never did it for Vivi—she said Vivien could fight for herself—but if I told her I wasn't happy about something she wouldn't hesitate to glide into the event and, with either charm or aggression, sort it out. Then I was labeled a sneak, which left me with the greater problem of judging what, and what not, to tell her.

Whereas Maud overcompensated for my unpopularity, Vivi clearly couldn't cope with it, so, during term time, I didn't see her much. When we did meet, it would be near the bins behind the changing rooms in the quad, or in the third cubicle in the central loos. Maud had hoped we'd help each other at school but Vivi didn't need any, and I understood that she couldn't possibly offer me the kind of help I needed. I didn't blame her for a minute but I missed her company terribly. Each time we traveled the bumpy country lanes to the far side of the county, packed between the poisons, I was saying goodbye to Vivi as well as to my parents for another term. I yearned for the school holidays when we'd do everything together once more. I never told Maud about Vivi's term-time desertion. Somehow I knew that she would have been devastated to hear of it.

OUTSIDE THE WINDOW I can see the fog creeping in. The light is fading even though it's mid-afternoon.

Vivien and her driver are talking upstairs. I can just about hear their muffled voices. I'm watching one of the last faint ribbons of steam funnel out through the teapot's spout and, I have to say, I've been wondering if she's planning not to come back downstairs at all. I had thought, briefly, of taking the tea up to her but I couldn't possibly. She's on the other side of the landing from my bedroom, through the glass-paned double doors, and I've not been in that part of the house for more than forty years. I doubt I'd even be able to. I wouldn't feel safe. It's not for superstitious reasons, I'm far too levelheaded for that. It's just not what I call the Normal Order of Things. I do like Order.

As the tea is made and I'm lost for anything else to do, I wonder if I go to the pantry and put my head against the door frame, I might be able to hear something of the conversation she's having. I try all sorts of positions and, although I can't hear her very clearly, I gather she's on the phone, a one-sided conversation in which I think she's thanking someone for their help. Her voice tails off as she walks away, her footsteps telling me she's heading down the corridor towards the small bathroom, just left of the landing door. I catch up with her movements as I get to the hallway beneath her and I hear her ask her driver if he'd "reach up for it." I'm surprised to find that as I creep between the two pantries, the back stairwell and the kitchen, straining to hear her movements and the other noises above me, I can visualize a little of what she's up to.

Now someone is coming heavily down the stairs and I hear Vivien shouting "Thank you" from the landing. I've moved back to the teapot and cups, and as the driver passes the kitchen doorway, he pauses, taking a firm hold of the door frame with one hand and leaning into the room. I'm focusing on his hand, wishing he hadn't put it there, thinking I'll have to scrub it pretty hard after he's gone to get him off it. Then I look up and briefly catch his eye. This might sound strange to you, but that fleeting contact unnerves me; I haven't looked a stranger in the eyes for an awfully long time now and it at once feels domineering, intrusive. Does he know I've been listening? Instinctively I drop my gaze to the floor, inherently apologetic, but a moment later I wish I hadn't as his other hand shoots up in a firm, friendly wave, and I realize I've misread him. He calls out cheerily, "Good-bye, then," as he passes. I want to answer but I'm not quick enough. I feel like a little girl again, back at school, waiting for the ridicule, the scorn, and never being fast enough to reply.

Did I tell you it was Maud who taught me the self-control that I desperately needed when I was teased? She told me about that place you can go in your head, a place you can walk into and barricade up so no one can come close and you don't need to listen and you don't get hurt. Of course, I had to learn to hold my breath while I ran down the tunnel away from myself. All I hear is the pounding of my footsteps, and their echoes, echoes of echoes chasing up my heels and the rushing of the dark wind screaming past my ears, blocking out all other sounds. Distant voices merge with the rushing wind; unidentifiable sounds, incomprehensible meanings in a constant faraway flow, like a ball of thunder yelling along the tunnel behind me, collecting and bulking as it rolls, gaining on me in speed and size and momentum. Until at last I reach the end, stepping into a room of my own, heaving the door closed behind me, shutting out the rushing wind, the ball of noise, the cascade of footsteps and echoes and nonsense. Safe and secure, I can bolt the door slowly. Confidently. One iron rod at a time, from top to bottom, slamming them firmly into their catches, unrushed and unflustered. There's an infinite number of bolts, so I am able to slide across as many as I want to give me the comfort I need in hearing them snap shut, one by one, until finally, when I'm alone, all I can hear is my own serenity. I have found composure. Peace. I can breathe again, silently and calmly. And I can check: Has it stopped? Have they gone?

I wait and listen to the car as the door is slammed, the engine starts and it purrs off along the drive, leaving Vivien and me alone. I hear the car reach the end of the drive, stop, then turn left into the lane, its engine straining up the steep hill and briefly becoming louder again as, at the top, the lane curves nearer to the house. Then it's gone, and as I glance out of the window, I see I am unable to make out the beech hedge just four yards away. The house is stranded in thick fog. And, apart from the sonorous ticking of the two hall clocks, silence.

Normally I would have welcomed this fog, by no means uncommon in the Bulburrow valley. As it swallows the house, it makes me feel safe, a blanket of warmth and security, asylum from the rest of the world. But today, it doesn't seem to bring me its usual solace, as if isolating Vivien and me from the rest of the world has made our own separation more stark. The thing is, I'm just not used to knowing someone else is sharing this house with me and, it might seem absurd to you, but I'm finding it most distracting. My concentration has shifted from its solitary focus on my life, to what each of us is doing in relation to the other. I could quite easily convince myself that Vivien and I are alone on this world, inextricably linked—nothing else exists and the other is our only hope of refuge. I'm waiting to hear her walking, talking, shuffling, anything, but I hear nothing. I'm transfixed by the silence, staring at the stagnant fog outside, empty of thoughts, existing in stillness, in a space somewhere else.

IT'S JUST AFTER four o'clock when I hear a lorry pull up outside the house. Vivien never came down to drink her tea. I wander into the library—with its walls of bare shelves—where I'll have a better view from the window, and finally hear Vivien on her way downstairs. Like an apparition through the fog I see the outline of a small lorry and can just about make out the hazy black lettering on the side, R & S FURNISHINGS, CHARD. Two young men jump down from either side of the cab, screech open the tailgate and carry a small single bed, in pieces, into the house and up to Vivien's room. Then they collect a small table, a basic rack to hang clothes on, two lamps—one of which they bring back and return to the van—and some other things that I can't see clearly. I spend the entire time listening and distracted, uncharacteristically preoccupied with a growing need to know what's going on.

They stay upstairs for a while, and from my listening post at the bottom of the back stairs I can hear them doing what I suppose is putting the bed together, muffled voices talking and, at intervals, laughing. I can't quite catch what is being said, but I feel strangely compelled to stay and listen until well after I hear the men leaving in their van.

"GINNY, DARLING, there you are," Vivien announces as she strolls into the library a while later. "I fell asleep earlier. Utterly zonked," she says. "It must be the country air." She's behaving as if she doesn't realize she's stood me up for tea. Perhaps she doesn't? I've forgotten how exhausting I find it to predict other people's frame of mind or to assess their general humor.

After my moment of thought, I say, "It's probably this house. I'm always falling asleep during the day."

"Well, we're up now. What do you say we make pizza? I've bought some bases and lots of different things to go on top. . . ." She fades as she walks back into the kitchen with me following. Should I have thought of what we'd have for supper tonight, her first night? How did she know I hadn't?

I've never made pizza before. In fact, I don't recall eating it either, although something holds me back from telling Vivien that. Her furniture outburst was such a surprise, I'm not so certain now how she might react. Privately, I'm thrilled we're having pizza. I've seen it so often on the leaflets that come and I've always wanted to try it. We spend as fun an evening as I can remember, deciding whether olives go best with ham or with mushrooms—or both—and how much cheese is needed. We also discuss our hands—she's got arthritis too, but not yet as severely as me—curious to inspect each other's, almost competitive to claim the harder time of them, and we exhaust the comparisons of pain and pain relief with which we've learned to live. We agree that we can't do buttons and that zippers are so much easier, and what we really need is a shoe horn with a really long handle so we don't have to bend over when putting on our shoes. She tells me she takes an aspirin every day, which her doctor told her keeps the knuckles symmetrical, and she promises to give me some anti-inflammatories she's been prescribed.

So we fuss and fiddle about hands, feet and pizza, all very pleasantly, and then we eat pizza, pleasantly too, sitting in lazy chairs in the small study behind the kitchen, warmed by a fire we've lit in the hearth and by the company we're offering each other. But now here's something surprising—neither of us refers to the missing furniture, or asks each other any of the more searching questions we know there's plenty of time to ask later. For instance, why it is now, after all these years, that she's decided to come home?

CHAPTER 5

The Monster, the Thief and Pupal Soup

TWO DAYS AFTER my sixth birthday I found a monster of a caterpillar among some dead leaves on the second terrace of our south gardens. He was extraordinary: as fat as a shrew and twice the length of my finger, mostly an apple green but splattered with blotches of white, purple and yellow, with a shiny black, sharply hooked tail. I watched him for a while, as I thought Clive would do. He looked gorged, fit to burst, taut in some places but flabby in others, and even then, at six, I realized he had the most unusual manner.

I'd seen the way caterpillars behaved normally on open ground. Prime and juicy targets for birds, they race purposefully along, stopping only sometimes to rear up on their hind legs as if to peer about, surveying the area for the direction of their next meal. My caterpillar, however, was sluggish, heaving himself across the ground oddly, first in one direction, then another, and when he tried to rear he'd get halfway up before his great, torpid body would come slapping down to the ground, exhausted by the effort. He was going nowhere and finally I scooped him up, together with the leaves he was on, and put him into the front of my jumper, which I'd shaped into a pouch. Holding the jumper with both hands, I ran back to the house to show my father.

Just as I got to his study door I stopped, so entranced was I to see that the creature was rearing up at me in a display, stretching itself to its full five inches and waving its legs, dancing in a sudden fit of writhing energy. Then, even as I stared at it—you're going to have to believe me—I began to see bulbous warts rising up along the length of its back, swelling and bubbling like thick boiling treacle, and within a minute I counted eight. Then the warts began to seep.

I've never been more afraid, before or since, and I was still riveted to the spot, holding my jumper stretched out in front of me, when Clive came out of his study. He saw me staring down, my face pale with horror, as if I were watching my insides spill out of my stomach. He peered over me. "Where did you find him?" he asked, neither alarmed by its appearance nor delighted.

"Underneath the lilac," I whispered, not taking my eyes off it lest the revolting creature start to shimmy up my jumper. Clive straightened and, rather than help by taking the damn thing off me, he started into one of his lectures.

"It's a Privet Hawk-moth caterpillar," he said. "They also like lilac. And ash. It wants to pupate and that's why you found it on the ground, rather than on the bush—"

"No, it's not," I interrupted sternly, astonished that an expert like Clive was unable to see the difference. "I've seen lots of Privet Hawks," I said, stretching my jumper to get it as far away as possible. Clive had even bred some in the attic last year. "And they're green with purple, white and yellow stripes," I said, "not blotches. And they're smooth, not lumpy."

"Well, that's why this one's so interesting," he said as, at last, he gently retrieved it from my jumper in a silver serving spoon. "He's shivering, he's sweating, and look"—Clive unfixed a needle from where he kept it in his lapel and pointed with it at some slime by the creature's anus—"he's got diarrhea," he said, smiling at me. He took it into his study and I hoped he might throw it in the fire, but instead he returned a moment later, carrying it in a biscuit tin lined with moss and covered with glass. He sat me on the stairs outside his study and put the tin on my lap so I could watch the caterpillar through the glass.

"If you want to see something interesting, don't take your eyes off it," he instructed.

I sat on the stairs outside Clive's office with the tin on my lap, entranced for the next two hours. The caterpillar gradually darkened and soon I watched it spontaneously rip itself apart, starting behind its head and continuing to split itself open, right down between its eyes, the skin on both sides falling away to reveal the shiny mahogany pupa underneath. As the skin continued to fall off, pairs of legs, a moment ago walking, became instantly inanimate, hanging down limply, a discarded costume. There was nothing unusual about that—I'd seen caterpillars pupate many times before—but it was midway through when I began to see something new. The caterpillar's shiny new underskin started to burst all over in tiny little uprisings, one at a time, a gash here, a gash there, and then all over, and out of the holes popped the writhing, tapered heads of a totally different creature's larvae, tiny translucent maggots hungrily eating their way out of the caterpillar, devouring the body alive, from within. I continued to watch, transfixed by the most sordid feast you could imagine, as these small larvae not only gorged themselves on caterpillar but also ferociously cannibalized one another whenever they met.

Before long those larvae, in turn, had pupated and the biscuit tin was swarming with flies under the glass, the huge body of the once Privet Hawk caterpillar half devoured by the flies' forgotten forebears. Later Clive told me they were ichneumon flies, that their mother had stabbed the skin of the caterpillar and laid her eggs within it, so that when they hatched they wouldn't be short of food. The caterpillar had become a living hamper.

Well, that momentous event at six years old thrilled and disgusted me so much that I have been fascinated by these creatures ever since. The moths didn't interest Vivi so it was always me, rather than her, who volunteered to help Clive during the busiest times of the year and it was me, rather than Vivi, who followed him into the profession. Clive often told me that I'd make a great lepidopterist. "It's in your veins," he would say. "Nobody can take that away from you."

It turned out he was right. But it wasn't until a few years later, at Maud's annual harvest drinks party, that I understood it was my vocation. I've always been taciturn and have never liked parties, so Maud, as usual, set me up offering people nuts from a tall glass dish and there I was, satelliting the room, hoping to be ignored. Even then I found eye contact with anyone outside of my family almost unbearable so, as I stuck out the dish for each little group of guests, I stared at the hands coming in to appropriate the nuts as if I was monitoring their takings.

When I came to Mrs. Jefferson, the rector's wife, I recognized her instantly from the waist down. She was a rotund, weatherworn, boot-and-skirt kind of woman who, when she had an opinion, let it be known. She would have thought it rude to ignore me, so, while she took four nuts in her fingertips, she asked what I was going to do when I grew up. I liked Mrs. Jefferson, and of course I would always have answered her, but I had no idea what I wanted to do when I grew up. I'd never thought about it. I was still studying the delicate frosted rim of the glass dish, searching for my answer, when Maud cut across me—she often talked for me—and said, "This one? She's going to follow in her father's footsteps."

Mrs. Jefferson bent down so I had to step back a little to give her room. "So it's moths then, is it, Virginia?" she asked at my ear level.

Is it? I thought.

"Yes, moths," Maud answered resolutely from above us.

Mrs. Jefferson straightened and I went on to offer my nuts to a huddle of people by the window.

From that day on everyone seemed to know that that's what I was going to do. Maud, having said it, had cast the future in stone. Many years later, when Vivi and I were expelled from Lady Mary's, it was a foregone conclusion, an undisputed assumption by everyone, even me, that I'd become my father's apprentice.

Vivi was fifteen when she was expelled for pilfering bananas from a box beside the fruit delivery van as it dropped off supplies to the school kitchens. She tried to argue that she simply had them a little earlier than she would otherwise but Miss Randal, the head, saw it differently. Randy had worked out that this must have been a long-term plan, with Vivi timing the delivery each week and taking notes of the man's progress as he went in and out with boxes. Vivi was not only a thief (Randy said you either are or you aren't, it's part of you, like your nose shape) but it was a premeditated heist and there was only a cursory difference between this and a bank robbery (one leading to the other sooner or later). It was all about principle, Randy said. She made Vivi stand up in morning assembly in front of the entire school and say ten times, "I'm a thief." Vivi thought it was funny but I cried for her in the back row and at the hopeless injustice of it all.

Maud received the letter expelling her lying, thieving daughter on a Monday morning and by lunchtime, having hurtled through much of the West Country's narrow, high-hedged lanes, she was banging on Randy's door and making such a fuss that Ruby Morris came running to class 6M to tell me that my mother was trying to kill the staff.

What happened next, and why I was also expelled, I'll never know the truth of. Maud said she'd been so enraged by the abominable way Vivi had been treated that she'd taken me away too, as a sort of punishment to them, she said. But Miss Randal told me that thieving was inherent and that the same characteristic might possibly show itself in me too, at some point, and it was part of her job to protect the school against the inevitability of future occurrences. When I looked unconvinced she told me that, if I wanted to know the truth, I was only there in the first place because Vivi was there. We'd come as a package, she said, so we'd have to go as one.

I was in her office and she was standing with her right fist on her desk as she spoke, her arm locked straight like a fulcrum for her stocky body, swaying back and forth with the pressure of a long and troublesome morning. Behind her hung a vast print of an oil painting, an elephant charging at full pace out of the canvas, and I was just waiting for it to hurry up and mow her down.

When I told Maud about Randy's sister package, she went berserk, said it was nonsense, that she'd never heard such tripe, and after that she swore rather a lot whenever Miss Randal was mentioned. Then she lectured me about how clever I was and what a lot I had going for me, which, I have to say, both my parents did frequently. They never seemed to offer the same compliments to Vivi.

What surprised me most was that Maud wasn't at all cross with Vivi for stealing the fruit in the first place. She said that seeing some bananas in a box outside school kitchens and helping yourself without asking was hardly an expellable crime. She accused Miss Randal of trying to find any excuse to get rid of us. She said the school was prejudiced.

So, according to the school, I was expelled too, but to the family I'd left in protest and in allegiance with my little sister. It's one of my most glorious memories.

Clive had said we didn't need any more schooling; we were clever enough as we were, so I knew that, after the long summer, I would at last become Clive's apprentice.

I haven't made many active choices in my life—I'm not that sort of a person—and I've never resisted anything that life's thrown at me, or even thought to steer it in a particular direction. I'm one of the lucky ones who are carried along and life falls into place by itself. It was as if my eventual success was printed at the beginning of time in the universe's voluminous manuscript, a very small part of the wider big-bang/collapsing-star theory. I was always going to be famous, even if I'd tried to resist it. Did I tell you I'm actually quite a famous lepidopterist?

Mrs. Jefferson would never have predicted it. Vivi was supposed to be the one to make something of the life she nearly lost when she was eight, not me. I just fell into it, and now my name will be heard for many years to come, whispered through the corridors of one eminent institution or other, citing my papers or my expertise in practical experimentation, the insight of my deductions or the acuity of my hypotheses. I hope you don't think me immodest to imagine that those praises would now have spread around the world within the most highly regarded entomology circles, in all the leading universities, societies and other elite academic establishments. Even here, in the small farming community of Bulburrow, they've heard of my reputation. I believe that here I am commonly known as the Moth Woman—after my late father, the Moth Man.

CLIVE DID NOT FOLLOW directly in his father-in-law's footsteps. The way I saw it, Clive was the first of a new breed of lepidopterist. He was *not* a collector and did not wish to be regarded as one. Collectors want to complete a collection. Some want to pin all the species to be found within an area, others want just one species, but from all parts of the country, while others still are rarity hunters. As long as the specimens can be grouped together in some sort of unified classification and the quantity in that categorization is a finite number, then, without doubt, that group will be collected.

Clive's goal was different from that of his colleagues. He didn't care about collections and—between you and me—he didn't care much for the insects either. Clive wanted to find out how nature worked. He was concerned with all nature, but he had chosen the moth as the subject of his research because, he said, it is an ancient animal whose evolutionary pathway is much older even than that of a butterfly, which, in biomechanical terms, is a lot more sophisticated. He wanted to know how a moth ticked, how all its intricate little processes make the thing live, die, breed, eat, move, molt and metamorphose.

There was a fundamental difference between the way that the collectors and Clive (and those like myself who came after him) studied these insects. Collectors have one goal in common: they are looking for the perfect unadulterated specimen, with flawless markings and anatomical composition. An insect with an aberration, say a spot too few or a spot too many, or any other imperfection or handicap, would be discarded at once. The point is, my sick Privet Hawk caterpillar, the one that I found on my third day of being six, would have been thrown, by a *collector,* straight into the fire in disgust.

To find out what makes a moth *a moth* it wasn't the perfect specimens Clive was attracted to. He appreciated earlier than all of them—Thomas Smith-Ford, Robin Doyle and the D'Abbrette brothers—way back in that slow postwar era, that it was nature's *imperfections* that we needed to study to discover the secret codes of inheritance and genetics and other biological mechanisms. Clive used to say you find out more about a machine when the machine goes wrong and, to him, that's pretty much what a moth was—a little robot that one day could be reduced to its biomechanics, a formulaic equation; every little piece could be pulled apart and laid out on the table, rather like the pieces in a construction kit. He wanted the moth's entire formula, such as

$$5x + 2y + 11z + \textit{(all other constituents)} = Moth$$

Clive was going to unpick a moth like a cross-stitch jumper, so while perfect insects weren't of the slightest interest to him, he became unbearably excited by a Six-spot Burnet with five spots, a wingless Fox Moth or tailless Lobster Moth, a blind Oak Eggar, a tongueless Convolvulus Hawk (which, I should mention, is a frequent deformity in that species). If you could work out, he said, how they'd gone wrong, you'd discover a lot more about how nature worked.

While most lepidopterists concentrated on breeding the perfect insect, Clive concentrated on breeding the perfect freak. Clive and I designed and manufactured more cripples than I can remember. Between our lengthy careers, we've set hundreds, perhaps thousands, of "malfunctional conditions," as I like to call them, during spring, when we'd dedicate a whole attic room to experimenting with deformities. Sometimes we'd set out with a specific goal, such as to create a particular aberration of the Lime Hawk, but often we'd just play around with adverse conditions and record the deformities that resulted from them, looking for patterns and clues to some of nature's secrets. Like an unapparent god, we've transformed their entire winters, or changed the conditions during their time of emergence, giving them early summers, late frosts, flash floods. We've used Vaseline to bung up their spiracles, blocking off their oxygen, pierced their horny casings, frozen them through winter, emerged them in unnatural spectrums of light. We've dipped, sprinkled or soaked them in every combination of every chemical from our lab, sliced off their wing cases, removed their twigs, their moss or their mud. Maud thought cripple experimentation was a sick sideshow of scientific perversion, and Vivi called it the Frankenstein Room.

A moth is such a simple machine in the animal world—the go-kart to the modern car—and it takes a lot of glitches to prevent it going. It's this intriguing simplicity, the idea that you could pull it into its constituent parts and put it back together in the same rainy day, that if you pulled back the skin, you could watch the inner workings, that makes a moth such an absorbing creature to study. Moths have a universal character: there are no individuals. Each reacts to a precise condition or stimulus in a predictable and replicable way. They are preprogrammed robots, unable to learn from experience. For instance, we know they will always react to a smell, a pheromone or a particular spectrum of light in the same way. I can mimic the scent of a flower so that a moth will direct itself towards the scent, even if I have made sure that in doing so it goes headlong into a wall and kills itself. Each time each moth will kill itself. It is this constancy that makes them a scientific delight—you do not need to factor in a rogue element of individuality.

Although a moth is complex enough to be a challenge, it is not too complex to imagine success at every stage. Reducing bits and pieces of it to a near molecular level, a series of spontaneous reactions, Clive convinced himself that it wouldn't be long before we'd be able to predict all their equations of cause and effect, then perhaps even map out each and every cell, and configure them in their entirety as robots, in terms of molecules, chemicals and electrical signals. So, in Clive's compulsive mind, it was not so unbelievable that one day, not too far in the future, we would know their complete chemical formula. And what fed this particular obsession was Pupal Soup.

If you cut through a cocoon in mid-winter, a thick creamy liquid will spill out, and nothing more. What goes into that cocoon in autumn is a caterpillar and what comes out in spring is entirely different—a moth, complete with papery wings, hairlike legs and antennae. Yet this same creature spends winter as a gray-green liquid, a primordial soup. The miraculous meltdown of an animal into a case of fluid chemicals and its exquisite re-generation into a different animal, like a stupendous jigsaw, was a feat that, far from putting him off, fed Clive's obsession. He believed it made his lifetime ambition easier because, however complex it might be, it was, after all, *only* a jigsaw, and to Clive, that meant it was possible. For all the chemicals required to make a moth were right there, in front of his eyes, in the Pupal Soup, as he called it, inside the horny casing of a cocoon. His fixation with the obscurity of a cocoon's contents peaked each winter and led him to endless hours in the attic dissecting and extracting the biochemical formulas for as many compounds as he could find contained within the cocoon and its changing molecular state during transmutation.

I think, in the end, the chemical composition of Pupal Soup crazed him, consumed him and eventually overran him. You see, Clive was in no doubt that he had been put on this earth to discover something, to educate us, to bring the world on in some way. It was inconceivable to him that his existence had no greater purpose, that it could be as worthless as he considered the lives of the creatures he studied. My family was fanatical. They all seemed to be consumed by something in the end.

SATURDAY

CHAPTER 6

Methodology

I'M AWAKE AGAIN, for the second or even third time tonight. Perhaps I never got back off. Nights, for me, are an endless enterprise of waking and half waking and wandering the landing in pursuit of sleep. I dread the start of them, knowing the lengthy path of insomnia I have to tread for the next eight hours. I only wish there were a clearly defined pattern, but instead it's made worse by its endless unpredictability: lying still, convincing myself I haven't *come to* yet, that I'm still drifting in a dream and can slip back there if only I shut out any wakeful thoughts; or getting up and out of bed, pacing the landing in search of the weariness that comes so naturally during the daylight hours; or trying to tire myself with things other than the worries of sleeplessness.

I heard the bell in the night, louder and clearer than ever before—and there it goes again, although I can't tell if it's real. Sometimes when a storm's up, I'll hear it even though it hangs on the other side of the house, not sounding like a gong, but a distant tinkling as the stick inside it glances the edge now and then. At other times I'll hear it in my sleep or when the air outside is calm and still. Then I know it's not the real bell, but the faint, relentless ringing in my ears, the reverberation of that single strike still trapped, rebounding in my head from when I was eleven, diminishing but never ceasing, never allowing itself to be fully absorbed; the strike I heard as I watched her fall.

I cannot bear to hear it. I find it helps to think positive thoughts like reminding myself of what I am good at, what I have a reputation for. Did I tell you I'm a fairly famous—yes, I think I can say *famous*—scientist?

This night has been unusually restless. First, I've woken up exhausted, as if sleeping and resting have made me even more tired. Second, my head has been invaded by a surge of long-forgotten memories that have scratched their way to the surface and crowded the front of my mind. As a rule, I don't like to dwell on the past. I've always thought that as soon as the past is permitted to fill more of your thoughts than the here and now, it precipitates old age. But I can tell you that since Vivien arrived yesterday I'm remembering things that happened half a century ago so much more clearly than what I did last week, as if her presence has given them the courage to crawl out of the past. I've thought of things I haven't considered again since they happened. Nothing of any significance, and often just fleeting, unrecognizable moments vying for my attention and becoming exhaustingly tangled and disordered in my mind. My childhood, my family, school, and then there are the games I've just remembered I used to play with Dr. Moyse, card games he'd made up himself. I can't tell you if it was real or something I'd dreamed, but I remember how the memories of it plagued me. I sense we played often. Different times, different places: in the kitchen and it's sunny outside; wrapped up in a rug in the drawing room while it's hailing or snowing; on the sofa in the library. I don't say it, but the games are a bit boring and Vivi's never allowed to play. It's private. She's not even allowed to watch. Maud brings me biscuits, she ruffles my hair, she looks over our shoulders.

Even though I know Dr. Moyse thought I wasn't very good at the games, he always enjoyed them more than I did.

IT FEELS LIKE Vivien's been home for ages, but she arrived only yesterday afternoon, precisely fifteen hours and thirteen minutes ago. I heard her during the night, twice I think. I'm sure I heard her go to the kitchen and then the kettle whistled so I can only assume she made herself a cup of tea. Milky tea, I've noticed. I couldn't possibly drink it the way she likes it, it's hardly got a hint of color. I wonder if Vivien is as restless as I am during the nights, and if one day we'll meet on one of our nighttime excursions and discover another trait that we share. Twisted fingers and night rambling. All I know is that, according to my bedside clock, she got up at 12:55 to make the tea, and then again at 3:05 when she went to the lavatory or, rather, when she'd finished in the lavatory. I didn't hear her get up that time, but from my bed I heard the water gushing along the landing pipes once she'd pulled the flush, as it raced to join the downpipe in my bathroom.

I REACH FOR my bedside clock, depressing the lime-green button on the top to illuminate it. It says 5:03 amid the ghoulish fluorescent glare of its face. A welcome advancement in the night. Any time past four-thirty and I feel I'm on the home stretch, that I will soon have the dawn to watch and listen to, propelling me to the start of the day. But before four-thirty I know I must try to take myself away from my conscious self once more before the night is over.

I may already have mentioned it, but I'm very keen on time. I never used to be, but as I've grown older I've realized how essential it is. Keeping time, being on time and knowing the time. I live by it. Time and order. All things have order and people should be ordered, and I find that in most instances order requires some element of time.

I have six clocks: a watch on each wrist (digital on the left and dial on the right), a bedside clock, a ship's clock in the kitchen, a longcase and a bracket clock in the hall (which both lose time, up to four minutes a week, and need to be reset and wound on Sundays). I like knowing I can find the exact time whenever I want to and, if I can't, it unsettles me and I worry about the next time Michael might come so I can check it. It can be a couple of weeks between his visits and I don't always see him. Michael's only ever been in the flagstoned areas of the house—the kitchen and the pantries—and he always comes in via the courtyard at the back, never through the front door. It's not my rule—it must be his own—but if I'm upstairs resting he won't disturb me, and I might miss him.

We all have our idiosyncrasies, especially at my age. Some people— on approaching old age—fear senility, others immobility, memory loss, confusion, madness. What I fear is timelessness, a lack of structure in my life, an endless Now.

IN THE HALF-LIGHT, I can just begin to make out the few shapes in my bedroom: the stripped pine chest with four deep drawers that I keep a change of clothes in; the mahogany bedside table (with drawer), which has almost finished shedding its veneer; and an old wicker nursing chair, white, which once had a green-and-white-striped cushion. It stands just outside the bathroom door, but facing the wall because I use the high back as a resting post on my trip from my bed to the bathroom on those mornings that I can't manage it in one go. The only other thing in here is this huge oak bed I'm in, which I inherited from Maud and Clive, high to my waist and with Gothic claws for feet.

The light is racing in now through the row of mullioned windows lining the south wall ahead. New tendrils on the Virginia creeper are in eerie silhouette, pointing at me with young, fresh attitude. It's exhausting having to watch them, all curled up like a chameleon's tongue, ready to unfurl and pounce towards the next foothold in their spring invasion of my room. Five diamond panes of glass from the top of the far right window (directly opposite my bed) are now smashed or have fallen out of their leads. I didn't see it happen. I just woke up one day last winter with an extra draft running through the room. It's as if all the elements of nature have come together to work slowly—imperceptibly even—on an old untended building to bring about its climatic downfall, with the rain and frost and wind somehow ensuring entry for invading plants.

IT'S TWO MINUTES PAST seven when I hear the faint squeak of the sprung double doors that separate her landing from mine, followed by their whisper as they pass each other on the backswing. In my mind's eye I see Vivien descending the stairs and, knowing where they creak, I judge her speed and her progress. A moment later I hear the water pipes banging and thudding round the house, as they do when you first turn on the cold tap in the kitchen. It's strange, after all these years, to have someone else in the house, and I'm too tired to get up and join her, too tired to negotiate another person.

I'm always tired during the day. Sometimes, more often in winter, I'll stay in bed all day, quite happy thinking my thoughts, undisturbed and unnoticed. Of course, the next day I'll pay for it arthritically. The flexibility of my joints each morning, I've noticed, and the pain within them, are directly proportional to the amount of exercise they had the day before, in the order of more exercise, less pain. And the weather, of course—the surges and the seasons, they all announce themselves deep within my joints. I swear I'm able to feel pressure changes long before the mercury, and my predictions never fall short. But my instinct for the weather is more than a physical modification. I've spent a lifetime necessarily predicting it as part of my profession—a moth's life is finely tuned to the forthcoming weather, and often it's the habits of the moths themselves that give me the first and most infallible indicator of an approaching squall or drought.

Even though outside all I can see now is a blanket of low cloud, believe me, I can feel that spring's on its way again, full of renewed energy.

. . .

THERE'S A KNOCK at my door.

"Morning," Vivien says, and without waiting for an invitation she busies round the door with two cups of tea on a tray. She flagrantly surveys the privacy of my bedroom. "I won't draw the curtains then," she says.

"There aren't any curtains."

She laughs throatily, then swallows it suddenly. "It was a joke, Ginny," she whispers.

Of course it was a joke. I'm quite surprised I didn't pick it up. I haven't joked for a long time.

"You really have lived on your own for too long," she says, as if she'd read my thoughts. Her face is neatly made up once again. Maud tried to teach me how to apply makeup, but I never understood why it was necessary. She used to say she felt naked without it, and I never once saw her venture farther than her bedroom with natural lips. They were always rose red.

"I've brought you some tea," Vivien says. I think of the tea as a peace offering, the furniture forgotten. She stops in the middle of the room and for a moment I think she's staring at me, but as I sit up, I realize she's not. She's studying the bed, the tall oak headboard behind me, blackened by years of polishing, with its heavy octagonal corner posts and fleur-de-lis finials. It's one of the very few old bits of furniture left and, though I agree that Maud and Clive's old bed is outlandish, I must say it's incredibly comfortable. It's very difficult to give up a bed you get used to.

"Where shall I put it?" she says, jerking her attention back to the tray in her hand.

"Anywhere."

"You need some more surfaces," she remarks vaguely, as she walks around the bed to put the tray on the bedside table on the other side. Then she sweeps her hand along the top of the chunky headboard and regards the fluffy dust collected on her palm. She pulls a disgusted face. "You might not like mess, Ginny, but you don't mind *flup*," she says, reminding me of Vera's pet word for dust and rubbing the flup onto her dressing gown. "I'll have to give the house a good clean sometime. Did you sleep well?"

"I kept thinking of things we used to do when we were children, things I'd forgotten," I say.

"Oh. I hope it was fun."

"It was," I agree. "But then I remembered playing card games with Dr. Moyse."

"Card games?"

"Yes, where me and Dr. Moyse are—"

But Vivien interrupts. "Goodness me!" she exclaims. "You're not still having those peculiar dreams about Dr. Moyse, are you?"

"I haven't thought about them for years actually."

"Well, I am sorry," she says, as she sits down heavily on the end of my bed. I'm slightly shocked. She did it without thinking, as if it had come naturally, but it's not as if I've had anyone sitting on my bed for the last forty-something years. I can't work out whether I like it or not. I want her to be there, but I can't help wondering how long it's going to take me to straighten the sheets. I'm finicky about sheets.

Vivien scours the empty bedroom that was once our parents'. It's a lovely room, south-facing, with tall ceilings and an oak floor that slopes west with age, so I've had to stuff three old *British Countryside* magazines under the bed legs to level it. Back then it was far from sparse. It was chock-a-block with antique furniture, paintings and photo frames, gilded mirrors, bowls of potpourri and varnished gourds, a stuffed sea-bird collection on a shelf above the picture rail, untidy clothes and all sorts of clutter.

The windows, now bare, were once dressed with thick green silk curtains, and the large burgundy snowflakes, which danced boldly across the wallpaper, have now faded pink, embellished under the width of the sills and in the corners of the room by a series of water-marks, as though a dog's been scenting his patch. In places the paper is peeling off altogether, exposing damp powdery plaster that every so often becomes unstable and comes crashing down in a great plaster avalanche. It's not an uninteresting pastime, looking at the progression of the damp through the walls, the peeling of the ceiling paint and the marching of the creeper up the wall and in through the window.

"Do you remember the chandelier?" Vivien asks, looking up at the lonely brass hook hanging down from the center of an ornate wreath of leaves and roses, the climax of the ceiling's plasterwork.

Even for such a grand bedroom the chandelier was enormous, raining shafts of providence into the room, collecting light from the windows and splitting it, directing it, combining and reflecting it, not shy to exercise its mastery of the laws of refraction. Maud had taken it from the even larger and grander drawing room downstairs, where she'd rightly thought it was hardly noticed and when, she'd said, the fashion was to have side lamps. Maud liked statements, not understatements.

"Don't you miss it?" Vivien adds, but before I have a chance to tell her I don't, she carries on, "Remember how Maud let us lie in here when we were ill? I spent hours gazing up at that chandelier, imagining that all the sparkly light was helping me get better."

"Were you? I was always thinking it was about to fall on me," I say. "I spent all the time watching the hook at the top, trying to work out if it was close to giving way. Exhausting." I sigh. "What about their fake-fur bedspread? Do you remember it?"

"Oh, that thing," she says. "Horrid. I'm very glad you got rid of that. I always thought it was crawling with lice."

Maud had been comfortable amid her clothes and clutter, so the room, like the rest of the house, was grand and shabby at the same time, full of warmth and belonging. Clive, being more of an exacting personality, had learned to ignore the mess or, rather, being on the verge—as he always was—of many important scientific discoveries, he preferred not to consider it.

BOTH MY PARENTS said they knew, the instant they met, that they were right for each other, even though, more often than not, they seemed complete opposites. When Maud's father enlisted a keen young chemist called Clive Stone as his new apprentice, by all accounts, Maud and Clive spent the following year conducting a clandestine relationship. When they married, my grandfather retired and, his wife having died some years before from tuberculosis, moved lustily to one of his hunting grounds—Brazil—where he lived out the rest of his days in pursuit of rare butterflies and beautiful women. Clive moved into his father-in-law's place, taking over the advancement of our knowledge of the moth world within the attics, cellars and outbuildings of Bulburrow Court. Maud sometimes teased him, saying he'd married the attic and got her thrown in too, considering the amount of time he squirreled himself away there.

They said it was their love of conservation—long before it became a fashionable affair—that brought them together, but I think even that they came at from very different directions. Maud loved nature. Each and every animal and plant was to be cherished and the miracle of nature something to be preserved. She was a pioneer of conservation and recognized, even in the 1930s, that, rather than assuming nature could take care of itself, we needed to assist the natural world by cultivating and planting natural habitats. Of all these, she spent the most time caring for her meadows and would discuss them at length with the gardeners: when to cut and where to shake the seeds, the grasses that were taking over and needed to be culled. Now and again she'd come home from the other side of the county, having procured some hay bales that contained the seeds of a new species she wanted, like wild carrot or yellow rattle, or a new type of dropwort. Then, on a windless day, she'd stomp around the meadows shaking the hay about, trying to infiltrate the grass with them.

Clive wasn't so much fond of nature as fascinated by it, as though he wanted to preserve the miracle just so he could unravel it. Together they transformed Bulburrow's gardens and grounds into an ecological haven, creating every possible type of habitat—marsh and meadow, wood and downland, heath and bog—and, over the years, stocked them with birch and alder and willow, elm, lime, poplar and plum, hawthorn, honeysuckle, blackthorn and privet. Every inch was given over to something that a moth, a caterpillar or a pupa might find useful or appetizing.

So the giants of the family, the great Hawk-moths, were enticed with limes for the Lime Hawk, pines for the Pine Hawk, poplars and aspen for the Poplar Hawk, and for the Privet Hawks, privet, ash and lilac. The eleven acres of meadow that ran from the gardens to the brook were assiduously laid out for grass lovers like the Ermines and The Drinker, whose black hairy caterpillars could easily be heard on warmer spring mornings noisily sucking the dew off the tall grasses. By the brook, bog plants were introduced to feed the Gold Spot and The Shark, willows were given over to the Kittens and the Puss, while copses and pockets of woodland, glades of ancient beech, elm and oak held the homes of the Lobster and the Scalloped Hazel, the Peppered and the Goat. Orchards of plums and pears were nurtured, not for their fruit but for the leaves that tempted caterpillars of the Grey Dagger, the Magpie and other fruit-tree lovers, and up on the ridge to the north you'd have found the brightly striped orange-and-black Cinnabar caterpillars in their thousands, and the Lappet, Yellow-tail, Sallow and Angle Shades flitting and fluctuating over willowherb and ragwort, bindweed and dock in the warmth of their short summer lives.

The fields were left wild and unkempt, smothered with weeds, and hedgerows a mess with sallow and bedstraw, brambles and sloe. A disgrace to a farmer but a haven for those species like the Prominents, the Tussock and the Eggars, whose ebbing existence is greatly worried by the taming of the countryside. And the suburban garden species were not forgotten. The formal terraces to the south were sculpted and manicured with lilac, buddleia and sweet-scented tobacco, urns of Mediterranean geranium and oleander, petunia and fuchsia, vine and balsam, all designed in the hope of sighting the Garden Tiger, the Elephant Hawk, the Dot, the Dark Dagger or the extensive tongue of the Convolvulus stealing nectar from the pink-tinged trumpets of the plant after which it is named. Even that rampant creeper outside my bedroom window, which in autumn paints the south wall a deep, aristocratic red, was planted primarily in the hope of encouraging the elusive Death's-head Hawk.

"CAN I GET IN, darling?" Vivien asks. "I'm chilly."

I nod. "If you like."

"I suppose it's really my bed too," she says, and I wince as she draws the sheets and blankets right back, pulling them loose from the sides of the bed to get in. It doesn't make an awful lot of difference now because, to be honest, it's just as difficult to straighten one part of the bed as it is to start over and do the whole thing again. The sheets are held to the blanket with safety pins along the top and have to be tucked in in a very particular way at the bottom. I hate it when they go saggy, when you can kick your foot at the bottom of the bed and not feel any resistance because they're loose. I'd probably have found myself taking off all the bedclothes and starting from scratch anyway. It takes fifty-five minutes and there's a definite method to it. I usually get away with doing it once a fortnight when I wash the sheets. I know what a bore it is so when I go to bed each night I make sure to slip between the sheets without drawing them back any more than is absolutely necessary. Once I'm in, and I've checked the pressure of them all over, I lie very still. In the morning when I get out—also very carefully—the bed hardly looks slept in at all.

I'd never have said no to Vivien getting into bed with me, not when she offers that sort of closeness. When we were young, she would often crawl in with me if she was sad or lonely or frightened of the wind, and things she needed to discuss had a habit of coming to her in the middle of the night, things that could never wait until morning. Back then I felt honored, and now, besides the tedium of straightening the sheets, I can't help feeling the same. Vivi always had a wonderful way of making me feel special by assuming that her world and mine were inherently each other's, without any barriers between them.

"Ginny and I are going for a walk," she used to announce, without asking me first, but it made me feel as if I'd been specially selected, out of a world full of people, to go for a walk with her.

So when Vivien asks if she can get into my bed, the privilege is all mine. She snuggles down on what used to be Maud's side, tucking her body into a ball, like the girl she used to be. Her head is resting on the upper part of her arm while her hand stretches up and her fingers feel their way childishly along the panels of Gothic tracery carved into the headboard behind her, reading it like a blind man would. For a moment she is far away in thought with her fingers. I can't help thinking that every minute I have with her, the less I see the old woman who arrived on my doorstep yesterday and the more I see the little girl I've always adored.

I study her lying next to me. It is her eyes that are most changed. Once they were a strong bright blue, scattered with natural shards of silver that made them sparkle as bright and vivacious and hypnotic as the girl herself. But now they're faded to a weak gray-blue, dulled by the life they've seen.

"Is anyone I know left in the village?" she asks finally.

"No, I don't think so. Michael's still here of course, still in the Stables."

"Well, he obviously doesn't do the gardening," she says, referring to the mass of tangled undergrowth and wild jungle that our once manicured terraces and meadows had become.

"No. He hires out those big tents in the peach houses for parties and he's made a fortune."

"He bought our glasshouses?"

"Years ago, with the Stables and the bit of land by the lower spinney. He stores the marquees in them." Vivien's eyes are shut, the lids flicker restlessly as she listens. "A few years ago he offered to buy this house and let me live in the Stables."

She opens her eyes quickly, bright thoughts rousing a remnant sparkle. "Swap with the gardener, darling? What is the world coming to?" She laughs. "Would you have to do the gardening too?"

I tell her that Charlotte Davis's daughter, Eileen, is now living in Willow Cottage. Michael told me she came back a few years ago, after her mother died. "I haven't seen her, though. Do you remember the Davises?" I ask.

"Yes, of course," she says, as she props up her head on an elbow. "Mrs. Davis and her beloved carthorses. What were their names?"

"Alice and Rebecca."

"Alice and Rebecca." She sighs. "That's right. Your tea's gone cold, darling."

"Never mind," I reply ruefully—but, to tell you the truth, I'd never have drunk it. It's far too milky and it's been spilt on the saucer. My tea needs to be the exact mix of strength and color, and there's a definite *method* to that.

CHAPTER 7

Breakfast

VIVIEN LEAVES my bedroom and I start the routine that gets me up and dressed. Then I take the cup and saucer to my bathroom and pour the cold tea into the washbasin. I manage to tip it directly down the plug hole without getting a drop on the white porcelain, and I feel satisfied to have spared myself the bother of rinsing it.

When I get down to the kitchen Vivien's not there, but a breakfast place has been laid for me at the table, with a couple of pieces of cold toast propped up against the sugar bowl. The butter and jam are out, and there's an egg in an eggcup with the egg toppers by its side. Is this what Vivien had for breakfast? I go to the cupboard to get my corn-flakes and a bowl, but even as I sit down I'm not the least bit hungry.

I watch Simon sleeping silently on a pillow in front of the dresser and wonder where she is. She's in the house, I know, because if she'd gone out I would have heard the door. She's had her breakfast and now she's gone off somewhere in the house. Even the birds outside stop singing for a moment to let me listen. Silence.

This house is more than thirty thousand square feet, including the cellars and the attic rooms. My parents were the first to trim the living space by gradually closing off rooms they didn't use. They shut off most of the north wing when we were still children and then the rest of that wing when Vera finally vacated it in death. Later, when there was only me, I closed off the rest of the rooms except the ones I still use—the kitchen, library, study, my bedroom and bathroom—and the hall and landing that connect them all. Forty-seven years ago I shut the doors and never went back, not to see the state of their decay and not when Bobby cleared them of their furniture and clutter. I didn't want to dwell on the past—best left alone undisturbed in the dust, sealed up, not to be rifled through. Live for today, I always say. It's dangerous to throw open the past. The deal with Bobby was he'd clear the lot and whatever he couldn't sell he'd get rid of to save me going through it myself.

As each of Bobby's trucks went down the drive I felt the burden of history lighten and float away after it. I'd watch it until it was well out of sight, taking with it not just our childhood and my life but one and a half centuries of the Bulburrow epoch. It was delightfully purgative. It's difficult for me to explain to you why, to put it into words. All I can say is that it feels reassuring to know that the rooms are empty, and if I don't see them again, I won't have to worry about what's happening in them, the dust and the dirt and the gradual decline. Perhaps it's that, on one hand, I couldn't stand to see their clutter, but on the other, I don't want to remember them any other way. Now it's strange, disconcerting even, to know Vivien is somewhere deep within the bowels of the house, infecting it.

I get up from the table and move to the hall door. I'm curious—I'll admit I'm almost frantic—to know where she's gone and what she's doing. Perhaps I could get some bearing on where she is by listening intently from certain parts of the hall. Bulburrow is a house of echoes, more so since it's been emptied of furniture. Sound travels through the air spaces—the beating of the weather on one side, a squeaking door on the other—so maybe I'll be able to hear the sounds of Vivien too. I need a prop. I return to the table and pour some milk into a glass, even though I don't actually drink milk, and then, glass in hand, I venture out into the hall. I know it's rude and it's none of my business and I really ought to stop myself getting fixated on Vivien's whereabouts, but I hope you understand that it's so new to me, so different, to have someone else here that I just can't help myself. Besides, there's no harm done.

I'm standing in the shadow of the kitchen doorway, looking out into the hall. Jake the pig-head smiles high up on the wall above me. Opposite me is the library, to my right the cellar door and then, farther along, the great curved oak stairs begin their gentle ascent. Off the first, wide tread there's a door to the little study behind the kitchen.

I walk straight ahead, as smoothly as my enfeebled legs allow me, passing the porch on my left and stopping in the wide architrave of the library door. I swap my glass to the other hand, aware of the fatigue in my fingers, which have been squeezing it too tight, and ready it to put up to my lips if Vivien were to appear from the library or the study, or at the top of the stairs. I put my head to the door—no sound—and then I move, crablike, along the edge of the hall wall, pausing at intervals to put the glass near my mouth and listen, but there's not a sound. I pass the stairs that run down the opposite wall and stop by the drawing-room door. I listen again. Nothing. Farther along there's another door, which leads to a different part of the house—the orangery, loggia, potting shed and out to the courtyard behind. It's another area that's off-limits, as it were. Could she have gone down there? What could she want there?

Right here and now it comes to me, with sudden understanding, that Vivien is *looking for something*. Well, it is rather odd, don't you think? Yesterday she tramped all over the first floor. At the time I thought she was just sorting herself out and settling in, but now I'm beginning to see it must be something else entirely. Vivien's come home with an ulterior motive, and it's one she's not telling me about.

Then I hear her. Footsteps, far away and above me, and then Vivien coughing. From here, I can see up the stairwell to the vaulted ceiling above, and beside it the vast stained-glass window that only comes to life with the evening sun. As I creep up the stairs I hear the footsteps again, and by the halfway landing I know she's in the attic. There are two ways up to the attic. The obvious one is via the spiral staircase behind a door off the main landing, but between you and me, I think Vivien must have secretly snuck up the back stairs by the pantry or I'd have heard her.

In fact it's not an attic at all, it's the second floor, but with so many rooms on the first floor for accommodation, it's always been called the attic and is entirely given over to moths. Three large "museum" rooms house the famous collections my intrepid ancestors amassed from around the world, all displayed in highly polished Brady cabinets. Then there are the larva rooms, hibernating cages, pupation troughs, net-lined emergence rooms, dry rooms, damp rooms, storerooms, a vast private library, the laboratory and a little workshop where Clive cobbled together his own boxes and breeding houses from crates and ammunition cases, jars and biscuit tins. I hadn't let Bobby into the attic so nothing's been removed.

But what's Vivien doing there? She's never been interested in the moths. This was something I never fully realized until the summer we were expelled.

Maud had asked us to seal her jams, ready for the harvest festival. Usually it was one of our favorite chores—melting a pot of discarded candle stubs and pouring the runny wax on top of the jam in the jars. But Vivi was silent and sullen, as she'd been most of the summer. I think it riled her that I was happy to have been sent home while she was so upset. She took up the ladle and nonchalantly scooped up the hot wax, dribbling it carelessly over the bench on its way to the first jar, then tipping in so much so fast that the jam's level was mucked up and some went down the side rather than settling on the top. She wasn't usually so slipshod. Then she dribbled it over the edge of the jar and across the workbench to the next, sloshing some into that one too.

"Do you mind if I have a go, Vivi?" I said as sweetly as I could.

"Is it not neat enough for you, Virginia?"

"I'd like to do it," and that was as much the truth as not wanting to watch her slop it about. She handed me the ladle. I dipped it into the wax and swirled it round, melting the last solid clusters as if they were chocolate. Then I scooped out the smooth wax, tipping the ladle backwards to catch the drips on its belly, then poured it carefully over a jam, watching it spread out and fill up the glass side smoothly. I poured slowly and evenly and cleanly before nodding the ladle to stop the flow and moving it over to the next jar. Vivi sat down and began to cut out squares of tartan cloth with pinking shears. Later, when the wax was cool, we would tie them over the tops of the jars with twine.

I'd found that if Vivi was very silent for a long time, it often meant she had something to say. I also found it wasn't always best to ask her: if I did and it turned out to be something I'd rather not have known, she'd always end with "You did ask. . . ."

She finished her cutting in silence.

"Ginny," she said, studying the pinking shears as she chopped at the air with them, "don't you ever feel you need to break out and get away, get your own life back? Maud and Clive make all the decisions for us, always. Why can't we decide what we want to do? It's not fair. Do you ever feel like that, Ginny?"

I knew I never did. "I don't think so," I admitted.

"Really?" She shook her head with resignation, as if she were disappointed in me.

I concentrated on pouring wax into the last jam jar.

"Isn't it obvious how unhappy I am here? Haven't you noticed?" she said.

"I knew you were unhappy about being expelled."

"Only because *this* is the alternative," she snapped, as if she'd been ready for my reaction. "This isn't a life, this house and Clive's damn moths. What am I supposed to do here? Grow old and dissect insects?" she said, as if his life was abhorrent to her. By answering I'd inadvertently given her the go-ahead for a small tirade. "I can't stay here, Ginny. I had friends at school. There's no one here but you and me. I'm not staying here to melt wax on top of Maud's jam. That might be all right for you, but it's not all right for me."

Vivi was in one of her moods and there was nothing I could say to change it. I skimmed off some of the wax at the top of the pot. It was just starting to form a skin so it creased a little as I drew the ladle through. I put the back of my hand out under the ladle and dribbled wax onto it, bit by bit, watching the little translucent domes turn opaque.

"Maud and Clive don't even try to understand me. I get so"—she searched for the right word—"lonely. Do you think there's something wrong with me, Ginny? I've been trying to work out what's wrong with me." She turned in her lips and rubbed them together to stop herself crying but tears gathered anyway along her lower lids and spilled over, running down the crease of her nose.

"I think they can be quite reasonable—" I started.

"They're reasonable to you," she butted in, sniffing herself together. "They don't listen to me. They only listen to you."

At the time I found Vivi's attitude surprising, but I realize now that she hadn't left school with the same advantage as me. You see, Maud had never got round to proclaiming Vivi's future to an interested neighborhood during a drinks party so, although it was generally understood I would now stay and help Clive with the moths, Vivi (along with the rest of the village) was at a loss for what she was going to do. Maud and Clive didn't seem the least bit concerned, and I could understand Vivi's frustration. They had this way of shrugging off her worries. "Vivien will be all right," they'd say. "Don't worry about Vivi." But, between you and me, I think they got it back to front: I was the one who was fine and Vivien the one who was always in some sort of quandary or getting herself worked up over the next life hurdle. After all, it was Vivi, not me, who had fallen off the bell tower and ruptured her womb, Vivi who had got us expelled and Vivi who didn't want to be here sealing jam.

Later that night, Vivi slid into bed beside me. I felt her search for my hand and entwine her agitated fingers with mine, playing with them, curling them and uncurling them with urgency, rousing me. I could tell she wanted to wake me, that she wanted to talk.

"Are you awake, Ginny?" she asked finally.

"Yes," I said, sitting up, befuddled. "What is it?"

"You do understand why I can't stay, don't you?" she said. "You know I have to leave, don't you?"

I wondered if I did. I'd never thought of myself without Vivi being somewhere in that thought too. I'd never dreamed a dream that she wasn't in. I only seemed whole when I was with her, as if she somehow made up the parts of me that were lacking. I couldn't imagine living without her.

"What about me?" I asked.

"You've got the moths," she said vaguely, as if she thought they could substitute for a sister.

Then she stretched up and kissed my cheek. "Thank you, sis," she said. "Even if Maud and Clive don't understand, I knew you would." She squeezed my hand again, and all of a sudden I felt very specially connected with my wonderful, spirited little sister, and everything seemed to make sense: we understood each other.

Then she told me the plan.

IT WAS AFTER SUPPER the following day when Vivi showed me where she would hide. She took me into the back pantry and shut the kitchen door. Climbing onto the workbench, she reached up to dislodge a rectangular panel above the architrave of the door. It was painted white, the same as the walls, and although I had vaguely noticed a square of beading there, we had lots of empty air spaces and access panels about the house and I'd never thought to take them off and have a look. Vivi obviously had. She crawled right in through the square hole. She'd already described—in the middle of last night— how, once she was in, she could crawl along the rafters in the empty space and end up behind the study wall, above the door to the kitchen.

I went into the study and waited until I heard her knock three times. I knocked back and went to call our parents into the study as a matter of priority.

"What is it, Virginia?" Maud asked, perplexed. I'd disturbed her on the telephone. She perched herself on the window seat, Clive sat at his desk and Vivi stayed very still on her hands and knees in the wall, listening to her scheme being put into place.

"I wanted to talk to you about Vivi," I started.

Maud glanced at Clive, narrowing her eyes.

"Go on," Clive said, but he seemed uninterested, opening the top drawer of his desk and fiddling with his pens.

"I think you should let her go to London to do a secretarial course," I blurted.

I think Clive was about to say something when Maud cut in. "You do, do you?" I thought she almost laughed. "And why is that?"

Clive only seemed interested in the leads of his pencils. He looked intent and serious as he took them out of the drawer one by one, pushing the tips against the pad of his middle finger to gauge their sharpness. I wished he'd join in and have an opinion for once on something so important to Vivi.

"Because she really wants to go and do this and I think it's unfair not to let her. She's not going to be happy here—and I won't be happy either, if she's so sad," I said.

"Oh Ginny, *reeeally,*" said Maud. "Don't you worry about Vivien. She'll be fine." That made me want to shout at her, to tell her to stop saying it, to tell her that Vivi was far from fine—had they not noticed how unhappy she was? But the words got stuck in my head and never made it out.

Maud looked at Clive again. "Vivien put you up to this, didn't she?" She sighed. Vivi had told me Maud would say that.

"No."

"Well, she's fifteen and she's not going anywhere," said Maud definitively.

I glanced up at the boarding above the door to the kitchen and imagined Vivi's hopes soaking into the rafters behind it.

"She's going to stay right here and—"

Maud was interrupted by Clive slamming his desk drawer back into place. "Sorry," he said, because the noise had broken off our conversation. "Virginia, thank you for coming to tell us." He stood up. "Now, if you could leave us, your mother and I will think about what you've said."

Of course I didn't believe him. He hadn't seemed interested in the slightest in what I was saying. I wanted to stay. Vivi would be disappointed I hadn't talked for longer; she'd say I hadn't tried hard enough. I wanted to think of a way to prolong the conversation, put forward a different viewpoint, anything to make them reconsider. But Clive had cut me short. He'd made it clear he didn't want to talk about it anymore. Perhaps he had blunt pencils to attend to, I thought unkindly.

I waited nervously in Vivi's room for her to come back and tell me what had happened next. The wall by her bed was plastered with posters and postcards and messages from her friends. The posters were an odd mix of animal pictures and film stars that she'd pulled out of magazines. A funny one of a donkey in a boater, with holes cut out for his ears, was right next to Ava Gardner drawing seductively on a cigarette.

When Vivi came back she told me she'd heard their entire conversation. Apparently Clive had told Maud to let Vivi go to London, although I couldn't imagine him being so forthright. They'd had quite a row about it, but in the end she said Clive had put his foot down. His decision was final, and he didn't want to hear another word about it. I was surprised. None of it sounded like the Clive I had seen, the one testing his pencil leads. I wondered if she was making the whole thing up.

Vivi leaned her head back against the wall next to a recalcitrant-looking James Dean in *Rebel Without a Cause*. She'd never seen his films so I thought it was extraordinary that she'd cried so hard—along with most of her friends—when he'd died in a car crash last month.

"What did Maud say?" I asked.

"She was worried about you and me not having each other, but Clive told her she should stop being so silly, we were going to have to go our separate ways at some point." She looked up at James Dean—

his jacket half undone and a defiant, ungovernable look on his furrowed brow—as if really only the poster could understand.

My room was painted yellow, and I'd not put anything on its walls. When, a few weeks later, Vivi left for London, I remember I felt that, somehow, her bedroom wall displayed how much I was going to miss her.

I AM STANDING on the landing, with my head bent as far back as it will go, steadying myself with my right hand on the dado rail and staring up at the ceiling. I'm following her footsteps above me. Now she's in the museum rooms, walking slowly, stopping. Something scrapes along the floor. Forty-five seconds later I hear her in the attic library, more shuffling and scuffing, then silence. The thud of a book landing on the floor. Now she's in the storeroom, which isn't above me but above the other landing, the one that's out of my boundary through the double doors. Faint, faraway noises. Now she's heading towards the laboratory, I think. A gentle tapping. Silence.

All of a sudden she's coming, walking across the ceiling directly above me with purpose, towards the top of the spiral staircase. I hurry down the main stairs, leaning heavily on the thick banisters as I go, and twice splash a little milk out of the glass onto the stairs, but she's coming fast. Now she's on the landing. I sidestep off the bottom stair into the little study, close the door and sit quickly on the padded leather seat of the fire guard, poised awkwardly with my glass.

Vivien opens the door and walks in. My heart is still racing. I am surprised that, only three years younger than me, she is so much sprightlier. She came down two floors almost as fast as I came down one. "Oh, hello," she says. "Well, you weren't wrong. It really has been emptied, this place, hasn't it?" She sits down on the window seat. "They even took the marble hearthstones in the drawing room and the main fireplace."

"Did they? How odd," I say, meaning it, and lower the glass of milk from my lips as if the thought had made me change my mind about drinking it. What had Bobby wanted those for? I wonder. He wouldn't have been able to sell them, surely. They were made for this house.

"The fireplace. The hearthstones." Vivien sighs in disgust. "Imagine that!"

I try.

"What does it look like? What's underneath the hearthstones?" I ask her.

"Well, it's just a great big hole. They must have been very thick slabs of marble. It's like . . . well, it's like a great big grave, darling," she says grimly. "I was wondering, Ginny, did you keep anything of Maud's, any little personal thing? I'd really like something of hers."

"No, I don't think so," I reply.

"Are you sure? How about a perfume bottle . . . or a gourd? Just something to remember her by." I'm studying the milk in my hand. My hand—and the outside of the glass—is wet from when I spilt it earlier so I hold it away from me. If it drips it'll do so on the floor rather than on me.

"A shirt you've kept to use as a rag?" she offers.

"There are lots of Clive's things, all his equipment and the observation diaries and recording books—"

"I don't want anything of Clive's," she snaps. "I'd rather not be reminded of him, thank you," she adds callously.

"Vivien!" I say, taken aback. "I know you think he favored me but he loved you too, whatever disputes you two may have had."

She looks slightly disgusted. "Don't be ridiculous," she retorts, firmly but not unkindly. "He spun a little silk cocoon around you like you were one of his specimens."

"Oh, that's absurd. We just worked together, that's all." I'm shocked she has such a wrong impression of our father.

"He made everyone roll over for you, Ginny. Even the world would have had to go round the wrong way if necessary," she adds.

I don't know what she's talking about. I never imagined we could have such opposing memories of Clive. I don't remember any times that he went particularly out of his way for me, or anyone else, for that matter. He was always too embroiled in his work. I think she makes things up in her head. I'd always thought Clive was impossible to dislike. He was such a passive person, quiet, I'd go so far as to say unnoticeable, most of the time. He never had a strong opinion on anything outside his work. Or if he did, I certainly didn't notice. He got on with his own business and didn't meddle much in anyone else's, and I couldn't see how he could have caused offense to anyone. I probably understood him better than Vivien because I worked with him and we shared more interests. That was what it boiled down to, different interests, and I'd have thought she'd realize that. I try to brush it off lightly. "Vivien, we both know Clive couldn't have made anything much go round. He was so entranced by his own little world."

"What do you mean?"

I thought it was obvious. "Well, he didn't have a clue what was going on anywhere in the house apart from his lab."

"What, Clive?" She laughs scathingly. "I'm afraid you've got the wrong person, Ginny. Clive could smell a rat in the pantry from that lab," she says.

"A rat in the pantry?"

"Give me that milk if you're not going to drink it. It's dripping over the floor," she says, changing the subject, and I'm glad; I don't want another pointless argument. I also don't want her to realize that I'm not drinking the milk, that it was a prop to help me spy on her, so I put the glass to my mouth and tip the milk up a little without actually sipping any. She's watching me so I pretend to take some more, this time tilting it farther, until I feel the milk covering my lips. I wish I'd used something I don't mind the taste of. The way she's looking at me, I think for a moment she might have guessed I'm only pretending to drink it, but when she winces and says, "Do you want to go and wipe off your milk mustache?" I know she hasn't seen through my milk prop after all, so I can stop.

Vivien follows me into the kitchen. "So, is there anything of Maud's?"

"No, sorry," I say. "Nothing."

CHAPTER 8

The Apprentice

MY OFFICIAL INITIATION into the world of entomology, as Clive's apprentice, in the autumn of the year that Vivi went up to London, was to accompany him to London to give a popular lecture at the Royal Entomological Society. It was called "The Response of the Barred Red to Differing Spectrums of Light." Clive instructed me on how and when to change the slides, and the cues he would give to let me know when to show an exhibit.

He wasn't looking forward to the lecture one bit. "Popular" meant that anyone could attend, and Clive didn't have much time for part-time enthusiasts. He himself, having had no significant further education on the subject—past his chemistry degree—and not working under the auspices of an institution, would also have been labeled an "amateur," but he liked to think of himself on a par with the academics. It was the only thing Clive was ever snobbish about. He had been given a doctorate and was awarded grants in the same way that university professors were, and although he hadn't yet made any astounding discoveries, he was well known for publishing a great many papers on wide-ranging subjects, from species dichotomy to the extraction and assaying of a great many of those minor biochemical compounds he'd painstakingly identified.

Clive said amateurs were made up of ex–medical men (who were, at the very least, educated), ex–military men (who were only interested in collecting beautiful specimens to display alongside their medals) and clergymen (who had far too much spare time, were all too often argumentative and dictatorial and at odds with everything—killing and collecting, evolutionary theory, the ferocity of nature). He told me he wasn't looking forward to the same old questions and arguments from this latter section of the audience, and within twenty minutes of the start, an eager, smooth-faced man with spectacles and a reduced chin challenged him.

"Are you suggesting that the moth has no say in whether it approaches the light or not? It doesn't make up its own mind, its actions are absolutely determined, and there is no decision-making process?" he said, in a much-rehearsed manner.

"Good afternoon, Rector," Clive began, and I wondered which one, out of all the rectors Clive had mentioned or Maud had laughed about, this might be. "Yes, I believe that insects are not capable of making a decision," he said.

"But . . . but, Dr. Stone, we've all seen a caterpillar making single-minded decisions, whether it's searching for a place to pupate, burrowing an underground chamber, spinning a silken sling or wedging itself into the nook of a rotten tree. Surely, before the preparation for its pupation, it must have *decided* to pupate," said the rector.

"No."

"No?" The rector appeared superficially aghast and looked about the room in a bid to rally support.

"I think you know, Mr. Keane, that I believe it is involuntary," Clive replied quietly. So it's Keaney, I thought. I knew all about him. He'd never made a sermon without reference to a moth hunt. He set light traps in his Cotswold church and would stop a service to check them, then enthuse to his congregation.

"Involuntary? What, like the muscles that pump our hearts? You really believe that insects are living automatons? They have no emotions, no sentiment, no interests and no mind?" the rector continued with practiced eloquence and feigned disbelief, his voice rising in volume and tone for crescendoing drama.

"I do," Clive said, as though it were a vow.

"Not even a conscious purpose, Doctor?"

Clive was on trial. He scratched the stubble on his neck with nervous irritation. "Actually," he said, "I'm not even sure *we* have a conscious purpose." The room broke up with appreciative laughter, but I knew it wasn't a joke. Clive didn't make jokes, and certainly not quick-witted, belittling ones like that. He continued earnestly, "Of course we'd like to believe it, to make our existence more meaningful."

I saw a group of people in the front row lean forward to exchange glances like naughty schoolchildren not understanding why they were having a telling off. I was sitting on a chair up at the front in the shadows beside the projector and took a long look at the entire audience.

Maud had told me once that Clive was a misfit among misfits. She didn't like these people. She said they adopted pet names and idiosyncrasies to make themselves more interesting. They'd hone the eccentric characteristic they wanted to be known for and, if they were lucky, it soon became synonymous with their name, to be cited in the same breath: "Ah, I know Dr. Toogood, he's the one who stirs his tea with surgical forceps." "Oh, of course, Lionel Hester, who pins his moths on his hat when he's out hunting."

Maud said they were often under the infuriating illusion that, as eccentrics, they might also be regarded as geniuses, or at least hoped to be mistaken for them. She said she had finally understood their collective affectations when Major Fordingly (who kept a pet seagull) once quoted grandiosely to her: "To distinguish between eccentricity and genius may be difficult, but it is surely better to bear with singularity than to crush originality." Well, Maud thought, *surely not.* She said it was better to admit who you were even if it meant admitting you were dull and had a dull little hobby, rather than covering it up in a pathetic attempt at some sort of singularity. Of course, Clive was different. Maud said Clive was the only one who didn't try to be eccentric and was.

From where I sat in the shadows of the stage, I looked at this room of charlatans and tried to spot any of their fabricated habits.

"So these creatures are just machines to you, are they?" someone from the midst of the bearded auditorium asked Clive.

"By definition not machines, no. They are living. But I believe every action an insect makes is due to a reflex, a taxis or a tropism. Their existence is purely mechanical."

"So an ant lion chews a struggling ant with no more emotion than a machine mangles a man's hand?" the chinless rector in the front eulogized loudly and poetically, still trying to elicit emotional outrage in the room.

"Yes."

The rector stood up to address the entire room.

"A caterpillar has no idea why it's spinning a cocoon or making a chamber for itself in the ground?" he continued, throwing up his hands with Shakespearean effort.

"Exactly," Clive replied in a quietly bored tone.

"So if a female moth saw her own larvae, she wouldn't recognize them as hers or even understand that they belong to her own species or class of animal? She has no parental feelings?"

"Love, you mean?"

"Yes . . . love."

"Oh, I don't know about love," Clive said, a little more roused. "I think many animals exhibit love for their offspring."

"Well, there you go," said the rector, sitting down heavily and slapping his hands on his knees in a show of triumph.

"It's just that I believe *love* itself is no more than a mechanical process," said Clive, once the rector thought his victory was settled.

"But love is an emotion, Dr. Stone," the rector replied with a certain asperity.

"Yes, and an emotion is merely the symptom caused by a particular chemical being released into your brain and central nervous system, which, in turn, acts on other parts of the brain to elicit this feeling."

"Your beliefs are more far-fetched even than I thought," said the poetic rector in a final irate judgment.

I could see Clive was glad that the matter was closed and he could continue with his lecture. He didn't want to argue with these people. He just knew what he knew, but, unfortunately for him, what he knew had always attracted impassioned opposition.

Afterwards everyone gathered for a drink, to discuss the lecture and to catch up with news of butterflies and moths the country over. I was glued to Clive's shoulder and he introduced me to everyone we came across. When he led me over to Bernard Cartwright I was relieved, finally, to see someone familiar. Bernard often stayed at Bulburrow—either to discuss his latest research with Clive, on his way down to the West Country for a field trip, or as a family friend for the weekend. Bernard was a proper academic. He was a professor at a London college, and a few months ago he'd isolated a caterpillar hormone, one that initiates molting, so he was now a household name in that very small and exclusive collection of entomology households. He was addressing a group of men as we approached.

"A gland secretes a hormone in our heads, which actuates a nerve, which then activates a muscle, all involuntarily, without us knowing," he was saying.

"Congratulations on your paper, Bernard," Clive interrupted, shaking his hand.

"Thank you, Clive. Good talk, very lively as usual. Hello, Virginia," he said to me, then leaned down to whisper in my ear, "do you like the way your daddy gets them going?" as if Clive had goaded them on purpose. Then he laughed loudly and I winced as a fine mist of spittle engulfed my face.

"So, Clive, what do you think makes the gland secrete the hormone in the first place?" said one of the men in the group.

"Most probably something that has not yet been discovered," Clive said.

"That's ducking the question, if I may say so." Another laughed.

"No. I could speculate if you like," said Clive, "that it was another hormone, one released as a coefficient of a mechanical process, like growth, perhaps. Before Bernard here"—he nudged his ally—"found the hormone that loosens and releases a caterpillar's skin at certain stages of its growth, you probably thought that a caterpillar *decided* to shed its skin—voluntarily—when it was getting a little uncomfortable, a little too tight? We now know it wasn't *thinking* of shedding its skin, and I'd say there's probably a lot more thinking that the caterpillar is given credit for."

"Well, I'm afraid I can't agree with you," said the same man.

"No, I know," said Clive, satisfied once again with a cease-fire, and the conversation drifted on to something else.

I looked towards the acclaimed Bernard. He was a truly ugly man. He was short with a pan-shaped face, a tiny nose in the middle and tiny eyes too. Bernard must have been slinking up to middle age but seemed younger on account of his plump cheeks and shiny-skinned complexion and his reputation for hailing round the countryside on a Triumph motorcycle. He had a loud, inappropriate laugh but, I thought, at least he was cheery and a friendly face. Whenever he visited Bulburrow he'd always take notice of Vivi and me, and make conversation or sit down for a game of dominoes, unlike some of Clive's more stuffy colleagues, many of whom would walk in and ignore us. (Maud said most of them ignored her too; they were weird about women, she said.)

When he saw me looking at him he sidled up, slapped his hand on my back and pulled me a little closer to him. "I'm glad to hear you've joined our team," he said privately to me, as he ran his hand down the length of my back. Then he caught my eyes and held them, his puffy face a few inches from mine, so I couldn't possibly avoid pitying the extent of his unnatural ugliness.

I assumed he was waiting for some response.

"I'm glad to have joined the team," I replied with a hiccuped laugh and an idiotic smile. It was all I could think to say.

"Great," he said. "Great. In this game you need allies, so remember I'm an ally."

"Thanks," I said, smiling again.

Then he ran his hand from the small of my back down over my

bottom, which he grabbed lightly and shook a little. And then he left it there. I didn't know what to do or say. I felt a little heat rise in my face and we both turned our heads back at the same time to resume being part of the group's conversation. His hand still lightly cupped my bottom but our bodies were too close for anyone else to notice. Was it familiar friendliness? Or a consequence of a tight space? Or was I being fondled? The answer wasn't as apparent as you'd imagine. We were squashed more or less into a corner so space was a little limited, and that confused my judgment for a start—the intimacy that's tolerated on a packed bus isn't on an empty one. All the options ran through my mind: He was protecting me from being pushed farther back into the wall. There was nowhere else for his hand to go. He'd merely forgotten it was there, as our familiarity over the years had deemed my bottom not a particularly personal place.

I was further prevented from reaching a conclusion by Bernard's own puzzling behavior. He seemed to be listening so intently to the conversation in the group, with his head strained forward, that I was convinced he couldn't possibly be thinking about his hand, so it was most probable that he'd just forgotten where he'd left it. A genuine mistake it may have been, but I couldn't help but feel a strange hand cupping my bottom was oddly uncomfortable. I clenched my bottom muscles a couple of times, hoping he'd feel the movement and realize his mistake—the equivalent of a sharp look of distaste—but he merely shifted it a little, so intent was he on the conversation going on in front of him.

"You think a dog has instinct, don't you?" a walrus-like man asked my father.

"Yes."

"So where do you draw the line in the animal kingdom between those that have developed instinct and those that haven't?"

"I don't. All animals have instinct. The difference is most of them don't know about it. The thing that sets us apart from other animals is self-awareness. And don't ask me where, in the animal kingdom, I'd draw the self-awareness line, because I couldn't tell you, but you can be sure it won't be distinct. It will be a question of degree, and there will be lots of animals with only a little self-awareness." Clive rattled off his thoughts without pause for breath, and I realized he'd said the same things many times before. He went on, "What do you think makes decisions for a pupa when it's in liquid form? There's no brain left. It's a primordial soup. Surely you don't imagine Pupal Soup can think. Its genetic coding orchestrates the proceedings, like a key opens a door. It's not a decision-making process."

A throng was now gathering round him, like a dissatisfied mob, and I could tell he was increasingly uneasy, as he stepped up the frequency with which he scratched his neck beard.

"So what exactly is self-awareness, then? Is it a soul, do you think?" someone asked.

Clive's trial was far from over.

"Well, that's an issue for a different kind of lecture entirely."

"I know, but I'm interested in your view. You seem very definite on all of it," someone pointed out acerbically.

"I am a reductionist, so I do not think that self-awareness is a spiritual attribute. I think that, perhaps, it is a by-product of evolution."

"By-product? Like a mistake?" came the reply.

"No. Well, I don't know. . . ." Clive paused, but it was obvious he did. "Perhaps," he continued tentatively, "as animals get more advanced in their biochemical processes it becomes too complicated to try to orchestrate everything in terms of reflex and reaction. It is, in fact, a simplification to make the creature's brain responsible for determining its own solutions, to be able to learn by memory and recognition, to compute its surroundings and make a decision for itself."

He said it all so quickly, as if he'd rehearsed it many times, that it sounded unbelievable, like an actor reciting lines his heart wasn't in. I was hot and uncomfortable and it occurred to me that it was as if I had dreamed up my worst nightmare and made it a reality: Bernard's hand was still on my bottom, and now he was moving his thumb up and down in a caress. Was it voluntary or involuntary? It was the same question to which the entire room wanted the answer. Did Bernard think this united us as allies in the team he had talked of? Clive looked exhausted. The crowd drew closer. I could hear the scoffs and general contempt for Clive's latest theorizing.

"I don't have the answers," he was saying with exasperation. "It is my hypothetical belief that everything, including self-awareness, can be reduced to chemical and mechanical reactions, and minute anatomical changes within our central nervous system."

The walrus-man looked askew at Clive in a mixture of pity and disgust. Clive scratched his beard. The group got bigger and bigger until I now saw swarms of people crowding in on us, encircling us, shrinking us. I couldn't think straight. The floor melted underfoot and I began to sway as if I were on a boat. The whole of The Hand stroked my bottom now, circularly. The ceiling started to drop, incrementally. The door at the far side of the room was now jammed full of men with beards and long necks all asking questions at the same time, and they were using up the air in the room, they were taking huge breaths of it, gulping it greedily. The Hand stroked harder in big, unrepressed, flat-handed circles, as if it were rubbing beeswax into furniture. Clive scratched his beard. All of a sudden I was naked. Bernard was a dog full of instinct, panting, dribbling. I couldn't breathe. I closed my eyes so I could go to that place in my head where I would be able to keep calm as I slowly asphyxiated.

At last I heard Bernard's sonorous voice, not right by my side, but in front of me, a yard or so away. It was unmistakable—he was discussing some sort of water heater he'd had installed in his house, then let out one of his loud distinctive laughs. I opened my eyes sharply and saw him—as I'd thought—two paces in front of me, waving his hands about as he spoke. *Both* hands. It was only as I looked at him that The Hand That Cupped My Bottom gently dissolved away. I glanced discreetly over my shoulder to check that there was *nothing there.*

I was still staring at Bernard's hands when someone else's passed him a plate of vol-au-vents. Rather than one hand taking one and the other passing on the plate, both hands reached out for a vol-au-vent, and both picked one up delicately between its thumb and forefinger.

While holding the surplus fingers aloft Bernard effetely popped them into his enormous mouth, one at a time, and after each I watched him rub the tips of his finger and thumb together to rid them of pastry crumbs. Nausea rose up my throat. Surely those same fussy fingers had been rubbing my bottom. Yet I'd still felt his hand there when I saw it wasn't. I was a little hot and very confused.

ALL THE WAY HOME on the train Clive was silent. When we finally got in, late that evening, Maud gave me a glass of sherry but I couldn't drink it. With Clive's gout prohibiting him, I think she would have liked me to have a drink with her, but the last time I'd tried it I hadn't liked it.

She had made an effort with supper. She'd made pork in cider sauce and put the silver on the table, and I knew she wanted us to sit down and tell her everything about our first lecture together as a scientific team. She had been so excited about it that morning, before we left, and had kept giving me bits of advice and thinking of things I should be ready to expect—listen, don't talk, keep well back and to the side of the stage so you don't feel daunted by a room full of people—and I understood she'd be excited to know how it had gone. Now, of course, I can appreciate that we should have given her the time, that we should have sat down and eaten her supper and told her the little details of the day that would help make her feel a part of it, but Clive and I were so weary that we went straight to bed. Maud stopped me as I was going up the stairs.

"Are you sure you won't have a quick drink?" she asked, pouring herself another.

I shook my head apologetically.

Then she asked me a strange question: "How many of them didn't have a beard?"

Funny, I thought. "All the men had beards," I said.

"Oh, I know that," she said, laughing. "What I really meant was were there any women?"

It was then that I understood the true position of my unchosen career. Not only would it involve a great deal of confrontation and debate, but I would have two ongoing battles: first, like Clive, to be accepted in academic circles without the certificates to prove it, and second, to be a woman in this men-only sphere, even though the famous Bernard Cartwright had welcomed me personally to the team.

CHAPTER 9

Another Trap

I WANT TO TELL YOU about what happened four or so years
later. It was 1959, the year that changed everything. It was the
year of the Plymouth Convention and the year—I'll never forget it—
that Bernard Cartwright threw down his challenge.

But first of all I should tell you about Vivi. While I was busy with
Clive and the moths, Vivi had molded herself into a new life in London, sharing a flat with two girls she'd met on her secretarial course.
She visited us irregularly, even though Maud was always trying to
coax her home, but she wrote every other week. Maud always got to
the letters first. She'd fetch the post the instant it arrived, then walk
back into the kitchen flicking through the envelopes, hoping to spot
Vivi's handwriting.

After her course, Maud had hoped Vivi would come home and
find a job locally, but instead she went to work in a London firm of
solicitors. A few months on she'd left and found herself something
more interesting, she said, in a newspaper publishing house, but even
then she was unsettled. She moved to a doctor's surgery, and then
became personal secretary to a freelance journalist. I lost count, after
that, of her different jobs. It seemed to me that each time she came

home she'd moved on again, and she always managed to persuade us that the next place would be so much better than the last.

I don't think Maud had realized when Vivi left home that it would be for good. But Vivi had wanted to make something of her life, and neither a crumbling Dorset mansion nor an attic full of moths was enough. One day, she wrote in one of her letters, she was going to work on a film set, perhaps even at Pinewood, because she'd met someone who knew someone who wanted someone.

During that time Clive and I had formed a remarkable partnership and our research enterprise at Bulburrow was saturated with work and grants. It wasn't all down to our brilliant teamwork. The fifties, you might remember, were a boom time for experimental science. They saw the invention of the electron microscope and the electronic chip, the widespread use of antibiotics and immunization, Watson and Crick's double-helical DNA, and then came genetics.

The moth, along with the fruit fly *Drosophila,* became the experimental animal of the moment, for all the same reasons that Clive had identified twenty years before, and by the late 1950s it seemed as if everybody wanted a little bit of moth. The traditional lepidopterists were swept aside as all the other scientific faculties—molecular biologists, biochemists and, in particular, the new evolutionary geneticists—hijacked the moth for their research. Kettlewell published his now famous illustrations of industrial melanism with the Peppered Moth, and the evolutionary geneticists Sheppard and Fisher used many species of moth to help interpret the laws of inheritance and the chromosomal behaviors that allow for continuous variation. Chemists took over the field, trying to find answers, equations and formulas to the questions that Clive, Bernard and others like them had marveled at for years: identifying the specific compounds that control its life cycle, instigate hibernation or emergence, the molecular events that attract a moth to light, that release volatile oil from a female's scent gland and the structures in a male that can detect it from a very many miles downwind. These considerations, along with the chemical assaying of every compound—pigments, hormones, pheromones, enzymes, neural inhibitors and stimulators—or, at least, an investigation into how they worked or behaved chemically, were suddenly up for grabs and it seemed like a race to be first there and first to publish.

Obviously Clive and I had a bit of a head start as Clive's solitary life's work, often derided in the past for being out on a limb between two scientific fields, was now being ambushed by institutional research looking for big business. We got busy. We published more than ten papers a year, gave twice as many lectures, and the grants rolled in steadily.

Finally I ought to tell you about the Robinsons trap. It was the only other real excitement that happened during those four apprenticeship years. It was Maud who first read about it in one of her subscription magazines, *British Countryside*, I think. The Robinsons were two brothers from Kent who launched a revolutionary new design of light trap on the market, and it was causing more than a small stir. I remember Maud specifically bringing the magazine up to the laboratory when it arrived with the post. She stood at the end of the workbench and sensationally read out the astonishing leader article: "A Robinsons set on a single night in Hampshire collects more than 20,000 specimens of the Setaceous Hebrew Character, Amathes c-nigrum L., Caradrinidae, along with vast numbers of other species."

I have never understood why Clive didn't rush out and buy one then and there but he didn't seem interested, even though stories of its success were soon to head up every entomological magazine of the season. The Rolls-Royce of moth traps, as it became known, consisted of a mercury-vapor discharge lamp set in a cleverly designed glass bell jar. It worked in a similar way to a lobster pot. From dusk onwards, when most moths are on the wing, they head into the top of the huge bell-shaped jar, attracted by the light, and, once in, they haven't the wit to get out. The Robinsons trap radically revolutionized the capturing of moths and—more shockingly—altered the current understanding of their national distribution and rarity. Moths that were once thought to be rare were suddenly shown to be abundant and others existed in places they had never before been found. So, you see, the entire bank of national statistics based on more than half a century's worth of scrupulously gathered distribution data was deemed invalid overnight and the auction rooms, which at the time made a good trade dealing in rare insect collections, were left reeling as prices plummeted overnight on those not-so-rare rarities that passed under their hammer. Not even that made Clive rush to order one.

When I asked Maud, she told me that of course Clive would like one but pride got in the way. She said he'd always made his own equipment, to his own specifications, which he'd perfected over many years, and he refused to believe that his own designs might not give optimal performance. I didn't believe her. Clive wasn't the conceited type.

OVER THOSE wonderful partnership years Clive never let go of his lifetime ambition—that of resolving the composition of Pupal Soup and, with it, revealing the secrets of metamorphosis—and as each autumn came, it led us, with trowel and chisel in hand, to the broad rides in the local woods or the sheltered borders alongside the furrowed fields in search of those small elusive pupae that had hooked themselves so deeply into Clive's fascination. Until the following spring we were thrown into this ambitious pursuit, analyzing the contents of cocoons at different stages of their development to try to find the pattern, the trigger, the golden key, to the miraculous process of metamorphosis. But it was frustrating and futile, and we found few patterns. A team in America had reported that pigmentation within the developing imago was affected by temperature, but from our own observations we found temperature had no effect either on the development of the pupa or on the initiation of the reorganization of the imaginal buds. Neither did we find it to influence or control the speed of destruction of the larval tissues and organs by the phagocytes, but that the process varied between a few days and a few years, depending on the species. We also saw no effect on the active phase of pupal life, the reorganization of the new insect or the time of emergence. Having discounted temperature, we looked for other triggers, such as hormones and changes in polarity or pH, but three years on we were no closer to finding the stimulus, catalyst or control that activates the onset of genetic reorganization.

Eventually we had some successes in other areas, especially on the subject of pigments. I particularly remember Clive's heightened enthusiasm when he discovered that the red pigment in red British moths—the Scarlet Tigers, the Burnets and Red Underwings—was not the same compound found in our red butterflies but, rather, one prevalent in continental species, which, Clive said, shed new light on the British moths' evolutionary pathway, the details of which he discussed at length in a lecture during an international entomology convention in Plymouth.

This convention brings me to the events of 1959 because it took place in the spring of that year. Clive culminated his lecture—unbeknownst to me—with a most impressive stunt that was to become the talking point for the rest of the three-day convention.

There are only two British moths, the Brimstone and the Swallowtailed Moth, to share a fluorescent yellow pigment in their wings, and they are both classified *Selidosemindae* because of it. But Clive dramatically illustrated the flaw in this universal classification, in front of the entire auditorium, when he passed an extract of the fluorescing compound from each of these two species under ultraviolet light. It showed—beyond any doubt—that the two phosphorescing compounds are in fact of a very different chemical makeup. With that redoubtable demonstration Clive then concluded by calling for a complete taxonomic overhaul of the entire genera based on new biochemical evidence. It became hotly debated: Should we, or should we not, reclassify when we find evolutionary pathways contradicting our observational classification and nomenclature? As you might imagine, Clive was punctilious when it came to correct classification.

The strangest part for me was that I had no idea, not even a suspicion, that Clive was going to perform this spectacle and challenge the entire classification system. I knew by heart the lecture he was going to give, I'd heard him practice it enough, but he'd never rehearsed this last little stunt. You'd have thought he would have mentioned it, but it was as much of a surprise to me as it was to everybody else.

The most memorable thing about the Plymouth Convention, however, was what happened when we got home.

We'd set off on a Tuesday afternoon and arrived back at teatime on Friday. When we walked in, the house was quiet and there was no one to greet us. I almost skidded on a pile of post on the hall floor. In previous years Basil might have been the first to the door but he'd died a couple of years before when his kidneys packed up. We called for Maud but, unusually, there was no reply. In the kitchen a great pile of washing up haunted the sink and the overloaded bin smelt sweetly putrid. It was most unlike Maud. In the library the cushions on the sofa were limp, the curtains half drawn. A saucerless cup and an apple core, browned with age, had been left stickying on the mahogany card table, sure to mark it. In other places things were curiously out of place: one of the ancestors had been knocked and tilted on the wall up the stairs, a small framed certificate had fallen off the paneling onto the floor and the whole house had a mildly shambolic feel.

Clive moved quickly now, checking the rooms downstairs one by one. I followed him. I felt the slow, sickening panic of a child who loses sight of its mother for a moment in town. Clive didn't speak but I felt his fear. It was in his short, sharp steps, in the way he swung open each door as if boldly standing up to his own dreaded imagination, in the curt, composed way he enunciated her name—"Maud"—as he entered each room, with intensity but not volume. My mouth was dry. My stomach was dancing. First we checked the downstairs—the potting shed, the shallow pond in the orangery, the steep stone steps descending from the loggia, round the back to the parlor where the meat hooks hang . . .

There was no sign of her downstairs so we made our way back to the hall. But just as Clive began up the stairs ahead of me, I saw, to my unimaginable relief, Maud at the top, sashaying elegantly down in a green and blue peacock-print evening dress.

"Hello, darlings," she called halfway down, glowing with exuberance. "Good trip?"

Her dress was cut high and rounded at the neck, and pinched her small waist with a sash. I hadn't seen her dressed up for a long time. Tight, lace-edged sleeves finished on her upper arm and two lengths of amber-colored beads hung in low loops round her neck, tied together in a loose knot. It was the kind of thing she had worn when she was much younger. Tarnished silver bracelets jangled round her wrists and a quarter-glass of sherry dangled off her right hand. She might have been neglecting the housework but she'd certainly made an effort with herself. Undoubtedly she was striking.

"It looks like you've had a party," said Clive, glancing into the kitchen.

"Oh, I did, darling. I've had lots of parties while you were away. And don't worry about the clearing up. It's all under control."

"I'm not worried," he said, meeting her on the stairs with a kiss.

I was still marveling at her appearance. I was sure I'd never seen her in that dress, yet it reminded me of something. I thought if I stopped trying to think of it, it would spill unexpectedly from my memory sometime soon.

"Did you really have parties?" I asked.

"No, I'm just *teasing* you, darling." She made a funny face and held my earlobe, shaking it a little. "Pulling your ear . . ."

She seemed animated, restless. "I've got you a present, Clive. It can be an early birthday," she said coquettishly, even though his birthday wasn't this side of the year.

She put her glass on the arm of the settle in the hall and pulled out from under it a large box wrapped in brown paper and tied up with string. She said, "There you are, darling," and smoothed down the waist, then the sides of her dress with her hands.

"What do you think?" she said. "Do you recognize it?"

He looked down at the parcel. "No. I have no idea. What is it?"

She laughed. "Open it," she urged. "Go on, open it."

Clive took out his pocketknife. Deftly, he sliced the string and split off the brown paper. I caught sight of the writing on the box before all the paper had come away.

"It's a Robinsons trap!" I exclaimed, as the paper fell away.

"So it is," Clive said plainly.

Then I remembered how openly he'd despised the idea of a Robinsons. He'd made it quite clear he didn't want one. I realized of course how much effort Maud would have gone to, tracking down the brothers' company in Kent and ensuring it arrived in time for our return, and I worried—as Clive casually undid the box and laid out the pieces—that he'd be ungrateful.

But he didn't reject the present out of hand, as I'd assumed. Instead he examined the parts to see how the structure had been designed and muttered disparagingly about any flaws that were instantly apparent to him. Then he set to piecing the thing together before he'd even consulted the instructions. It wasn't long before he was completely immersed in the assemblage, studying the dynamics and durability of each little part before fitting it into the structure. I began to realize that, in actual fact, Clive was excited. But even then, as he assembled the device, he swore at the ill-fitting bulb and the tiffany of the surround, cheaper than he himself would have used.

Maud offered to fetch him a glass of bitter lemon but I don't think he heard her. I remember how he stood back, trap partly assembled, almost suppressing a laugh as he said, without taking his eyes off it, "This really is beautiful, beautiful. Thank you, Maud." He walked round it, at arm's length, like a dealer checking first the head and then the flanks of a horse he'd acquired. "Look at this. It's exquisite. Really stunning." Maud couldn't have wished for a more effusive reaction or more obvious gratitude, but she went into the kitchen to serve up the supper as if she'd gone off the whole thing.

I followed her in to see if I could help. It was funny to hear Clive next door, muttering half sentences to himself: "Oh, I *see*." "Yes, that's how they did it." "Interesting . . . but I can't believe it stays put." "The wind'll whip that." Sometimes he swore in frustration, I presumed when something wouldn't fit, and at other times he'd let out a little pitted laugh. The sounds and words came from him unrestrained, as though he were the only person in the world.

Clive was so thrilled with his new Robinsons that, in fact, it turned out to have been a mistake to give it to him before supper. It seemed Maud had worked that out already, the way she called him halfheartedly to the dining table. After we'd sat there for ten minutes it was quite apparent that there was no chance of Clive joining us.

Maud and I sat together and ate. She'd set little posies on the table and dressed it with the family silver as she had years ago. I'd forgotten how good-looking my mother was, even though the dress she wore didn't suit her age. The neckline was too prim, the waist too pretty and the dainty, lace-trimmed sleeves cut into the baggy skin at the top of her arm, leaving the rest drooping loosely out of it and juddering as she cut up her food. Still, it was easy to see how lovely she'd once been and, even now, I was impressed by how handsome she was with a little effort. She'd given her face some extra color and her eyes were lifted with blue shadowing. She'd pressed her lashes with the lash curler, forcing them upwards, curly and girly. But Maud's earlier exuberance had subsided. She was quiet and unhungry. She opened a bottle of wine.

EVERY NIGHT I'd ever known, Clive had unfailingly set a moth trap, a simple homemade device, on the slate sill outside the drawing-room window before he went to bed. He called it the Night Watch. It wasn't for serious collecting, just a daily reference to see which moths had visited during the night, to note what sort of weather and temperature had brought them, or even, in some cases, to forecast weather that was on its way.

The evening that Maud gave him his Robinsons, he set it on the drawing-room sill, replacing the one that had kept the Night Watch for more than a decade. During the night, at times of lighter sleep, I was plagued by anticipation of the rare visitors we would find in this new miracle trap, and in the morning I rushed down first thing to have a look. Clive was already there and he was giving it undue attention. True, the jar was reasonably full, but I could tell in the instant I scanned it that there were no great surprises, no jewels. It might seem insignificant now—as it did to me at the time—but that morning Clive did something I found extraordinary.

Most mornings he scanned the Night Watch quickly, jotted down anything of interest, then released the lot. Very occasionally he found a scarce one worth breeding, or one with a pigment he wanted to assay. Then he'd drop a couple of grams of tetrachloroethane into the jar to sedate them all and pick out the ones he wanted. But that morning he chased around in it with his hands like an amateur, wrecking—I was sure—a number of beautiful specimens. Garden Tigers, Underwings, a Bordered Beauty, Scalloped Oak, some Small Black Arches and several species of Pug were disregarded in the wake of his unfathomable mania. I thought he must be after the Light Crimson Underwing for a source of that iridescent pink, but why not anesthetize the jar first? Instead he spent at least a minute rummaging about, crushing some and damaging others until finally he had hold of a small, unremarkable gray micro-moth that I hadn't even noticed.

There are nearly one thousand species of larger moth in Britain, but more than three times as many small—and sometimes tiny—micro-moths. Far too many for them all to have names, so that when Clive had hold of that one, at the time I didn't even know what it was. All I could think was, What an odd calculation to damage lots of beautiful large ones in order to catch such a dull, possibly nameless, tiny one. His strange behavior didn't stop there. He pinched it neatly through the thorax with his thumb and index fingernails, which is a way of killing that usually you'd use only as a last resort—say, when you're in the field and haven't brought any killing fluid with you, or if you're specifically trying to avoid the side effects of some of the poisons, such as the discoloring of ammonia or the stiffening of cyanide. Pinching is bound to mash the body a bit, and it's certainly not the way I'd have chosen to kill a little moth like that. I'd have pricked it in the belly with a nitric acid needle.

"It's *Nomophila noctuella,*" Clive announced finally, arranging it in a small pillbox.

I wasn't to find out for two more years, on the day that Maud died, why he was so unusually interested in it.

CHAPTER 10

Bernard's Challenge

A WEEK AFTER the convention, Clive received a simple telegram. It was from Bernard, who was, by that time, head of biological sciences at a northern university. It read simply:

YOU DO BRIMSTONE STOP
I'LL DO SWALLOW-TAILED STOP
IT'S A RACE STOP
BERNARD STOP

"Silly games," Clive tutted, tossing the telegram dismissively into the wastepaper basket in the hall. "He's supposed to be a professor now," he added, walking through to the kitchen.

I had thought that would be the end of it so at first I didn't take much notice. But—now here's the funny thing—it turned out Bernard understood something about my father that I didn't: that a challenge of this nature had an irresistible lure for him, that even against all rational judgment and time pressures on our mounting deadlines, he would never ignore it.

A moment after he'd dismissed it as frivolous, I saw Clive scribbling calculations on the notepad he carried with him in his jacket pocket for "observations," but it was only after lunch, when he laid out his entire stratagem for assaying the Brimstone fluorescence, that I realized he was picking up the gauntlet. He still professed irritation at Bernard's message, so I can't think why he decided to waste valuable time and energy on it when we were already up to our necks in the grant-backed research.

To make all this perfectly clear, what Bernard was challenging us to was a race to assay the fluorescent compound in the two species of moth—him doing the Swallow-tailed and us the Brimstone. First we'd need to extract the compound, a fairly simple process of emulsifying the animal with a pestle and mortar and putting the resulting slurry through a series of alcoholic distillations. Assaying the compound would be easy too, if a little laborious: it's a series of strategically devised chemical tests, the results of which would lead, by a process of elimination, like laboratory Cluedo, to the type of compound we were dealing with, if not to its specific empirical formula. There were lots of tests to do: the murexide test for uric acid; litmus test for pH; chromatography for solvency; hydrogenation, distillation, oxidization and acid/alkali reactions.

So what was the difficult bit of the enterprise? The challenge, as Clive put it, was not in the chemistry but in the cooking. It was a problem of quantities: to get enough of the fluorescing compound to do the assay, Clive had worked out that we were going to need to crush more than twenty-five thousand Brimstones.

So that was it. We went headlong into Bernard's challenge.

YOU CAN'T JUST set up a light trap night after night and hope you'll catch lots of Brimstones. By the time the hunting season is over you'd have only a few hundred. We needed thousands, and quickly, and for that some cunning was required. Clive devised an ambitious plan. First, we needed virgins.

Moths share our weakness for sweets and alcohol, and the Brimstone is no exception. If you take the time to make their favorite recipe, mix it in a little treacle and smear it on trees or fence posts, they will come from miles around to feast and, at the same time, get stuck to the treacle, ripe for collection. So Clive went into the pantry and, like a witch at a cauldron, set about mixing together a potion of exquisite attractiveness to Brimstones, whose particular tastes are for wine, fermented bananas and rum. In time he reappeared with a sticky, gloopy pot of sour-smelling treacle.

Clive knew when and where the Brimstones would be on the wing and want a little something sweet. Each morning and night, he consulted his barograph and plotted the hygrometer recordings, patiently awaiting the perfect conditions. Moths won't come to sugar when the air current is northeast or easterly, or if the atmosphere is not to their liking. For the first three weeks the weather was lazy and calm, too clear, too hot or too dry, but in the middle of the fourth there was a sharp rise in the mercury. It was overcast at dusk, and the night became a little thick and heavy, tight and threatening, hot and thundery, not a breath of wind. . . .

"Tonight," said Clive, like a conjurer, "but the Brimstones won't fly 'til ten."

Just prior to the ten o'clock news on the wireless, we slopped the treacle in strips onto six of the lime trees down the drive, and just after the news we returned to collect fourteen fresh yellow Brimstone females, two pregnant and twelve virgins.

It was the virgins we particularly prized. Back inside, I squeezed their bottoms one by one, and out dripped the most powerful aphrodisiac known to nature. Males will seek it out from up to five miles away, even from within a closed smoke-filled room upwind. It was with this powerful potion that we were going to persuade all the male Brimstones in southwest Dorset to flock here to take part in our experiments.

As well as light traps, which we set along the hawthorn hedges, we hung the scent of virgins in lures all over the grounds and began to collect the Brimstone population of the surrounding countryside.

They came each night in their hundreds and each day I had the laborious task of anesthetizing them in batches and sampling through them, gassing the males, saving the pregnant females, which we could breed from, and squeezing the virgins for more potion. It was like a military operation, the mass execution of the local Brimstone population, and I sat from dawn to dusk, for days and weeks, during that long deathly summer, separating those who were to be immediately gassed and those who were of more use to us alive.

THAT SUMMER Clive and I were both so involved in our work that we'd break for a quick meal at seven, then work long into the night. The autumn that followed was particularly dreary, bringing days when the mist refused to lift, as if a daylong dusk had come forever to the Bulburrow valley. Looking back, I can see how I got caught up in Clive's unhealthy obsession with his work but—you must believe me—I'm not about to make excuses for the problems that arose from it.

One early autumn day Clive and I were busy killing and counting the second-generation Brimstones from the night before. It had been the best catch of the season, the trap such a shimmer of iridescent yellow it looked as if we had caught a single celestial being, which writhed in protest in its jar. It was while we were jubilantly counting them, more than two thousand in one trap, that we considered showing the result to Maud. That is when, to my disgrace, I worked out that we hadn't seen her for two days.

Eventually we found her camped in the library. She had moved in, she said, in high spirits. The room stank. The customary smell of old books and beam oil was now suffused with burnt toast, stale breath and pure alcohol. She was lying on the floor in front of the sofa, her head propped up on her hand, her usually temperate hair loose and angry. Various books, with some issues of *The Ideal Home,* for which she had a subscription, were strewn about. Within her reach there were two plates with crumbs, a yogurt pot and a Kit Kat wrapper. Letters from Vivi were scattered across the floor with an array of varnished gourds usually displayed in a bowl on the window seat. The Hoover was on its side under the window as if it had dashed out of its cupboard in the hall in an independent attempt to help but at the last moment keeled over in horror at the sight of it all. I counted five bottles of Garvey's sherry at various levels of empty, and seven tumblers. It was just after ten-thirty in the morning.

"Did you discover how to make a moth?" She grinned.

Clive tutted and walked out.

I was shocked. "Not yet, Mummy," I said, appalled at the state of her and the room and my own selfishness not to have seen what had become of her. A sick thrust of guilt and love and shame and overbearing failure churned through me.

"I'm so sorry, Mummy," I said, kneeling to hug her. "I'm so, *so* sorry." I started to cry, taking her in my arms, and I felt her stiffen a little as if the role reversal was too unnatural for her.

"What on earth are you sorry about, darling?" She giggled, her chin digging into my shoulder. "I really don't give a damn if you haven't discovered the divine secret of moths," she slurred. "I never have," she whispered. "Just don't tell Daddy that." Her elbow slipped, her head hit the floor and she laughed at the ceiling in pure enjoyment.

"No," I said, straightening up. "I'm sorry about *this*." I gestured to the room around me.

"What?"

"Well, the room. And you lying here like this and—"

"You mean all the crap, darling?" she said, with her arms outstretched as she lay on the floorboards. "Oh, we don't need to worry about that, my love, just a little dust and a sweep and a . . . you know, we can do it anytime," she said, breaking into a sort of singsong.

She'd lost sight of herself. What was the point in trying to convey to her what I saw? What a shock the real Maud would have if I could lead her into the room and show her *this* Maud as I saw her now. Maud, one of the most respectable people in this village. It struck me suddenly that it was partly my fault. The real Maud would have put enough trust in me to ensure it never came to this. I'd failed her, even though she'd always been there for me. I'd let her down because I had been too concerned for too long with my work and my own life to see what needed to be done.

"What's the time, darling?" she asked, sitting up again.

The shutters were closed and I shouldn't have thought she knew the time, the day or the year. Maud was not there at all. I checked my watch. "It's just gone ten-thirty." I went to open the shutters. "In the morning," I added.

What happened next came as a bolt from the blue.

"What do you mean by that, Virginia?" Maud barked aggressively at my back. "What do you mean by *in the morning*?"

I turned slowly. I wanted to say that I hadn't meant anything by it, but when I opened my mouth nothing came out.

"In the morning," she repeated, imitating an enfeebled voice. "Don't you dare patronize me, my girl. Hear me. I won't stand for that behavior from you. Do you understand?" She was shouting now and had pulled herself up to sit with her back against the sofa.

"Look at me," she ordered, and stared straight into my eyes in the most frighteningly direct way, a look I'd never seen in her before, her eyes keen, wild and vivid. She pointed at me and went on, "You might think you've got all big and clever because you've joined Daddy in his work, and you might think what you do makes the world go round, but, Ginny"—she stopped shouting, stayed pointing and deepened her voice so low and gravelly that it shook—"you've still got a hell of a lot to learn, my girl, and I don't want to *ever* hear you talking to me like that again. I don't care what you might think I am, or how remarkable you think you are, but you *will* respect me because I'm your mother. Do you understand? Do—You—Understand?" she repeated, shouting once more.

CHAPTER 11

Arthur and the Cannibals

I TOOK THE REST of the day off to look after Maud and straighten the house. After supper Vivi phoned. Maud was fast asleep on the sofa in the library where I'd left her, wrapped up in a blanket like a battered sausage. If Vivi had been here, I thought, she'd never have let Maud get into that state. She'd have confronted the issue early on. She'd have picked Maud up by the shoulders, given her a good shake and told her to pull herself together. That's what a good daughter would have done.

Vivi was talking to me but I wasn't listening. Had it been obvious? Had all the signs been there that Maud had started to drink so much? I must have been blinded by my own ambitions. It had suited us to be left alone to our work that summer. Then I remembered a promise I'd once made to Maud, after Vera died. She'd made me promise I'd hit her over the head rather than let her die a death like Vera's. She'd said, "Ginny, I want to die quickly and with dignity. I want you to remember that." I was sure that Maud would have applied "dignity" to how she wanted to be seen conducting herself in life too, and it was there that I knew I'd let her down.

Vivi said she was coming home the weekend after next. "And I've a little surprise," she said.

I wondered if it could be anything like as surprising as the things that had gone on in this house recently. I wanted so much to tell her about Maud shouting at me that morning but I stopped myself, partly because I knew Vivi would storm in and make a scene about it, and partly because I knew I was to blame. I suppose I had patronized Maud, even though I hadn't meant to. And I had failed to help her before she'd got herself into such a state, and for that I deserved a dressing-down. But Maud was wrong about my arrogance. I'd never thought of myself as arrogant.

"I'm bringing Arthur," Vivi said. "Arthur. My boyfriend," she added after my silence.

I HEARD MAUD stirring and decided that the news of Vivi's forthcoming visit would cheer her up. As I walked in I was assaulted by the acute smell of rancid vomit. I walked across the room and folded back the shutters round the box bay window, allowing the day's silver light to streak across the floorboards and leap onto Maud. She'd hardly moved. Her face was loose and relaxed, her mouth open and her cheeks sagging, temporarily released from the pressures of life. But she'd been sick in her sleep: a dried crust ran down her blanket, spilling over to scurf the yellow silk sofa and down, pooling in the gap between the floorboards below. I went to get a bucket and mop, and when I returned she was sitting up, looking bewildered.

"Hello, Maud. You've been a bit sick," I informed her as I busied about, unable to look her in the eye. She stirred slowly back to the here and now.

"Oh. Oh, darling, how disgusting, oh, you are a sweetie. I must have . . . I don't feel too well," she said. She looked dreadful—old, even. She stuck out her hand, signaling to me not to clear up the mess, then grabbed my arm and held it tight. "What happened, darling?" she said. "I don't remember." Her eyes pleaded for comprehension. I led her gaze with mine to a Garvey's amontillado bottle lying empty on the floor a yard away.

"Oh. Oh, yes," she said and let go of my arm, leaving a little bleached band where her fingers had squeezed it bloodless.

"Vivi's coming home soon—the weekend after next. And she's bringing Arthur," I said.

"Arthur?"

"Her boyfriend."

"Vivien," she said. "Oh, no." She crashed back onto the sofa, defeated by the day before it had begun.

I knew what she was thinking. "Don't worry, Maud, I'll help you," I said, putting my hand on her arm.

"Would you, darling?" she asked. "Would you really?" Right there and then there passed between us an unsaid secret. We both knew what kind of help she needed. If she was to keep her dignity, she must have an ally. She could no longer control the drink's hold on her, so she needed me to do whatever was necessary to cover it up, to hide her ignominious habit. That I should know it she could bear, but that anyone else—most of all Vivi—should discover it would be too humiliating. So, not having found the courage to help her stop, I would become her accomplice instead, standing guard between her and the outside world, protecting her against giving herself away.

VIVI AND ARTHUR arrived just before lunch on Friday, a day earlier than expected. Vivi looked exhausted. She hadn't been home for almost six months and it seemed that so much had changed. As soon as I saw her, I realized I could never tell her about Maud. It wasn't only that I'd promised Maud not to, but also because of the unexpected wedge that lodges itself between people once one of them moves out of the house, as if they've swapped teams. Even though she was a daughter and a sister, Vivi was now officially a *visitor* and it seemed natural that the message should be we were coping just fine without her. So it was that the allegiances of the people within the house, however unstable, far outweighed all external bonds of love and friendship. When Vivi left Bulburrow, she had given up the right to be party to its authenticity; she had visitor status now, so that week I'd made sure I'd scrubbed the house clean and unreal.

When they arrived, I made soup with some courgettes I found in the pantry, and I dragged Clive from the attic and Maud from the library to sit and eat with us all: a pretend family.

I felt a heavy responsibility to everyone to ensure it went smoothly: to Maud, to cover up her secret; to Vivi, to make Arthur feel welcome; and to Clive, to translate for him between his own world and the real one. It felt like I was orchestrating a grand performance. I was protecting everyone from everyone else, and some of them also from themselves.

ARTHUR MORRIS WAS A BAKER, or rather, he helped his father run a business that supplied bread to shops all over London. It was a difficult topic to talk about if you knew nothing much about bakeries or the new self-service stores that Arthur told us were coming from America.

Vivi had first mentioned him to me about four months ago, but I hadn't appreciated until recently that they were actually stepping out together. Arthur had short wavy black hair and two overblown freckles on his forehead. Dimples dug into his face to frame his ready smile, and you could see that his teeth were a little crossed at the front. He was very enthusiastic, about practically everything, and he seemed extraordinarily appreciative to be with us, as if he'd won a golden ticket. He talked a lot, about shopping schemes and shoppers' habits, although during lunch, Clive was patently more interested in the habits of a slothful hornet that had landed on a slice of bread near his elbow and was walking slowly round the edge of it. All in all I thought it was very lucky Arthur was helping himself to conversation because he wasn't being offered any.

It struck me that none of us had any common ground with Arthur, not even Vivi. He had hardly ever set foot outside the city and she had only recently stepped into it. Arthur knew everything about convenience shopping and nothing about insects; Vivi knew little about shops and lots about insects. Arthur was full of optimism and eagerness; Vivi was forever finding obstacles.

I was clearing the soup bowls as Arthur set to with a lengthy description of his baking premises, which, he said, were out to the west on Wainscot Road. Clive sprang on the name as if it were the punch line to the entire luncheon conversation.

"Wainscot Road? How interesting," he said, more animated than he'd been all day. "Why's it called Wainscot?"

"I have no idea, actually," said Arthur, tilting his head, giving the impression that now it had been asked it was an interesting question.

"You don't know?" Clive said incredulously. "You work in a bakery on Wainscot Road—"

"I don't actually work in it," Arthur corrected him—politely and without arrogance. "I run it."

"All the same," Clive said, flipping the comment back at Arthur with his hand as if it were a fly, "you run a bakery on the road but you've never bothered to find out how it got its name?"

"Clive!" Vivi exclaimed, but he ignored her and went on to get assurances from Vivi's boyfriend that he'd go back and find out the origin of the road's name. Because, did Arthur know?, there was an entire family of moths called the Wainscots, so he would be extremely interested to discover if the road was named after these moths or— which he thought more likely—if it was named after the very famous family from whom the moths had also got their name. Arthur agreed cheerfully that it was important, as well as profoundly interesting, that he should find out how the street had got its name, but I had the impression he didn't think Clive was being altogether serious.

Once that conversation was over and agreed on, I was about to prepare for an uncomfortable silence when Vivi saved the moment in one swoop, as easy as a stroll in the park. "Clive is very clever, aren't you, Clive?" she teased.

"Well . . . ," Clive started seriously, missing Vivi's playful sarcasm.

"But the thing, Arthur, that he's particularly clever at is bringing absolutely any conversation round to moths. Most people find it incredibly difficult to put anything about a moth into a conversation, but Clive finds that most conversations naturally come to moths in the end, don't you, Clive?" It was only when Maud and I started to giggle that Clive understood he was being gently teased and braved a small smile. Arthur was gazing at Vivi adoringly.

"Clive," Vivi continued bossily, "why don't you show Arthur some of your specimens? He'd love to see them." She turned to Arthur. "Clive's got moths from all over the world. Some are bigger than your hand."

I relaxed a little, letting my responsibility lighten. Vivi was taking control. She was pure, fresh air, and slowly she was filling up the house with it, resuscitating the space and pulling us all back together.

CARING FOR CATERPILLARS is like caring for the young of any animal. They require constant attention. Our attic and our drawing room and, incidentally, much of our south terrace were full of larvae boxes housing our self-created plague of Brimstone caterpillars. Once we'd given Arthur a tour of the museum, he volunteered to come on our rounds of the caterpillars, helping to clean them out, give them fresh food and check them over.

The Brimstone is a shady brown caterpillar tinged with green and spends much of its time clasping a twig with its back legs, sticking its body out in front of itself, rigid yet crooked, looking uncannily like the twisted twigs of the bramble it's most often found on. To complete the general effect, it has two growths midway along its back that look exactly like a pair of buds. It took Arthur a while to find one, but once he caught sight of it he was so thrilled that he made a game of seeing how many others he could spot in each cage. He asked a torrent of questions with boyish enthusiasm so we were spurred into explaining to him the basics of their daily care. Clive gradually assumed his lecture voice, giving Arthur tips—their leaves should be fresh but not the youngest and most succulent in case the richness gave them diarrhea.

"The onset of diarrhea spreads through a box of larvae like a virus and it's nearly always fatal to the whole batch," Clive informed him. I could see he was beginning to warm to Arthur. "You also need to check for flu, fleas, parasitic flies, wasps, mites, and, because caterpillars are little more than a bag of fluid, they're particularly susceptible to desiccation, drowning, sweats, salt—"

"The odds don't sound good for a caterpillar," Arthur interrupted gamely.

"And their worst enemy—*earwigs,*" Clive replied.

"Earwigs?"

"Terrible. Terrible," Clive said, shaking his head vehemently. "If I could destroy an animal species on earth forever it would be the earwig. They manage to invade even the most indestructible box to ravage my caterpillars—"

"What's this?" Arthur interrupted him. He'd picked up a jam jar of leaves and was peering into it, searching it for a less upsetting subject than the earwig one.

"Why's this poor fellow all on his own?" Arthur asked once the occupant had been spotted.

"He's a cannibal," said Clive, almost proudly, a parent blind to his offspring's antisocial habit.

"Oh?" Arthur said, regarding the jar now as if he might drop it.

"Some are born with a taste for their brothers and sisters. All of them eat their shells once they've hatched, but some then carry on and eat through their siblings."

"That's quite disgusting," Arthur said definitively, placing the jar down carefully.

"Well, it's all good protein," Clive reasoned. "Some species, like the Privet and the Death's-head, the whole lot of them are cannibals and will never let up on a chance to gnaw into each other, but with the others you might get just one or two in a batch. The trick is to spot them before they start because once they get going that's it, they'll finish off all the others pretty quick."

"So you have to sit and watch them once they've hatched, at the ready to pick out the cannibals?"

"Well . . . yes."

"But how long do you have to watch them for? I mean, how long before you know they're *not* going to start eating the others?" Arthur asked, obviously worrying that too much time was spent on this one exercise.

Clive looked at me and smiled wearily. I knew he was thinking that such details were a little tricky to explain.

"No," I butted in abruptly, "you don't really need to watch them at all. You can usually just guess—instantly—which ones will be cannibals."

Arthur raised his eyebrows and I realized that wasn't a sufficient answer for him. He was genuinely interested.

"You just *know*," I tried to clarify. "They've got a look about them."

"Vivi!" Arthur shouted playfully to her in the next room. "You're going to have to clear this one up for me."

"How can you tell a cannibal?" he asked her as she glided into the room.

"Well, they're the only ones left, silly," Vivi replied cheekily.

"No, *before* they've eaten the others," he said.

"Oh, that," she said, affecting mystery. "They've just got a look about them," and Arthur and I, we started laughing.

I FOUND MAUD keeping herself busy in her potting shed. I'd hidden her sherry today, as we'd agreed, and as soon as she saw me she said—very politely—"I need a little drink, Ginny." I didn't say anything. It was half-past four. She was trying to separate some bulbs as she said it, and I remember watching her shaky hands, which looked like mine do now, swollen round the joints and bent at the knuckles. All they were achieving was to strip off layers of the bulbs' papery skin, as if her fingers couldn't get a proper grip. Now that I know how hard my own hands are to manage I realize her arthritis might have impeded her, but back then I was shocked by what I thought were clearly withdrawal symptoms.

It was only after supper, when Maud seemed choked with desperation, that I finally helped her into the library. I was proud of her, like a nurse might be proud of a patient, and I told her so. She said nothing. She sat stiffly on a small upright chair by the window and looked at her feet, lifting them up and down to exercise her ankles.

Since I'd become her official collaborator, we'd normally have gone through a little role-play at this point: I'd ask her if she wanted a drink, she'd say, "Go on, then, just a small one," and chide me for not joining her. We'd talk about whatever sprang to mind, and for a while it would seem a most congenial affair. Then, when her sense started to leave her, I'd go and let her slip inside herself to reflect on the darker side alone.

That night, however, she sat there on the chair, loosening her ankles and rubbing her clenched hands up and down her legs to encourage the circulation. When I asked if she'd like a drink, she didn't answer. Her jaw was taut and I wondered if she was even capable of speaking. Then, when I poured her drink, she couldn't muster the coordination to hold it steady, so I wrapped my hands round hers and together we lifted the glass to her mouth and tipped it. At that moment I felt us take another secret leap together. The role-play, the polite ceremony, the pretense, it was all gone now and her crude addiction was laid bare between us. By the third glass she'd refueled and discovered a moment of equanimity. She relaxed into the chair.

"Ginny," she said, "what would I do without you? Thank you." This was the first phase—I called it her lucid phase—when she was replenished but not too drunk, when the sherry had loosened her tongue, but not her mind, and she would pour out funny stories and scrutinize the world.

I'll tell you something now, something I'm ashamed to admit, one of those honest little secrets that are hard enough to admit to yourself, and I can only hope that you'll try to understand why I felt it. You see, I began to covet the intimacy that Maud's reprehensible secret brought us and I really enjoyed—looked forward to, even—the entertaining moments her lucid phase would bring. One minute she'd have found a way to relate the pattern of Mrs. Axtell's flower borders to her personality, the next she'd have taken on one of Clive's pompous colleagues in a make-believe row. Maud had never talked to me in that way before. It was like some of the conversations she used to have with Vivi.

The second phase was when Maud *turned*. I was usually out of the room well before she turned, but that day she'd drunk too much too fast, and the lucid phase skipped by too quickly. Something trapped and dissatisfied was gathering buoyancy, pushing its way to the surface. She transferred herself to the sofa to sit next to me.

"Well, what do you think, darling?" she whispered hoarsely.

"Think of what?"

"The boyfriend. Bit stiff, darling, don't you think?" Maud said, discarding the whisper. "Tight-arsed, don't you think? Tight-arsed," she said, even louder. Her head flopped against the back of the sofa and she laughed.

"Bloody London bloody little tight bloody arse," she said, laughing at her moment of inspired rhapsody.

I didn't say anything.

Then she turned on me, her mood switching suddenly. "What's wrong with you? Can't you talk?" she snapped.

I didn't say anything.

"You can wipe that bloody look off your face, Ginny," she said. "You've really got some cheek, you know. You're not so damn perfect yourself." She'd consumed an entirely different personality.

Just then we heard Arthur's laugh burst out down the hall and luckily her attention was thrown back to him.

"Tight-arse," she shouted to the ceiling. Then her eyes searched me out again. "Well, don't you think, darling," she said more softly, "bloody tight-arse?" I glanced nervously towards the door, as if to judge how far through it her voice might travel. Maud caught me. "Oh, Ginny, darling, please don't be so bloody pathetic. I'm just telling the truth, darling," she complained peevishly. "Can't you see he's a bloody tight-arse? God, I think I might have to go and live in Spain, yes, that's not a bad idea, is it? What do you think? Get away from here for good and sit in the sun and look at the sea, darling, what do you think?"

I knew I had to leave.

"Tight. Arse." She laughed again, as if it were just saying the words that she found so enjoyable—therapeutic, even.

"I'm going to do the washing up and then I'll be back," I said quickly, and left before she had a chance to protest. I knew the only possible way to extricate myself was on a promise to return, and I was relieved when I'd closed the door behind me. I stayed to listen. It was my responsibility to make sure no one saw her drunk.

There was silence for a second, then the clanking of glass on glass. Maud was going to make trouble tonight. I took a deep breath and rubbed two fingers along the key in the door's lock. I balanced the risks: I could faintly hear Vivi and Arthur chatting in the drawing room farther down the hall; Clive was either in the cellar or the attic; Maud's sherry supply was plentiful and I doubted, anyway, that she'd be able to get up from the sofa for the rest of the night. My mind was made up.

I held my breath, pulled the door tightly towards me so the lock wouldn't click and, very slowly, very quietly, turned the key.

It felt good. A problem locked up for the night.

I went to clear up the kitchen. Tonight's outburst had been less manageable and had felt more sinister than any of the previous ones. It was not only my job to hide her behavior from Clive, Vivi and the rest of the world, but also my solemn promise to the other Maud, my mother Maud. Vivi was in the house and I would have to be on guard all night. All at once the house, and everything in it, felt extremely precarious.

I HAD NEARLY FINISHED the dishes when I heard a dreadful thudding at the library door and Maud shouting, her voice distorted with rage. "Ginny, come and open this door at once!"

I could hear the pounding and crashing of books being flung at the inside of the door. What had I been thinking to lock her in?

"Ginny, do you hear me? How *dare* you lock me in."

I was outside the door now, silent—and uncertain whether or not to open it. I wasn't sure that anyone else could hear her. I didn't want to enrage her further but I didn't know what I would be faced with if I opened it. I was weighing the options when she whispered through the door. Surely she couldn't have known I was standing there.

"Ginny . . . I promise that if you don't open this door right now, I promise, *I'll kill you,*" she threatened in a low growl.

I turned the key, the door flew open and three large hardback books hurtled towards me, glancing off me as I ducked. Then more books came, one or two at a time, as I cowered on the hall floor.

Vivi opened the door to the drawing room and stuck her head out. "What the hell's going on?" she said. "What *are* you doing, Ginny?"

Thankfully she hadn't witnessed any books in flight. She saw me kneeling in the hall with books scattered around me and I quickly busied myself with collecting them up and sorting them into piles. As soon as Maud heard Vivi, she had shut the library door on herself.

"I'm just chucking out old books. We're finally sorting the library," I lied impressively.

"Well, you don't have to throw them around, do you?" Vivi said, slightly irritated, and went back to Arthur.

I pushed the books against the wall and went to bed. I was relieved that Vivi would be gone tomorrow and we could get back to our normal routine without any added constraints.

THE FLYING BOOKS marked the start of violence that seemed as addictive as the drink. When she was drunk Maud looked for a fight—only with me—and the more I tried to appease her, to say the right thing, to tell her what I thought she wanted to hear, the more aggressive she became. It was a good day when I suffered merely a little shouting, and increasingly normal to suffer worse. I didn't resent her for it. I felt sorry for her. I saw how she couldn't help it, how she went away and something else filled her place that didn't resemble her old self in any way at all. It took hold and possessed her, gaining in strength daily, feeding off her weakness. At those times she wasn't my mother: she'd been ravished by a demon, overtaken by uncontrollable anger and aggression. Strangely, she was physically far stronger too, than my mother ever was. I found her lifting tables, smashing doors, throwing chests, things Maud would never have been able to move, as if her muscles, during those rabid moments, received a secret gift of strength. But it was her eyes that were most severely altered. They quickly became another's. Clear, hard-edged and determined. Eyes that saw everything darkly. And I knew that Maud would never conquer this thing. Its force and ambition grew more palpable each day.

But one thing I could never understand. Even though I'm sure she was, for the most part, oblivious to her attacks, she would always stop the instant she heard Clive coming, and switch to a task close at hand. She was like a five-year-old who, even if she seemed completely out of control, still knew somewhere in her heart that she shouldn't be behaving as she was.

When I closed my eyes at night, I'd remember my mother, the sober Maud, who'd hold me in her more lucid moments, stroke my hair and tell me she loved me so much it hurt. And then she'd thank me for being me, and I'd almost imagine her eyes were wet with tears, and I'd wonder if she was ever aware of the terror that daily turned in her.

CHAPTER 12

I Spy

VIVIEN'S BEEN HOME for a day now, almost exactly twenty-four hours. I've been lying on my bed all morning. The last time I saw her was earlier this morning, when I was holding my glass of milk as a prop and it had become quite obvious we had very different memories of our late father.

Since then I've been trying to shake off this awkward, irrepressible feeling that has crept over me ever since she came home: the need to know exactly where she is and what she's doing. As time goes on the urge grows stronger. I've managed to get through the last forty-seven years without knowing her whereabouts, yet now, since twenty-four hours ago, I'm liable to panic if at any point I don't know where she is. It's completely illogical, I know. Perhaps it's because I'm used to knowing exactly where and how things are in the house, because my surroundings are fixed, a constant if you like, and that, until Vivien came home, I was the only variable.

Luckily she doesn't realize I've been spying on her. I know this house so intimately that I don't need to be right on her heels. I've been developing a system whereby I can track her movements by listening to its sounds while staying within my own boundaries. I know all the views from the windows. I can recognize the doors that creak, the boards that squeak and the pipes that rattle. I can interpret the echoes that reverberate through the air spaces, the windows that shake when certain doors are opened and closed and the sounds that old ventilation pipes bring me from all directions. It is as if the entire internal workings of the house have been transformed into a vast communications network, carrying to me the sounds of Vivien, wherever she may be.

For instance, I might look through a window on the first floor to see her pass by another in a different wing or on a different floor, and I know if I move to a back room on the ground floor I will be able to hear her footsteps above me. Then, with the creak of a door, I can judge where she's headed. I've been following her routine (at our age you always have a routine, it's impossible not to—your body dictates it): last night she got up to go to the lavatory twice, and this morning to get her—and my—tea. All these noises are brought to me by this loyal house, as though it's alive and throbbing and I am in tune with it, or even part of it, as Vera once said she was. It's on my side.

However, it means I'm always trying to make sure she doesn't see me, so our paths haven't crossed as much as you might imagine they would, and there seems so much that is still unsaid between us.

LISTEN, I can hear her again. She's bashing about loudly—in the hall, I think. I pull myself off the bed and creep onto the landing. She's rattling the door to the cellar, trying to open it. She's got various keys in her hand that she must have found in the house and she's trying each in turn. I'm baffled as to why she wants to open it. I tread as quietly as I can down the stairs and finally step out behind her.

"Oh my God, you gave me the fright of my life!" Vivien gasps, as her hand shoots up to her chest.

"Sorry."

"I never know where you are or where you come from. It's always so quiet and then you appear out of nowhere."

"I saw you were trying to open the cellar door," I say.

She looks at her hands as if to remind herself that that's what they've been doing. "Yes I was, as a matter of fact. That's exactly what I was trying to do." She puts them back on the door latch and gives it a demonstrative yank.

"What do you want from there? What are you looking for, Vivien?" I want her to know that I've guessed she's come back to look for something.

"I don't want anything. I just want to take a look, but the damn thing's got stuck," she says, pulling at it again. She stops and stares at me. "I'm allowed to, you know," she says testily, although I didn't say she wasn't. "Sometimes I think you forget it's my house too."

Her saying that surprises me a little. Of course I've always known it's both of ours, but she's right. I never really think of it as hers.

"I've had the door locked," I say. She might as well know her labors are futile.

"But I've unlocked it."

"You've unlocked it with the key but there's a bolt on the inside."

"On the inside?"

"I got Michael to put it on the inside, then climb out through the window."

She looks at me strangely.

"Why on earth would you want to do that?"

"It was years ago, after Maud's death. I never wanted to see the damn cellar after that. I didn't want to be reminded of it or have it happen again. The problem is, it's completely dark and the stairs are so steep and they're right in front of you. It's easy to see how you might step out into nothing as you reach for the switch. And that would be it."

"So that's why you locked it?"

"Yes."

"Because Maud fell down the steps." She eyes me carefully, uncertainly, as she has many times the past day. It feels intrusive, as if she's looking right through my clothes to my nakedness.

"Yes," I say impatiently, and even as I say it I can tell that Vivien has planned, in her mind, the entire future of this conversation, and I don't like it.

"So you still think that's what happened?" she says, to my astonishment.

It's been years since I've felt someone's goading me. I thought I'd long grown out of it, but here I am now, feeling tight as a coil, like an adolescent, remembering with irritation how Vivien had a way of obfuscating everything, and how Maud had to tell her to stop it because I never found a way to react that didn't make it worse.

"Yes, that's what happened," I reply, with mild indignation.

She considers, and nods.

"Never mind," she says, stepping back from the door and turning to leave.

Is she really going to end the conversation right there, like that? She can't do that. You can't start a revolution and then go home for tea.

"I was here, Vivien," I say. "I saw her. I phoned for the ambulance."

"Were you, Ginny?" she says, stopping to look up at Jake. "Were you standing right there? Did you see her fall?"

"Where were you?" I retort, more sharply than I'd imagined I could.

She shakes her head and turns to go, another of her most maddening teenage tendencies. She had a habit of introducing an infuriating idea or a niggling suspicion, and then she'd refuse to explain herself, presumably because she couldn't. And even if the whole thing was complete and utter rubbish, she'd still have left the tiniest doubt to nag away at you for years.

"Vivien, you can't walk away. I asked you a question. I said, 'Where were *you*?' "

She seems a little surprised.

"Where were you when Maud died?"

"In London," she says.

"Exactly." But she doesn't seem to understand the relevance.

"So who is better placed to say what happened?" I say, spelling it out for her.

She is clearly stunned that I'm fighting back. I feel myself redden. I don't remember standing up to her like this before. By all logical reckoning I've won the argument, but for some strange reason it doesn't feel like a victory. She stares at me for longer than I like—as if, for the first time ever, she's lost for words.

"Well," she begins slowly, "I think that depends on who is able to see things as they really are." And then she adds glibly, "Was the cellar door always left open?" Again, a question to which she already knows the answer.

"No. It was left open accidentally and Maud mistook it for the kitchen door."

Now she laughs. Not a real laugh, but an affected, condescending one, emanating superiority. Is it really us having this conversation, exactly the same adolescent girls battling it out with infuriating pauses and omissions, leaving everything unsaid? Why should she make me feel small in my own house?

"Mistook it for the kitchen door?" she says with ludicrous disbelief. "Ginny, how I would love to have your cozy view on life, everything slots into place. You never question anything, do you?" She pauses.

Of course I should be infuriated by her belittling strategy, but instead I'm bewildered. I can't begin to work out what she's getting at.

"She wasn't an *idiot*, Ginny. Why on earth would she mistake it for the kitchen door?"

Now, suddenly, I understand. I've just remembered, *Vivien doesn't know.* She's never known. I'd made sure of it. Of course I'd *like* to tell her the truth. I'd like to scream at her, "No, your mother wasn't an idiot, she was a *drunk*," but I can't bring myself to tell her, to shatter her untarnished memory of her mother. But now I realize that by ensuring that Vivien never knew the truth about Maud's drinking I'd inadvertently led her to question the manner of her death. If only I could tell her that Maud was raving and rampaging at the end, that she could easily have walked into the greenhouse thinking it was the bedroom, or the pond for a bath. Mistaking the cellar door for the kitchen wasn't the least bit difficult to imagine but only, of course, *if you knew.*

"But, Vivien . . ." I sigh, and then I'm stuck for words. The knowledge that I have stood by my promise to Maud gives me the composure to rise above all this. She can patronize me as she likes, but after years of protecting her from the truth about Maud it wouldn't be fair to destroy her perceptions of the past at life's final hurdle, just to prove a point. I won't do it, not only for Maud's honor, but also for my little sister's sake.

"Well, they're right next to each other," I say feebly.

Perhaps she's still not got over Maud's death. Perhaps it was Maud's death that stopped her coming back for so many years.

"I'm sorry," she says, and I let her bring me close until my head is buried in her shoulder and she holds it there firmly. It's her way of finding support.

"No, I'm sorry," I say.

CHAPTER 13

The Ridge Walk

I'LL NEVER FORGET the winter that followed, the same year Vivi brought Arthur to meet us for the first time. It came in quickly. I like winter. I like its contradictions: cold but cozy, sparse but beautiful, lifeless but not soulless. The fences were smoothed with ice, the ground white, crunchy. The trees shut themselves down, skeletons standing firm against the winds, and the ones that line the top of the ridge, exposed and bent like wizened old men, were said in these parts to bear the souls of the dead.

Inside the house winter had come too, for all of us, bleak and desperate, but here it was worse—soulless but not lifeless. Clive continued his feverish pursuit of small-world fame. Maud turned more often to the dark side, her rampages more and more extreme. And I was a wretched bridge between them and the world. I felt liable.

Maud didn't go out anymore. She wouldn't have been able to go through the necessary procedures to get herself ready. For the next few weeks and months, I took her phone calls, answered her letters and when anybody called, Maud was either very busy or fast asleep. Sometimes the villagers would quiz me about her and I'd feel the sweat gathering on my face as I lied, hoping they wouldn't see through me.

Mrs. Jefferson came up to the house on a number of occasions when she realized we'd stopped making it to church on Sundays, and asked if we needed any help. Each time, before she went, she tried to pin me with her small powerful eyes and told me that if ever I needed her she would always be there.

Maud's drunken habits became stranger and less predictable. All of a sudden I'd find out about something she'd been up to for a while, things she'd done covertly so that I'd not known about them, like the time I discovered she'd been telephoning the operator. Apparently she'd insisted on interviewing him for various positions in the house or gardens, even though we weren't looking for anyone in the house and we already had the Coleys for the garden. The operator got so irritated with her disturbing his work that he telephoned one morning and told me he was very happy in the telephone exchange and if we insisted on trying to reemploy him during his working hours he'd have to report us to his supervisor. From then on, I had to remember each evening to pull the telephone cable out of the wall, disconnecting the line into the house.

That winter everything deteriorated, along with Maud. We had the worst storms I could remember, and the cold and the wind and the wet had finally got underneath the vast slated roof on the north side. Clive wasn't interested. He told me to board up the top two floors, Vera's old rooms, of the north wing rather than investigate the leakage. The house was far too big for the three of us, anyhow, and Clive said it wasn't worth maintaining a wing that would never be used again.

Then, late in January, Vivi let in a bit of warmth by coming to visit us, just for a day. She demanded a walk on the ridge. She and I saw walks in the way that most people regard teashops: the perfect environment in which to relax and chat. This walk and talk seemed more urgent than most. She rushed me out of the house, grabbing our coats and hats, and was halfway up the hill at the back, shouting for me to hurry, before I'd even started. There was something on her mind.

It was past midday and the low valley fog had only just lifted, unveiling a layer of soft white sherbet sprinkled on the fields and atop the bare hedges. The chill was ready to be burned off by a weak winter sun, low in the cloudless sky. It's always been the perfect weather in which to admire this part of the country.

We'd reached the top, from where you could see three valleys meeting, rolling and falling, as they'd done for generations. I stopped for a moment, but Vivi went on ahead, following the path along the top of the ridge, drawing in the fresh icy air she missed in London. I stood admiring the village and the patchwork of bleached fields beyond, the solitary farms and homesteads, the hamlet of Saxton perched on the valley's rim and the windy interlocking roads and pathways that bind all these places together, linking one life with the next, in a tangle of shared stories.

I was about to start off again, when I noticed a Fox Moth caterpillar rolled up into a tight black hairy ball and strapped with silk to the side of the fence, hibernating. It would be frozen solid, I mused, as hard as rock, probably too hard even for the birds to eat. It shuts down so spectacularly during hibernation that it's unimaginable there's life left somewhere deep within it, a tiny epicenter with a remnant pulse. But spring always works its magic, bringing it miraculously back to life. Even if it was frozen solid all winter, spring would revive it; if it were submerged in a pool all winter, it would survive; if it were submerged for five years rather than one, those restorative ingredients of its first spring would be able to return it to the world. What was it, I thought, that enabled it to adjourn life so effectively, and how is it that something as simple as the warmth of the sun can restore it, can get the tiny valves pumping once again, to shunt along its cold, stagnant blood? How is it that it can send an impulse to awaken the clusters of nerve cells in each segment of its body? If it doesn't breathe all winter and if its neurons are inert and uncharged, is it theoretically dead? Is this, in fact, a resurrection? I marveled: all this inherent ingenuity, yet it doesn't have the slightest idea that it's doing any of it. Its nervous system is far too simple to *know*, to *think*, to be self-aware. It doesn't even have a brain in the way you'd think of one—a single central command center. Instead it has a loose knot of tangled nerve cells—a ganglion—in each segment of its body, a sort of beaded string of early brains. People see the cleverness of nature and suppose it's the cleverness of the animal itself but it was obvious to me that each and every segment of the animal isn't *aware*. How much I'd hate to live totally unaware of myself, I thought. What would be the point of living, of existing, if you weren't ever to know about it? I looked at the Fox Moth and pitied it, poor unconscious creature. But then, I supposed, at least it wouldn't be disappointed. It would never find out.

I heard Vivi marching up behind me, breathing heavily. She had been far ahead so she must have turned round and come back.

"Ginny," she said, "knock, knock." She tapped my head gently. "You're playing statues again," she said in a childish singsong. I said nothing. I was still thinking: If you were born unaware, at least you'd be blissfully ignorant. It's not as if you're going to wake up one day and suddenly discover yourself.

"Ginny?" she said more seriously. "Ginny, you're not moving." I felt her put a hand on my shoulder. "Giiiinny?" she called, as if she were summoning me from a different floor of the house. Why's she doing that? I thought. I'm right in front of her.

"Ginny!" firmly now, like a mother telling off a child, and she gave my shoulders a little shake.

I looked round at her.

"Oh, God, don't *do* that, Ginny," she said.

"Do what?" I asked.

"Your absence thing. You haven't moved an inch for fifteen minutes."

She was exaggerating, of course. "It's not an absence thing, I was thinking."

"I know, but it does seem like you've gone away sometimes. It really does," Vivi said. "You need a back-in-twenty-minutes sign," she joked lightly.

"I'm just concentrating."

I have the best concentration of anyone I know. I can concentrate so hard that I block out everything around me. My family used to get completely flustered by it but it's perhaps my only natural gift. It annoyed me when Vivi called it being absent. She would say she'd seen me stay as still as a statue for hours at a time but she always exaggerated. In fact I can only ever keep it up for a few minutes.

"I've got something to ask you, Ginny," she said suddenly, as if it were another ploy to pull my attention back to her. "Are you there?" she asked annoyingly.

"Yes."

"Okay," she continued. "I want to get married." She said it quickly, almost as if it were a question.

I stopped, surprised. I'd already thought, over the last few months, that she might marry Arthur. It wasn't what she said that came as a surprise, just that I hadn't expected it right then, or that that would be the manner in which she'd say it.

"Oh, Vivi, that's wonderful," I said effusively. I tried my best to give her an uncustomary hug and sort of grabbed her around the middle.

"Oh, no, he hasn't *asked* me, Ginny. We've just talked about it."

I should have guessed she'd have found a complication. Vivi always managed to fill the simplest ideas with ambiguity. I should have trusted my instincts. Had she actually got engaged, telling me would have been a far more elaborate affair.

"But I can't marry him," she continued, squeezing her eyes shut. Only Vivi, I thought, could start you off assuming this was a happy event and, in moments, twist it into a sad one. Infuriating as it could sometimes be, her overflowing emotion was also part of her appeal, and I hated to see her sad. I could cope with pain and disappointment, but somehow Vivi wasn't built to shoulder anguish. Her fragile body would crumble under its weight. She needed shielding. She should live free of suffering, and in return she'd give so much back in happiness and vibrancy and fun.

"I'm sorry, Vivi. I thought you were saying that you were getting married," I said finally.

There was a long silence. A jay landed on a rusty tin barrel that had been discarded at the edge of the fence by the farmer. It hopped along to the end, jerking its head this way and that with robotic, watchful movements. I knew I wasn't the most ideal comforter at times like this. I was a practical person, not well equipped to offer emotional support. I tried anyway. "So do you think he'll ask you?" I asked cautiously.

"I suppose he has, sort of."

"Well, that's great, isn't it?" I offered.

"But, Ginny, I don't want to."

I was certain that a moment ago she *had* wanted to. As always, with Vivi, I had to expect the unexpected. Often I saw no point in trying to understand her and the puzzles into which she tore her life. I watched the jay as it leaned down over the edge of the barrel, doubling back on itself to inspect the inside. Then it jumped to the ground and skirted warily round some fungus that foamed out from beneath, then hopped sideways and disappeared into the darkness within.

"Don't you want to know why?" Vivi asked.

She'd buried her head in her jacket but I could hear a note of annoyance. "Why?"

"Why do you think, Virginia?" she barked confusingly. First she'd wanted me to ask a question, and then it was a stupid one.

"Because I can't have children," she continued. "I can't have children so I can't see the point of getting married. I mean, if you can't have a family then it's not a . . . It's just not the life I'd want. I can't think of anything more depressing than a childless marriage."

She started to cry properly now and she looked fifteen again. I took her by the shoulders and supported her as she sat down on the icy grass, trying to pull her jacket under her bottom to protect it from the wet. Then I sat down next to her. Her not being able to have children wasn't something we'd ever discussed properly. It had seemed such a small price for her life. I'd never felt any desire for them and had assumed she felt the same. I tried to take an authoritarian stance.

"Now Vivi, you might not be able to have children, but you're alive, aren't you? And you've found a man who loves you and that must be wonderful. You can't have everything always," I finished, just as Maud might have.

"Everything? I don't want everything. I just want a child. I've always wanted a child," she sobbed, "ever since I couldn't have one."

"Well, it's not going to happen, Vivi, and that's that. It's pure biology," I said. I didn't want to make her any more upset but there was nothing else to say. It all seemed pretty miserably final to me. Poor Vivi, I thought. She'd be more stable with the security of marriage. She was the type who needed constant assurance that she was loved. "He loves you for you, Vivi, and not being able to have children is just part of you," I said after some thought.

It stopped Vivi crying. "Rubbish. It's not part of me at all, Ginny," she rebuked me. "I wasn't born unable to have children. It's something I lost. It's a part of me that's missing, not the other way round."

"I'm really truly sorry, Vivi," I said, meaning it sincerely, and put my arm tightly round her. "You poor thing." She sobbed loudly on my left shoulder. I was the stronger, self-sufficient sister and it was at times like this that Vivi really needed me.

When we'd been expelled from school Vivi and I had spent two hours crying in a lavatory cubicle in the kit room with Vivi's best friend, Maisie (who'd apparently requested some bananas in the first place). We'd cried and cried, sobbing as if our lives had fallen apart, and Vivi scratched "Fuck Bananas" with her hair clip three times across the black and yellow harlequin floor tiles and declared she was an anarchist. But to tell you the truth, I wasn't upset. I was just pretending. Instead I felt invigorated, revitalized and valuable. I was at the center of something with my sister. We were deep in it together. After a time I asked Maisie if she could leave us alone for five minutes because, I explained, she wasn't in the same situation as us so she couldn't fully understand what we were going through. Vivi had needed only me then, as she did now, and now, like then, my role as her elder sister suddenly felt crucial.

The jay finally hopped out of the barrel into the light, carrying a snail in its beak like a prize. Vivi looked up and stared at me. Her face had puffed up and—

"Will you have my baby?" she asked.

I laughed.

"No, I mean will you, you know, have my baby?"

CHAPTER 14

Vivien's Day Out

VIVIEN'S WALKED OUT. She's gone. She didn't tell me where she was going or when she was coming back. She didn't tell me she was going out at all. It's all rather odd, don't you think? It's almost like she *sneaked* out, and if I hadn't been watching her I'd never have known. I happened to be in my bathroom, from where I could see her dark outline pass back and forth across her bedroom window. Then I heard her go onto the landing and down the stairs, so I ventured out myself and, halfway down the stairs, I glimpsed the back of her long winter coat as she shut the front door behind her. I wanted to follow her but I knew that by the time I'd changed into warmer clothes, of course I wouldn't know which way she'd gone, so instead I hurried back up the hall stairs to my lookout on the landing and peered close to the leaded window so that I could see which way she was headed. Perhaps, I thought, I could hurry from window to window and keep her in view. I was surprised. I thought she'd retrace one of our old walks; I thought she'd skirt the house and go up the ridge or down through the meadows to the copse. But she didn't. Instead I've just seen her stride off boldly down the middle of the drive, headed for the village, straight into the arms of its whispering houses.

Here's a strange old thing: I didn't want Vivien to go, and as I watched her walking away I was desperate not to lose sight of her. The farther she went, the more I hoped she might suddenly turn round or go right and follow the brook, where I could see her from the house. But—and this is the unexpected part—now that she's gone and I've finally lost sight of her, I'm not craving for her to turn back at all. To tell you the truth, the twisting anxiety that has wrung my stomach ever since her arrival has evaporated, and now I'm overtaken by a delightful sense of relief and freedom. It's the same feeling I had when I watched Bobby driving away, the furniture and all that clutter disappearing down the drive in his van. I have respite from her being continually in the house, and a reprieve from my constant vigilance. I can wander about without worrying where she is, and what I should do or say if I come across her. I can shut a door and know it will stay shut. I can put my tea blends back in the right order in the kitchen cupboard and throw out the greasy butter paper she's been saving in the fridge.

I walk downstairs into the hall, in part to exercise my newfound freedom but also to check she hasn't left any doors open to the empty rooms. I don't like them open. For me they're not part of the house anymore. It's like leaving the front door open. Luckily I find them closed, but it's as I wander through into the kitchen that I notice that Vivien's left her handbag on the counter by the Kenwood mixer. It's a soft green leather one with heavy brass buckles and no zip or fixings so that, as it lies in a saggy pile, the top flops over, showing me through its wide-open mouth, the contents of its belly. A lipstick and a book of stamps peep out near the entrance and, as I come closer and lift up the edge, I see inside a messy world of receipts and slips and paper clips and safety pins, a nail file, the face of a wristwatch with the strap broken off. . . . I am distracted briefly by the inside lining, a thin loose material, unattached to the leather. It is light gray and evenly punctured with tight rows of pinprick holes. Its recurrent pattern mesmerizes me; I can see the dots as rows or as columns, or diagonals, triangles or squares, and then as shapes with depth, stretching away from me until I've lost perspective entirely. Eventually I have to reach out and touch it to feel how far away the material really is and bring me back from my wildly distorted visual field. It feels silky and, as I caress it, it shimmers in the light—like silk, but I know it can't be silk because it catches on the rough dry skin at the tips of my fingers, sending a queer shiver down my back.

I lift the handbag and pour it out, its contents spinning and skating over the smooth Formica work top. I don't know why I'm looking in here or what I think I might find. Perhaps an insight into the new grown-up Vivien or a clue as to why she's returned. I collect up her things, one by one—three pens, her mobile phone, a bunch of keys (what for?), a pocket sized *London A–Z,* six loose bobby pins—and put them back into the bag, aware that she could come back at any moment. There's a lipstick, a powder compact, a fold-up comb, a magnifying glass, three safety pins that I pause to look at (I'd like to add them to the eight I have on my bed to keep the top sheet from shifting against the blanket, but I wouldn't dream of taking them).

I try to put everything back randomly, messily, as chaotic as I found it, but my natural disposition is to order things—it's the scientist in me—and I find it terribly difficult to resist. Once or twice I look the other way, shove my hand into the bag and whiz it around to mess it up more than I am capable of doing deliberately. I envy her the bobby pins and it's as I'm trying one out, sweeping some fringe hair into a parting, that I spot the gold brooch that must have skimmed to the far edge of the counter and come to rest under the shadow of the wall cupboard. It's about the size of a small bird's egg, a similar shape too, oval, but flattened. As I pick it up I see there are small colored stones encrusted in the gold on the front and, in the center, a large bloodred ruby. Its heaviness surprises me. I weigh it in my hands, rolling it over and over. On the back, under the big pin, one edge is beaded with tiny decorative gold hinges, and opposite these is a small catch. I ping the catch open with my nail and catch my breath. It's an old photo, scratched and faded, of Vivi and Arthur gripping each other tightly. They are sitting on a low stone wall and Vivi is holding one hand splayed protectively across her rounded tummy. I peer more closely at the photo. There's no doubt: Vivi looks pregnant. They appear to be a beautiful example of an adoring young couple, a new baby on the way to bond them into a family as well as to each other. I bring it closer to my eyes, trying to fill in the scratches and faded parts as best I can. Vivi is looking at Arthur. Her happiness is transparent. It makes me smile to see it, and she's clinging to Arthur with her other hand as if she's worried he might fall off the photograph. He is upright, stiff and sober-looking, and stares straight at the camera—a proud new parent perhaps? But I find it baffling. I can't remember seeing this photo. I don't know how on earth it could have been taken.

I snap the brooch shut and plop it into the green handbag. I decide to go to the landing, to my lookout, and wait for Vivien to come home, but I can't get the image of her and Arthur out of my head. That young, spirited Vivien was the one I had clearly remembered for all these years, before she turned up again yesterday and started to replace it with the older, less recognizable version. But it's seeing Arthur again that's thrown me. I've never forgotten the snatched time we spent together, but over the years my memory must have distorted his appearance. I've been remembering a fully grown, self-assured man, as if his image had grown old with me, but I'm mistaken. Seeing that photo has made me realize that the only man I've ever been intimate with was little more than a boy.

I remember clearly the first time Arthur and I had sex.

NINETEEN SIXTY. An easy, breezy summer's day, almost two and a half months after Vivi and Arthur were married, Arthur was sent to me by train to try to make Vivi a baby. I watched him alight from the far end of the nearside platform at Crewkerne station. It was only then, while he walked the length of the platform and I studied his long slim legs striding boldly towards me, hugged in corduroy, that I felt a small slight panic of reality: I was going to have sex with this man and his long slim legs. Arthur didn't mention it—and neither did I—as he greeted me, or during the fifteen-minute car ride home from the station, or when we parked the car in the drive, or as he greeted my parents. We didn't mention it while I showed him to the small burgundy spare room off a half landing in the west wing of the house, with its high single bed and pretty window overlooking the sunny silky meadows below. But, of course, all that time it was the only thing I was thinking about.

In 1960 people hadn't started to admit freely that they couldn't have children. The boom in fertility treatments, which changed all that, didn't happen for another twenty years. If you were married and couldn't have children, you either said you didn't want them or you got them from somewhere else and often no one was ever the wiser. It was always a private affair, at times a dirty little secret. It wasn't that surrogacy was a *bad* word; it wasn't even a word yet, though up and down the country private agreements along those lines were being forged, as they had been for generations, among close family or friends.

I was never going to disappoint Vivi up there on the ridge that day, however much her suggestion had surprised me. It wasn't so much that I'd decided, out of compassion, to give my sister the baby she so desperately wanted. I didn't even consider turning her down. She'd made me feel so honored: Vivi had chosen *me* to be the mother of her baby. In the same way that I'd never have stopped her sharing my bed this morning, despite the intrusion and discomfort, I wasn't going to turn down the chance of securing that everlasting kinship with Vivi by having her child.

Vivi was adamant that the surrogacy must be kept secret from everyone—apart from the three of us—so that there could be no possibility of the child stumbling across the truth of a lifelong lie and hating us for it, or of anyone else finding out for that matter. She said that having a secret from your child for their own good was one thing, but for a child to grow up amid a secret that everyone else knew was wrong and unkind.

Vivi especially didn't want Maud and Clive to know yet. Of course, they knew she couldn't have children but, for reasons I have never understood, she felt they'd be opposed to the idea.

"I said they *might* be against it," she corrected me, as we huddled together in the cold on the ridge that day. "I don't think they would necessarily," she said quickly. "I don't know what they'd think."

She wanted us to get pregnant, before we let them in on the secret, in case they tried to stop us. She said at best they'd give us lots of opinions that would confuse us, and it should be for us, and us alone, to decide.

"I can make up my own mind, Vivi, and I've told you already that I'll do it," I assured her.

"Thank you, sweetie, I love you. You're my best friend as well as my best sister," she said in a pure rush of love that made me feel dizzy. "I just want it to be our secret to begin with, Ginny," she said pleadingly. "We'll tell them as soon as anything happens."

"As soon as I get pregnant?"

"Yes, of course," she said. "When you're pregnant they can't put us off." She laughed.

I decided it came down to the difference in how we viewed our parents: Vivi had always seen them as working against her, while I always thought of them as on my side. If I could tell them once I was pregnant, I couldn't see how it would make much difference to do as Vivi wanted. So it was agreed.

"Promise, cross your heart and hope to die," she'd said.

"I promise." I'd sincerely crossed my heart with my right hand to secure the pact and seal our fate.

We were still up on that frozen ridge when she told me her entire stratagem. Ostensibly Arthur's visits to Bulburrow would be on business—an idea for a new wholesale bakery to supply the area— although they'd happen to correspond with my monthly estrus. She'd got it all worked out, as always.

So THERE WE WERE, Arthur and I, alone for the first time in my bedroom, which was farther down the landing and on the opposite side to my parents' room. It was the afternoon, just before teatime. Maud and Clive were busy in other parts of the house.

The first thing Arthur said to me, almost formally, was, "Ginny, I need to know that you understand what you're doing, that you know you're giving the baby away. It will not be your baby. You will not be its mother. Vivien will. Are you sure you want to do that?" He said it so very s-l-o-w-l-y and c-l-e-a-r-l-y, as if I were an idiot.

"Yes," I said, my single-size iron bed looming between us as an overwhelming symbol of the enforced intimacy of the very near future.

"But you need to think about it," he said, rather puzzlingly.

I find it a struggle to understand the complexities of people I know best, let alone decipher those I don't. Surely in giving him the answer I'd already thought about it. I've learned that it's futile to challenge anyone about why they say what they say, or mean what they don't say. Mostly I try to humor them, saying and doing what will please them most, and hope it all becomes clear later. So, on the other side of that bed, which was glowering up at us in the hope of unification, I tried to act like I was "thinking about it" for a few seconds, as if "thinking about it" was something you did rubbing your chin and gazing skyward, but what I was really thinking was how odd it was that I'd never discussed the surrogacy with Arthur directly, not once. I'd only ever talked about it with Vivi. Occasionally she alluded to Arthur's opinion on this and that aspect of the arrangement, but mostly she talked about it furtively and covetously, as if it were only our secret, which made me almost forget that Arthur was involved at all. She'd talked about how we would watch the child grow and progress, how she would teach it about the city and I would teach it about the country, so that I'd come to regard it as Vivi's and my baby, not his. I'd considered him an inert part of the process, a catalyst—necessary for the reaction to happen but remaining unchanged at the end.

So until that moment I'd never actually considered Arthur's feelings. I wondered if this last-minute deliberation meant he wasn't as keen as Vivi on the idea. Perhaps he was looking for a way out, but I didn't know whether it was because of the baby or because it meant having to have sex with me. Then I said, as thoughtfully as I could feign, "It's not my baby. I will not be its mother. I understand that."

He considered my response slowly and, for whatever reason, decided it would do. "Good," he said, and relaxed. "Shall we get undressed?"

I quickly stripped off my skirt, underpants, blouse and bra and stood naked by the bed. When I looked up I found Arthur with his back towards me and a towel fastened round his waist. He was struggling to undress beneath it, as if he were changing on a crowded beach. Modesty about our bodies made no sense to me when we were about to do something as intrusive and intimate as sex.

"Oh," he said simply, when he turned back to me holding, with one hand behind his back, the towel that covered him. He was looking intently at my face, as if he didn't want to be caught ogling my body, but I couldn't help staring at the towel. I would have liked to see the equipment we had to work with before we got started. This was sexual reproduction for reproduction's sake only, so surely we could be matter-of-fact about it. We stood there uncertainly, hovering in hesitation.

"Are you nervous?" he asked.

"A bit," I lied, my eyes shifting from the carefully placed towel down to the floor. I should have been nervous, I know, but I was far too preoccupied with the practicalities of the situation, and once I get an idea in my head I find it difficult to think of anything else until I've resolved it. How, exactly, from this position, the bed between us, him covered up, were we going to end up with his penis depositing sperm into my uterus? I was more confused than nervous.

"Well, don't be," he said kindly.

My room was a bright daffodil yellow, richly augmented by the late afternoon sun stretching gloriously through the window. I'd selected it—the daffodil—when I was too young to know better and insisted that the ceiling as well as the walls should be done in the chosen color. Maud had painted it herself, directly over the Victorian wood-chip paper, which had raised swirls all over the ceiling.

When I was little I liked it because when I stared up at it from my bed and half crossed my eyes, enough to make them lazy, it was easy to lose my focus in the swirling ceiling. It would take a minute or two to get my eyes into it, to lose perspective and start to see the shapes and patterns in other dimensions. Once I'd got my eye in, it was quite impossible—without looking away first—to see the ceiling as flat again. Sometimes the swirls would be shooting away from me, and at other times they were spiraling out of the paper towards me so that if I reached up I could put my hand straight through them. I'd lie there in the light evenings or the early mornings of my childhood, moving them about and watching them dart in and out of the room.

Sex didn't hurt, as Vivi had said it might, and it didn't give me any pleasure, as I'd wondered it might. Instead, as I lay as still as I could under him, I watched the yellow spirals on the ceiling above me, dancing in and out like lively springs, and was astounded that this frenetic, mediocre act was what we were made for. This, apparently, was what men and women craved, not just when they wanted a child but for the act itself. After all, it's all we're required to do in life—by the laws of nature—to ensure the continuation of our species.

I can't think why but at that moment I thought of a stag beetle with his shiny black armor and huge, fierce-looking antlers, as long again as his body. With such an outfit you'd assume he was a great warrior, yet his fearsome appearance is a mystery to naturalists. He doesn't fight once in his monthlong life. He doesn't even eat. His sole purpose is to lug his cumbersome body around in search of a mate and, once he's mated he dies, his formidable weaponry an unnecessary encumbrance.

Arthur's head was buried in the pillow beside me, his mouth close to my ear. I smelt his musk and listened to his strained irregular breathing and I thought of all the forces driving him to do this. His arms were on either side of me, solid in rock-hard tension, his elbows locked at right angles to give him a little height, and I could see his sinewy upper body immaculately taut, powerful. Every slender muscle had a job to do and I marveled at the force in the thrust of his bottom, even for a thin man.

At last I felt Arthur's whole body go rigid in involuntary spasm and wondered if there was any other moment, apart from ejaculation, that so many of a man's muscles contract at the same time. I imagined the little packages of ATP and lactic acid being busily shunted and exchanged deep within the filaments of his muscles, a powerhouse working at full capacity.

When he'd finished and withdrawn, I flipped my legs to the head of the bed and stuck my feet and bottom up on the wall above me.

"What are you doing?" he asked then, rolling off the bed.

"I'm just helping them."

"Does it?" he said. "Help them?"

"Vivien thinks it might. It's on her list," I said, referring to a list of helpful hints and instructions she'd sent me, but Arthur was looking at me strangely, at my legs. "It's not one of the things I *have* to do but just something I can do if I want—"

"Ouch, what happened to you?" he interrupted. "Did you have an accident?"

"Those?" I tried to sound casual. "I always have bruises," and I tugged at the sheet to cover up the marks of Maud's outbursts.

"Sorry." He looked embarrassed, as if he'd just pointed out a deformity he shouldn't have mentioned, and went into the bathroom.

I felt his sperm trickling inside me and along the inside of my thigh. I checked that he was out of the room before I felt between my legs with my fingers. I had an urge to rush to the lab upstairs, smear the glistening liquid onto a slide, drop over a coverslip and push it under the X1000 lens. I'd have liked to see them swimming.

We did it once more that day and three times the next. The rest of the time we actively ignored each other, not only aware that we had to keep our baby-making plans secret from Maud and Clive, but also, perhaps, in a subconscious effort to balance out the impossible intimacy we were to have three times a day.

I'M SITTING at my lookout on the landing, staring at my toes protruding from the ends of my slippers in their thick woolen socks.

Did I tell you that three months ago I had to cut the tops off my slippers, at the very end, to let my toes stick out? My feet get so swollen that they felt as if they'd been crammed into slippers two sizes too small. Every step made me wince with pain. It's such a relief to have them out.

It's while I'm sitting here on the window seat, trying to wiggle my toes up and down, exercising them, that I finally catch sight of Vivien, walking back up the drive. At the same time, I hear the faint *whirr* and *chink* of the bracket clock in the hall as it passes the half hour. Something inside the workings has become misaligned. It used to strike the half hour properly, with one full, rich note, but over the last few years it's been muffled and the sound shortened, stripped of its echo; a chink, not a chime. Luckily, I can still hear it from the parts of the house I frequent, and when I do, I always check it against both of my wristwatches to make sure they're all keeping time. Right now, they are in agreement: it's four-thirty in the afternoon, and Vivien's been out since five past one.

Three and a half hours since she left the house—without a word—and the light is fading, but here she comes meandering slowly up the side of the drive, close to the beech hedge. She stops awhile to bend down and fiddle with her boot, then starts off again, dusting the beech hedge casually with her hand as she goes. Where has she been? I try to imagine all the places she might have been but, to tell you the truth, I can't even think of one. There's something strange about the way she's walking, a manner that I can't quite put my finger on or explain in words. She's running her hand along the side of the hedge as she walks, childlike, knocking off some of last year's crumpled brown leaves that seem to cling tightly to beech right through into spring.

I hurry down the stairs, giving myself plenty of time before she reaches the house, and shut myself into the study behind the kitchen.

The study has two doors off it, one to the kitchen and one to the hall. I've decided that if she goes into the kitchen I'll time my entrance to happen upon her there, and if she goes straight upstairs I can pretend I'd just decided to leave the study as she starts up the stairs. Either way I'll be able to ask her where she's been. I plant myself by the bookcase, equidistant from the two doors, ready to go one way or the other. Vivien goes straight upstairs. Once she passes the study door, I count her footsteps up five stairs, then open the door.

I freeze, hit by the unmistakable stench of sherry. The smell unleashes a little remnant of fear and unease that burrows its way out onto the skin of my arms, crawling between the hairs. It's the smell of Maud. I back away from the door and close it again, quietly. I wait until I hear Vivien's footsteps pass above me to her room before I go quietly to my own.

CHAPTER 15

In Remembrance of Pauline Abbey Clarke

ONCE I'M IN MY ROOM, I rearrange the pillows at the head of my bed, stacking them up so I can sit and admire the sleepy Bulburrow valley through the south windows. Outside the breeze leads the tips of the creeper's new shoots in a quivering dance, each one searching for a partner to entwine. Maud said she'd planted the creeper because it was my namesake—Virginia. She said she liked the idea of me creeping all over the house forever, and I remember that then she laughed a lot because I asked her what she meant by that and she said I shouldn't be so serious about everything.

I can't help thinking what a shock the smell of sherry has just given me, and the memories it's inflamed. I'd forgotten how fearful I was of Maud when she was drunk. There'd be so little warning. One moment she'd be humming to herself, happily inebriated, and the next she'd have grabbed a weapon—a mug, a brolly, a book or whatever else was close to hand—and lashed out at me in unrestrained fury. But—I think I've mentioned this before—I always forgave her for what she did, I knew she couldn't help it and, somehow, she more than made up for it when she was sober, with her sublime reassurances of love, when she'd lay her head on my lap, or squeeze me tight and kiss me. It was at those times that I thought we'd never been so close, and that we'd never needed each other so much.

I could cope with the violence. That was easy—I could rationalize it. It was the incessant insults I found hardest to bear. I knew not to believe a word of it, I knew not to listen and, thanks to Maud herself, I knew how to lock myself in that place in my head where I can go and not hear. But there was one that came up over and over again, the one about how I'd ruined her life.

"You'll never know how much you've ruined my life," she'd shout, grabbing my face in her hand as if she wanted to grind it to dust. I always thought how lucky it was that it was me, not Vivi; that I was able to detach myself from it in a way that Vivi's mercurial personality would not have permitted. But it was this theme, that I'd ruined her life, that came up the most, that all the others would culminate with, the one she'd repeat over and over in different ways and, by the end, I couldn't help but believe—in a little part of me—that she truly thought I had.

Once or twice I let myself wonder what on earth I might have done to make her think it, but mostly I knew it was nonsense. Her life would have been ruined without me to cover up her every misplaced step, to shield her outbursts from her husband and her other daughter. She couldn't have coped without me.

I made sure Maud never knew that her gibes got to me. I remained impassive and unaffected, even though I saw the danger in that too. I saw the pattern but I couldn't stop it. The more resilient I appeared, the more Maud wanted a reaction and the more vicious her behavior became. Only now, looking back, can I see that a clash was spiraling out of control.

I stretch over to pull out the drawer at the top of my bedside table. It lost its handle many years ago so I have to pull on the screws that once fixed it and stick out two inches apart. The drawer is stiff, but once I wangle it out enough to slip my fingers into the top, I can wrench it all the way. There, lined up neatly, are two full rows of cannabis tea bags, each like a perfectly crafted marble with the muslin gathered in a spray at the top and a length of cotton thread for manipulating it in the mug. I don't like to use them unless it's absolutely necessary and I've exhausted all the other ways to alleviate the pain in my joints. It's not that I'm moderating myself. It's just that I so much prefer the two rows in the drawer being full. When there's a gap the bags slide about as I open or close the drawer, upsetting their careful alignment.

I lift up a bag and smell it. I like the idea of the smell more than the smell itself. My favorite thing is to take them all out and line them up on the bed. Then I pick up each one in turn—as I'm doing now—and roll it in my fingers, admiring the handiwork, the immaculate rows of small, even stitches along the seams. As I study it I picture Michael working at his late mother's kitchen table, his fat, practiced fingers carefully folding the muslin, gently pulling the stitching to gather and tie it at the top.

I like to believe he thinks of me while he's stitching. I feel that he and I have a small connection and not only because our families go back for three generations in an employment partnership. We are both quiet and, I should imagine, similarly misjudged. Besides, I've known him all his life. Soon after his birth it became evident Michael was a near clone of his mother, missing out on all his father's failings. He was born big and gentle and calm, and soon disclosed a big heart and a small intellect. But, like his mother, Michael was a grafter, and after she died he took over nursing his father patiently through his final ailing years. No other son would have put up with the childlike tantrums of that cantankerous man, until one glorious cold and cloudless day when Michael was collecting blood-blue sloes from the hedges along the willow walk and his father was choking slowly to death at home. For many years Michael was haunted by the ghosts of guilt, believing they were the actual ghosts of his father's celestial fury.

It took Michael several years to understand that he had, in picking the sloes that day, secured his freedom. He rebelled gently, admitting his hatred of gardening—the only education his father had given him. I released him from his duties in the Bulburrow grounds and allowed him to continue living in the Stables in return for nothing. With the scrapings of a lifetime savings his father had forgotten to, or not got round to, spending in his own lifetime, Michael bought a big motorcycle and a small tent, about the size of our hanging pantry. He hired it that first year to the Jeffersons at Christmas for mince pies and carols, and for some yearly gathering at the Liberal Club, then to Ethel Phelps in the gatehouse lodge to extend her conservatory for Stan's seventieth. And then he bought another slightly bigger tent— about the size of the kitchen study. Throughout the following summer, he hired them out for events and parties in the neighboring villages, Saxton, Broadhampton and Selby.

I could swear Michael showed no sign of strategy, cunning or business, but now he has sixteen marquees, enormous ones, the size of the drawing room and library put together, with all the trimmings for weddings and funerals, and all of life's ceremonies between. Michael never needed or cared for anything but that which he couldn't have: a loving father. He still lives at the Stables, he still rides his bike and he still looks as if he works in the vegetable patch, but I know that he's now the wealthiest man in the village. His late mother would have laughed and loved him just the same, but he would never have been able to make his father proud.

He had acquired some cannabis seeds from his biker friends and, with the expertise in tending plants that his father had drummed into him from an early age, he used the remaining peach houses in the walled garden to grow a celebrated line in skunk, as he calls it. Like me, he lives alone, and although I wouldn't be so bold as to claim a friendship, Michael and I have a long-term connection. He visits me irregularly—about twice a month—to deliver my groceries, take out my rubbish, block up new drafts, tell me the briefest of village news and, if necessary, to top up my supply of his personalized brand of herbal remedy.

THE SECOND TIME Vivi sent Arthur to Bulburrow, he telephoned quite unexpectedly from Crewkerne, an hour and a half before his train was due in. I wasn't ready for him. I'd had a long bath and scrubbed myself clean. I hadn't yet peeled the potatoes for supper or finished rearranging the dried flowers in his room. I shoved aside the vase and the oasis I'd been piecing together in the back pantry, grabbed some King Edwards from the sack and threw them into the sink to remind me they needed to be sorted. Thankfully the place wasn't in too bad a state. Recently, I'd been spending much more time on the housework than my moth work, much to Clive's disapproval.

One of my biggest regrets is not talking to Clive about Maud at this time. If only I had, he might have done something before it was too late. I didn't know to what extent he thought she was drinking. He'd seen her drunk, of course, but he couldn't have known how badly she'd deteriorated. At the time I was trying to avoid the subject so that I didn't find myself having to pretend I knew less than I did. Maud was relying on me.

Arthur was waiting for me by the station entrance as I pulled up in the Chester. The passenger seat was overloaded with Clive's boxes and tools, so Arthur volunteered to squeeze in beside the apparatus in the back with his bag on his knees, facing the back windscreen.

"I'm sorry you had to wait," I said.

"Not at all. I got an earlier train," he shouted, competing with the full choke as I turned over the Chester's engine. "So, how's it all going?"

"Everything's ready," I shouted back. "I'm sure the timing will be right this time."

"What?"

"I'm sure I've got the timing right," I yelled, trying to throw the words over my shoulder while I watched the road. "Maybe this time is going to be *it*." In the mirror I saw Arthur craning his neck round stiffly, apparently still aware that he was in a chemical factory, to look towards me in the front.

"I didn't mean that, I just meant how are you?" He half-laughed. Our eyes met briefly in the mirror before I flicked mine back to the road.

"Virginia . . . ," he said, seriously now, like I was about to be told off. I wanted to move the mirror: it had brought him too close. "You do know it could take years?"

"Oh, no! I'm sure it won't," I said, a little appalled. I kept my eyes fixed on the road. I'd never imagined that these illicit meetings between Arthur and me would go on long. I'd never thought they might become less detached, less functional, that we might actually begin to get to know each other, that we might form a bond of our own, a friendship.

"Really? What makes you think it won't take long?" Arthur asked.

The truth was I hadn't thought about it. "Well, Vivi has worked out the chart really carefully and I've checked it as well. We think we're right on timing so there's nothing stopping—"

"Ginny," he interrupted, "there's more to making a baby than preparations and timing control."

"Well, that's if the sperm are—"

"I didn't mean my sperm." He laughed loudly. We were coming down the hill into the village, passing the new bungalows on the left. "Ginny, let's go for a drive. Let's not go up to the house yet."

"Drive? Where to?"

"Don't you have a favorite place?" I didn't answer. "Somewhere with a view?"

"No."

"Come on, Ginny. *Anywhere* . . . ," I slowed and took the right-hand turn between the ivy-clad stone pillars, into the corridor of yellowing limes that escorted visitors up the winding drive. "A beauty spot?" he added, with gentle impatience.

I had lots of favorite places: places I'd go caterpillar or moth hunting, places I'd walk and think and breathe and study. Or treacle the trees. But they're rarely beautiful: behind the mobile homes on the cliff walk between Seatown and Beer, where at this time of year I'd hunt through the thorny scrub to find the Oak Eggar caterpillar hibernating in its hairy orange-and-black coat; the bog at Fossett's Bar, where two streams meet and overflow, and marsh reeds grow in thick unsurpassable clumps, and I'd wade in to find the long silky cocoon of The Drinker tapered to the stems; the railway station, the one we've just left, to the disused square of land behind it, where the tall wire fence has fallen in so you can squeeze through and be in the company of some of the rarest wildflowers in the West Country; better still, the dump behind the Esso garage on the A303 at Winterbourne Stoke where, on a day of good fortune, I'd find the distinctively bulbous cocoon of the Elephant Hawk-moth tangled among the moss and litter on the ground, or Golden-rod Pug caterpillars, starting on a feast of ragwort. These were my favorite places, my beauty spots. Like the insects I studied, I've never been attracted to manicured beauty. To us, weeds are wildflowers and untended scrubland a rare and forgotten paradise. Dorset's true wildernesses have quietly become the disused dumps, the unworthy wasteland, the boggy, the bleak and the barren. Certainly not a place to entertain guests.

"No," I said again, "not really." The truth was, I didn't relish the idea of walking and talking with Arthur. I could cope with our monthly sessions being purely clinical, impersonal, but I didn't want to get to know him. I was happy to have this baby for Vivi if Arthur remained a catalyst, an inert part of the process. I'd have preferred him to be a total stranger.

"So you don't have a place you go to be alone sometimes," he said, softly now, so that I had to strain to hear him. In the mirror I could see he was looking straight ahead, out the back window, but it felt as though he was peering right through me, inspecting my every secret.

"Or a place that you like to walk?" he suggested. We'd reached the final bend, just before the house came into view. "Come on," he pleaded finally. "Let's not go home yet. Let's just stop *here* and walk."

I pulled up at the side of the drive and turned off the engine. "We can walk to the brook if you like," I said.

"I'd *love* to walk to the brook," Arthur replied quickly, enthusiastically, and opened the rear door.

I smiled for the first time since I'd picked him up, but so that he wouldn't see it. Something that was tight within me relaxed a little, something I hadn't known had been tight until that moment. Much later I came to realize that Arthur had a wonderfully natural way of putting me at ease. Looking back now, I might have known—by the end of that first walk—that he was never going to remain, for me, an inert part of the process.

I led Arthur behind the line of fir trees that run along next to the fence marking our eastern boundary. The lowest branches reach a foot above my head and splay out over the top of the fence so that between it, the tree trunks and the dense layering of branches above us, a dark walkway has been created, which I've always called the Tunnel Walk. It was dim, but shafts of light collided through the trees in pretty spectacle and it was good to walk. I looked up, privately scanning the branches, increasingly taunted by the desire to stop and shake them and examine the fall. I'd not have hesitated had I been on my own, of course, but I knew it might seem an odd sort of habit so I refrained. Instead I guessed at the fall; mostly needles and cones, with a smattering of beetles and bugs. I'd look for any wasp apples, preferably without an exit hole so I could watch the wasp emerge *in vitro* back in the lab. But what I'd really be hoping to spot was the Puss Moth chrysalis, cocooned on the tree trunks and expertly disguised within the surrounding bark.

I was proud that Clive had taught me to see the world around me without the blind ignorance with which most people must wander it. Where others see a small, dreary spider crawling up a fence, I might see a wingless female Vapourer; where I see an exquisite, harmless Bee Hawk attracted to sugary jam, others swat a pestilent wasp coveting their picnic; where I see a hibernating Eyed Hawk, others might step on an old dried-up leaf.

At the end of the Tunnel Walk we emerged into the glare of daylight beside the brook, which languished thickly through the mud. Four ancient crack willows stood woven together, huddled at the water's edge. I picked up the end of a wispy branch that stuck out a little over my path, holding it up first above my head and then Arthur's, as though I were disentangling his path. But my expert eyes had already scanned the underside of the leaves for the fresh-feeding signs that told me the Eyed Hawk had already hatched.

I LED ARTHUR over the beech tree bridge—a weeping copper beech that had split down the center of its trunk, sending one side to traverse the brook.

"You must have had great fun growing up here," Arthur declared, his arms outstretched as he walked across.

I'd never thought about it as a particularly unusual place to grow up. He followed as I jumped off the beech onto the narrow footpath, overgrown with brambles, which follows the brook to St. Bartholomew's church.

"Where did you grow up?" I asked.

"Lancaster Gate," he said. "Pure Londoner."

"Lancaster Gate sounds exciting."

"It's beautiful. The houses overlook Hyde Park. But *this* is the place for children." For the first time I wondered what sort of childhood my child would have, what sort of space it would find to play in and how different its life would be, compared to mine, if it lived in London. It was as if Arthur was thinking the same.

"I think children should be brought up in the country, with all this," he said, waving an arm in the air. He was in the lead now, picking his way. Whenever he came across a bramble that spanned the path he untangled it and held it back for me, like a gentleman opening a gate, then let the thorny sentinel spring back after I'd passed. It was just a little endeavor, I know, but it made a big impression on me. No one had ever shown me such courtesy before.

"Do you think you might move out to the country, then?" I asked.

"I'd love to, but Vivi's such a city girl, isn't she? I don't think she'd ever want to move out. She'd go crazy."

Vivi, a city girl? Did he know Vivi had hardly stepped into a city until five and a half years ago? Did he know that she knew as much about the country as I did? That she knew the name of each bird that sang outside her window, and whether they sang for a mate, a territory or as a decoy? That she knew which animal had eaten a nut by the way the discarded husk had been opened? Did he not know how quickly she'd assumed a city personality and denied the country one?

We reached the tiny graveyard, bound by the brook on one side and the church on the other. It was another of my favorite spots, but I didn't want to let on that I frequented the local graveyard, so I stepped among the headstones looking, as if for the first time, at the inscriptions, names, dates and epitaphs, that I knew already by heart. Since its first occupant, PAULINE ABBEY CLARKE (Forever Remembered, Forever Missed), died in 1743, I should think the tiny graveyard was filled pretty quickly with Pauline's family and friends. In any event there had been so much pressure from the village that the rector had had it extended into a section of his garden next door. All the new dead now went through a gap in the hedge to the garden extension, but even that seemed to be filling up fast, leaving the elderly with the great dilemma of vying to outlive each other, yet at the same time competing for a spot in the ever-diminishing allotment.

But—as I was telling you—in that original bit of graveyard that Arthur and I were in, there were no gravestones as late as the twentieth century, so neither Pauline Abbey Clarke nor any of the other dead there had actually been missed or remembered for an awfully long time and, luckily for the wildlife, that meant nobody had taken too much care of the place. In spring it was a refuge for unruly weeds and insects, and on a warm evening, the moths emerged from their winter capsules in such abundance that although a moth is near silent, the air would shudder with the throbbing of fresh wings.

"I love graveyards," Arthur said, to my surprise, as we stood side by side reading Pauline's inscription.

"Do you?" I wasn't surprised he loved them but that he admitted it so easily. I'd never allowed myself to say it for fear of what people might think. I knew that the villagers had spotted me there at dusk. Sometimes moth hunters need to be nocturnal, like their prey. But when I was spotted after dark in a rarely visited place, not least an eerie place like St. Bart's graveyard, clutching a halogen lamp, a tin of treacle and a rug to keep me warm, I knew that the next day Mrs. Axtell and her friends conjured up all sorts of sinister stories. I could tell from the way the children looked at me that they had been scared at bedtime, their eager imaginations fed with tales of the numinous qualities of my character.

But Arthur was an outsider and didn't come with prejudice. He was a townsman and didn't think like the neighbors.

"Do you want to see inside the smallest church in the country?" I offered.

"Yes, please. I love churches too"—he paused—"but I can't explain why."

He didn't need to. I'd stopped going to church for services, even though as a child I'd never missed a Sunday, but now and then I'd go in secret, on my own, just because I liked that eerie, nostalgic, adrenaline-fueled feeling that you can't help sensing, after a childhood of churchgoing, when you walk into a spiritual place and wonder whether you've made a terrible and timeless mistake in rejecting God and letting down your soul.

It was more a chapel than a church, tiny but disproportionately tall. It had three rows of wooden benches either side of the aisle and windows so high that they didn't shed much light on the proceedings far below. At the front stood a simple wooden altar and behind it, screwed into the brickwork, was a near-life-size painted carving of Christ wrapped lithely round his cross, crowned with a gold wreath, his pink skin shredding off in long thin flakes down his legs. At the back, on the dusty floor, there was a small stone bowl used as a font, and next to this, taking up a disproportionate amount of room, St. Bartholomew, carved in stone, rested in a coffin pose, hands crossed on his chest, eyes closed and peaceful, robe perfectly arranged and sandals pointing neatly to the roof. A wooden pew was pushed up next to his feet. When Vivi and I were children the prime spot to sit was right beside him, so you could rest your elbow on his toes.

"Look over here, Arthur." I was sitting in the prime seat and

Arthur joined me. "The sole of St. Bartholomew's left sandal." I nodded towards it.

He leaned forward across my legs to peer more closely at the effigy's foot, and I was uncomfortably aware of his chin brushing my lap.

"V . . . I . . . V," he read slowly, then laughed, pulling himself up. "Naughty."

"It was *my* hair clip, though. Over many Sundays," I informed him. "She had short hair then. Sometimes I wonder if she grew it only so she could have her own readily available supply of hair clips for desecration."

"Really? Did she do it a lot?"

"Oh, she's left her mark everywhere around here."

"I'd like to follow that trail. It would be fun." He opened his palms, as if they were a book he was reading. "An insight into the life of the young Vivien Stone through her vandalism," he read dramatically. "Nobody's going to file down St. Bartholomew's feet now, are they? Her mark will be here forever. There'll be children in two hundred years time saying, 'Viv used to sit here,' and trying to imagine what sort of person she was."

I had the vague impression that Arthur himself was trying to work out what sort of person she was. As we sat in the church, thinking and talking about the one person we loved so much, studying the marks she'd once inscribed, sitting upon the seat she'd once touched, I felt as if the sister I'd known so intimately all my life was becoming less tangible, less obtainable, that she had evaporated into an ethereal, almost divine presence to be remembered and worshipped. For a surreal moment I imagined that the altar and the hymn books and the small dim windows high above us had all been designed for Vivi, that unattainable of gods. Also, in our shared silence, I thought of how at ease I was feeling with Arthur and how, in so many ways, we were similar—our love of the country and of churches, his genuine interest in Clive's and my research.

We made our way home and he continued to ask questions about Vivi, and although they weren't particularly probing, something made me wonder if I ought not to be answering them. Somehow I felt that if she knew about our walking along the brook and talking about her in the graveyard, and finding her graffiti in the church, she would have added them to the list of things that were very much not allowed.

"Right," Arthur said, as we approached the house. "It's about time you told me your family secret." Although I could see he was smiling and I should have guessed he was teasing, I thought for an awful moment that he was going to question me about Maud's drinking. "I want to know," he continued authoritatively, "how you can tell a cannibal caterpillar? That *look* you were all talking about."

"Oh, that," I said, relieved, and I had to think for a moment how to put something I'd only ever known by instinct into words. "Well, they're usually a lot less hairy than their brothers, and sort of . . ."

"Sort of?"

"Twitchy," I decided finally.

"Thank you," said Arthur, courteously holding open the front door for me.

As I said, that was only the second time Arthur had come down to try to make a baby for Vivi, and after our stroll to the church, I relaxed in his company. More than that, I began to enjoy it. Neither Maud nor Clive questioned why Arthur came, or how long he was staying, and for the next few months his visits melded calmly into the pattern of normal life. With Maud drinking more heavily each week, and Clive and I up to our necks in research, Arthur's visits became, for me, a respite from the predictability of Bulburrow life. I thought of him when he wasn't there, and looked forward to his arrival, counting the days until he broke the interminable cycle of routine. When he came, as well as our baby-making sessions, we'd walk and talk and I even felt him inch into some of the space that, until then, Vivien had always filled in my small circle of life. And, to tell you the truth, I believed, even though he never said it and I never asked, that he looked forward to seeing me too.

At the same time I increasingly despaired that my days had

become embroiled in deceit. On the one hand I had the baby to keep secret from Maud, and on the other, I had Maud to keep secret from the rest of the world. My life took on the form of a treacherous board game, the people within it the counters. But I was playing on my own, for and against myself, discreetly moving the counters, making sure each one was winning while ensuring that none of them were aware that they were being played.

DURING THE SEVENTH month's visit the trouble started.

Arthur and I had sex twice that day and I went to bed early. It was around ten o'clock in the evening when I woke up thirsty and went, sleepy-eyed, down to the kitchen to get a drink of water. I switched on the dim kitchen light and moved to the cupboard for a glass. As I bent to reach for one someone grabbed my hair, jerking me backwards. I yelped, doglike, as I was dragged away from the cupboard and onto the floor. I was still half asleep and slow.

"You little whore!" Maud shouted. "You fucking little whore! What do you think you're doing? How dare you? You *slut*." She was wearing the same clothes she'd been wearing all week—her green wool trousers, which were designed to have a stiff crease down the center, and a sloppy blue jumper of Clive's, now heavily stained.

"*Whore!*" she shouted again, as she tried to rip out my hair and punched my head.

"No." It was all I could manage to say. I tried to tuck my head between my legs.

"You've ruined *my* life and now you'll ruin your sister's too. Oh, no, you won't!" she screamed. "I'll kill you first! I'll kill you!" She pulled me by my hair towards the Rayburn.

"No," I said again, weakly, groaning at the pain in my scalp. But she didn't mean it: her mind was distorted. It was the drink talking.

"Whore!" she yelled again. I'd curled up into a ball, burying my head into my body, but she was kicking me, I think as hard as she could, big, unrestrained swings aimed for my head and stomach, but instead striking my hands, forearms and shins as I protected myself. She was shouting throughout, but I didn't hear any more of her words. I was focusing on the blows, each adding pain to the last, and ensuring that she didn't break through my defenses to my head. It seemed to last forever and then, all of a sudden, the lights went out.

Maud stopped kicking.

"Look! I've something to show you!" I heard Clive's urgent and unusually enthused voice. It was pitch-black. He was in the room and I heard him moving towards us.

"Everybody, look," he continued. "Can you see it? Virginia? Maud?"

Neither of us spoke.

"Is it not glowing? Can you see it glowing?" Clive urged. I'd grown a little more accustomed to the light and could now make out the figures in the room. I was sitting up on the floor in front of the Rayburn, leaning on my right hand with both legs casually out to the side, as if I had been caught at story time. I congratulated myself on my quick recovery and repositioning. Maud had slunk at least fifteen feet away from me, near to the pantry door. She had her back to the wall and was relaxing heavily against it. Her hair was bedraggled, her face rouged with anger and, in the dimness, she looked little more than a wayward child.

It was then, as my eyes grew accustomed to the darkness, I began to make out what she was holding. It was the heavy iron skillet, which she must have picked up from the stove just before Clive had walked in. She was holding it downwards in both hands, arms extended, resting it on her knees. I'll tell you now, when I saw that skillet in her hands, I truly believed that had we not been interrupted she might well have carried out successfully her earlier death threats. Clive was in the middle of the room, by the table, thankfully between Maud and me. He was holding something at eye level, a test tube. He had his back turned slightly to me and directed himself at Maud.

"Maud," he said gently, "can you see it?"

Maud said nothing. She wasn't looking at him but at the skillet.

"I said, 'Can you see it?' " he repeated vehemently, and when she didn't answer he said, "Maud, I'd like you to concentrate on this for a minute."

She didn't move.

"Look up!" he demanded.

Maud lifted her head slowly, but as soon as she saw him, she dropped it again. She couldn't look at him.

"What is it, Clive?" I asked, intrigued.

"Well, Ginny, my dear"—he turned to me—"I thought it was the Brimstone fluorescence, although it doesn't seem to be working now," and it was easy for us all to see that not a glimmer of hope radiated from the test tube. He'd failed, poor Clive. But—now here's something that might surprise you—Clive should have been bitterly frustrated, angry, disappointed even; months and months of pedantic work and effort, all for no result. Instead, he said glibly, "Oh, well," and then, "Shall I take that, Maud," as he removed the skillet from her hands, "or are you about to cook us some steak?"

I would have laughed but I didn't. It was rare for Clive to make a joke, although he'd probably thought she *was* about to do steak.

It was the most merciful coincidence that Clive appeared when he did, not a moment too soon, although quite what he was doing there at that time with his tube of nonfluorescing fluorescence I have not been able to fathom to this day. Inadvertently, he had saved me from the skillet in Maud's grasp and yet he still seemed oblivious to the tension in the room.

"Lights!" he barked, as if we'd just finished a rehearsal, and they flicked on, whipping away the secretive screen of half-light and flooding us with stark reality. There was Arthur at the entrance to the kitchen, stage-managing the switch. Arthur too? What was he doing in the room? I thought. And when had he arrived? I was confused. I can't put my finger on why, but the whole episode had an air of performance.

I started to fumble around on the floor, pretending I'd been interrupted in looking for something I'd dropped. I needn't have worried;

nobody seemed to think it odd that I was down there. Then I saw Clive throw the skillet into the sink and along with it—to my utter amazement—his test tube of precious nonfluorescing fluorescence, then go to Maud, who still looked fixed to the spot. I watched as Clive put his arm round her waist, lovingly, I thought, and half escorted, half carried her out of the room.

"Good night," he said cheerily, but I was a little disappointed. I couldn't believe that Clive, of all people, would throw away half a year's hard work on a whim in the middle of the night. Perhaps we just needed to purify it further. Perhaps the Woods glass was set incorrectly? I was looking at the sink and deciding whether or not to go over there and save what I could of the substance when Arthur strode up to it and ran the cold tap. That was it. Anything that might have been saved a moment ago had now been washed away. I had to stop myself thinking about it.

Arthur helped me up from the floor.

"Are you all right?" he asked.

"I'm fine," I replied, but I had to bite back the pain that shot through my legs and arms, all the while pretending to search the floor anxiously, dreading him asking what I was looking for, knowing that if he did I'd be completely flummoxed. My face was hot and stung, my cheek tight with swelling below my left eye.

"But poor Clive," I continued. "He'll be really disappointed, after all that hard work. It didn't even fluoresce."

"I'm sure he'll get over it," Arthur said rather dismissively. "Would you like a glass of water to take to bed?" he asked, holding one out to me.

"Yes, please." I took it and, looking down intently, wished him good night into the water.

Later, in bed that night, I understood that I should have told Maud about the surrogacy. Either that or I shouldn't have presumed she'd be too drunk to notice. Of course she thought I was a whore. What else could she think? It was my own fault.

CHAPTER 16

A Nuclear Test and Titus

ON GOOD FRIDAY, just two days after the skillet incident, my mother, Maud, died—at fifty-four years old—shortly after five in the afternoon. She and Clive had spent the entire day together. Clive had packed a picnic all by himself and they'd driven to a little cove on the Dorset coast called Seatown, which isn't a town at all but a beach full of pebbles with high limestone cliffs rising up on either side of it and a lone guardhouse perched halfway up the hill. It had been their favorite picnic spot during my childhood summers, but that day was still wintry and they drove the car almost onto the beach and picnicked looking through the windscreen at the stormy sea and beyond. I don't know what they did for the rest of the day but they were out in the drizzle in the car until midafternoon, while I worked alone in the laboratory upstairs.

It happened around teatime. I was iodizing some white-mantled Wainscot caterpillars in prep to section them, when I heard Clive shouting my name. "Virginia! Virginia!" I knew something was up. I'd never heard Clive shout before.

"Virginia, quickly!"

I raced downstairs and found him at the bottom of the wide hall stairs, clutching the thick oak newel post for support. His breathing was heavy and he was staring at the floor by his feet.

"It's your mother," he said. "She's fallen down the steps." I looked about me, not understanding. "The cellar." He tilted his head in the direction of the cellar door, which I now saw was open.

I walked over to it and peered down the steep stone steps. I could see only the darkness. I looked back at Clive. He was very still, very quiet, leaning on his post. Was he too shocked to go to her? Was Maud really there?

"Down here?" I asked softly.

He nodded.

I flicked on the light and illuminated Maud at the foot of the steps. She was lying perfectly still on her back, her hands and legs splayed out wide to the sides, like a child acting dead.

"What does she look like?" Clive asked quickly. "Is she moving?"

"No."

I knew she was dead, but I went to her anyway, listened and felt, unsuccessfully, for any sign of life. Clive clutched his post. I called for an ambulance, then tried halfheartedly to resuscitate her, but she reeked of so much alcohol that I became light-headed with the vapor.

Finally I went to Clive, prised his hands from their post and held them. He was in shock.

"She would have died instantly, Clive," I told him, "and she wouldn't have known a thing about it. She was too drunk."

"Thank you," he said.

There was a long silence. Poor Clive, I thought. What a shock it must be to face, so suddenly, the end of nearly thirty years of marriage. Then a really strange thought popped into my head. I have no idea why, and I'm sure you'll say there were far more appropriate things to think at the time, but I was simply hoping that they'd enjoyed their car picnic a few hours before.

Then I thought of the stories of their early love affair, when they'd had to keep it a secret from her father. I thought of them in the photograph on the table in the drawing room, the one taken before I was born on what looks like a Parisian balcony (although I'd never thought to ask them), and the adoration with which they are gazing at each other.

I think almost the instant that you hear of somebody's death, it's a bit like when someone comes back again after a very long time: all those moments you've had with them pop immediately into your head, all the most loving moments, from a more distant past. And never the more disturbing ones since.

"Virginia," he said, "I left the cellar door unlocked. She must have mistaken it for the kitchen one."

"It's not your fault, Clive," I tried to reassure him, but he didn't look up.

"Go and phone Moyse," he said. "Go and phone Dr. Moyse."

"Clive. There's no need—"

"Just phone him, please, Ginny. I want him to see her." With that, he took himself off and locked himself into his small study behind the kitchen.

I'M NOT PROUD of it—far from it, believe me—but I think you should know that from the moment I saw Maud's lifeless body splayed out on the cold stone at the foot of the cellar steps right up to this very day, I have not shed one tear for her, nor felt one pang of sorrow. At first I thought it must have been the shock. Her death was so sudden that I thought perhaps I hadn't yet given myself a chance to believe it and feel it. For years afterwards I searched for my grief, thinking it had somehow become trapped within me and just needed a nudge to be released. Each day I waited, and when I felt that rather than getting closer it was moving farther away, I'd spend hours thinking of her, of my childhood, reminding myself of the comfort and love and wisdom she'd given me. I'd think of picnics by the river, the lardy cake she'd make on our birthdays, the smell of her hairspray, the feel of her skin and her lips, and I'd insist that the tears and the grief should pour out of me. But they never came, and it wasn't because I didn't love her, miss her and want her.

I must have been too busy. I understand that now. I'm too practical, that's my problem. It's the scientist in me. Until I forced myself to reflect on her, I remember thinking less about Maud and more about how everything was going to work now, the house and the family; how it would all fit into place. More so as, believe it or not, Maud's death wasn't the only life-changing thing that happened that day. I haven't yet told you the extraordinary thing Clive did when he'd finished up in his study.

BUT I'LL START where I left off. Clive locked himself into his study. Dr. Moyse, of course, came "as quick as he could," which was all a bit too quick for my liking and, once he was there, he wouldn't leave me alone. He stuck to me like a limpet, taking me to a quiet room upstairs so that, he said, I didn't have to see my mother's body being covered up and removed, or get involved with the other proceedings of her death that Clive was busy dealing with. I wouldn't have minded. Perhaps it would have helped me grieve.

Four hours later—almost ten in the evening—after the police had taken their statement, Maud had been taken to the mortuary, the cellar door had been firmly locked and the house had finally fallen silent of strangers, Clive emerged from his study and sat me down at the kitchen table. He put four hard-backed A4-sized notebooks on the table and on either side of them three piles of typed papers and letters. Then he handed me a binder, opening it to reveal its first immaculately typed page. It was titled: BULBURROW COURT: TERMS OF . . . DEPENDENTS, ESTATE HOLDINGS, ACCOUNTS AND RECOMMENDATIONS OF . . .

Before I had a chance to read any further Clive made his shocking announcement: "I'm leaving Bulburrow and my whole estate to you and Vivien. I am moving to the Anchorage retirement home on Paul Street in Crewkerne. The address is in the last section of these notes." He talked as though it were a recitation. He didn't look at me once but concentrated on the paperwork in his hands or on the table. "I have organized my affairs so that you can easily take it on from where

I've left off. I've written you a detailed list of recommendations in here to cover most eventualities in the years to come. As I've put here"—he flicked a few pages over and pointed to a section; I saw his hands were trembling—"first of all, you need to sell the glasshouses to pay off some outstanding debts. I've resisted selling them for the past few years but now I've determined there's no other choice. I've already had one conversation with Michael about it and I think you'll find he's able to offer you a good price. I've written to my colleagues, letting them know of my retirement, and to the Royal Society, the British and Natural History museums in London. I've instructed them to address all future research to you. I'm leaving in the morning."

"But . . ." I had no words. I stared at the neat piles in front of me. I didn't believe a word of it. He was still in shock. He needed a good night's sleep.

"I think you need time to think about this," I managed finally.

"I've thought about it for a long time," he said—but he couldn't have. He didn't know what he was saying, what he was doing. "Here is my paper." He handed me the last few sheets he held in his hand. The article was headed: "*Nomophila noctuella,* a West African Visitor."

"It's in *Lepidopterologist–Atropos* this week and the *Journal of the Society for British Entomology* in two weeks' time. And it's being considered for *Nature.*"

"*Nomophila noctuella*? That tiny moth from the Robinsons on the drawing-room sill?"

He nodded. "It was radioactive. That's why I didn't poison it. It would have invalidated the results."

"Radioactive?"

"Yes, contaminated by radioactive dust from a French nuclear test in the Sahara desert. The half-life was exactly the same. It had to have been there," he said unenthusiastically.

I'll admit I didn't understand the significance at first, not until I had scanned a little of the opening statement: "Micro-moth *Nomophila noctuella* . . . definitive proof of the staggering 3,000-mile migration from West Africa by its contamination with radioactive dust by French nuclear test," it read dramatically.

Radioactive! Who would have guessed? I didn't presume to understand the ways in which Clive worked sometimes but it was impressive. *Fairly* impressive. No one had yet proved that any moths or butterflies, weighing in at a maximum of around two grams, were able to fly the vast distances they were suspected of flying. But Clive had proved it—with this little moth, at any rate.

"Congratulations," I said, but I too was finding it hard to muster enthusiasm. He stuck out his chin and scratched the hair at the top of his neck.

"Well, I did it, so I thought I'd retire," he said halfheartedly.

"Yes, you did it."

He was already three years past retirement age, but whenever the issue had been raised he'd always refused to contemplate it. He wouldn't retire, he had said, until he had made his mark on the world. Clive had lived with an overdeveloped need for recognition. Maud had said it was a man thing. I looked down and scanned his neatly constructed paper. We both knew it wasn't important enough for *Nature,* and proving one journey of a little-known moth hadn't exactly fulfilled his lifetime's ambition, but perhaps we also knew it would have to do. Besides, it's possible to feel very important indeed, for a time, within the world's exclusive community of lepidopterists, as the first person to have used radioactivity as a tracking device. It might also have been of interest further afield, perhaps even to the entire entomology world. If he were to walk through the corridors of the Royal Entomological Society in London during the next couple of weeks, I'm certain he would have attracted more than a few outstretched hands and passing praises.

"What about the Brimstones?" I demanded, thinking of all the work we'd done over the summer.

"I ran out of time for that," he said.

I was amazed at how easily he was giving it up.

At that moment a car screeched up the drive and we both knew it was Vivi. She'd left London as soon as she'd heard and we'd been expecting her. We went into the hall to greet her but as soon as she stormed in I could see, beneath a face bruised by sorrow and tears, that she was livid. She marched straight past me and followed Clive into his study without greeting me. Now I think of it, I don't think she greeted Clive either. She didn't say anything, didn't even look at me, although I was standing right in front of her. I'm not sure why I'm bothering you with such a trifling detail, but I do remember thinking how odd it was. I know memories shouldn't be trusted, that two people's recall of the same event can be unbelievably different, that even their perceptions at the time can be paradoxical, so I accept that my own recollections may be distorted, but I remember it as being the strangest entrance. As soon as Clive saw Vivi he turned his back to walk towards his study, without a word, as if he knew she was going to follow him, as if the entire movement had been choreographed.

Dr. Moyse, who'd been lurking about since he'd arrived and making himself scarce at what he considered the necessary moments, latched on to me again with his unnecessary comforting as I went upstairs. I suspected he and Clive had agreed not to leave me alone in case I collapsed beneath the weight of my grief, which they hadn't realized was eluding me. At times I could hear Vivi's voice from the study, puncturing the silent aftermath, sometimes strained and sometimes angry, and then her bursting into tears. I presumed Clive was informing her of his rushed retirement plans and her reaction, as expected, was a little more explosive than mine.

I didn't get to see Vivi at all during her visit, which lasted well into the night and early morning in discussions with Clive. The last thing I overheard before I finally fell asleep was an argument, not between Vivi and Clive, but between her and Dr. Moyse. They were in the hall and Moyse, who had been discharged from his duties, was at the front door, about to leave. I think it must have been lack of sensitivity on his part, but I heard him say something like, "Even your mother would have understood, Vivien." At that, she hit the roof. I've never heard her yell so loudly and I was scared.

"Don't you presume to come in here and tell me what my mother would have wanted. She damn well wouldn't!" she screamed.

By the time I got up the next morning, Vivi had gone. And that, I can tell you now, was the last time she ever set foot in this house until yesterday.

THE FOLLOWING MORNING, a Saturday, Clive carried out his itinerary to the letter and by nightfall, just a day after Maud's accident, Vivi and I had acquired our parents' entire estate, along with its outstanding debt.

I spent the next three days from dawn to dusk scrubbing the house, closing and locking the rooms that, on my own now, I wouldn't need. I'd left lots of messages for Vivi. I wanted to see her desperately but Arthur had said she was too shaken to come. Finally, on Tuesday, she phoned and said she'd gone to see Clive at the Anchorage but she still wasn't coming to the house.

On Wednesday morning I got in the car and drove through the high-hedged lanes, up Bulburrow hill and down again to Crewkerne. I parked outside Gateway and walked the short distance to the cobbled square, where the town hall stood in the center with a huge bronze statue of the man who had founded the town's first paper factory. According to the inscription, Titus Sorrell turned round Crewkerne's ailing economy in the mid-nineteenth century. I'd arranged to meet Clive there, on the bench outside The George. When I sat down an elderly man joined me, planting himself at the opposite end. I looked at the clock tower. Eleven-thirty exactly. Titus surveyed his empire smugly while pigeons fought to perch on his shoulders, desecrating him front and back.

At 11:33 Clive arrived. He sat down next to me and we both looked ahead at Titus and his pigeons for a while. Finally he said, "I've been thinking that if you could find a way to tag other species radioactively you could make some great progress with migratory patterns. There's been so little research in that area, Ginny. The society might like that."

I didn't reply. At that moment I didn't care what the society might like and I could hardly believe that he could.

"Yup," said the man at the end of the bench eagerly, and for a few seconds I thought, perhaps, that I'd walked into someone else's conversation. The man and I exchanged a pleasant look. Perhaps he'd only worried it was *his* conversation because no one else had replied. I glanced at Clive, who stared distantly at the cobbled square and the statue. He seemed altogether older—a real *old man*—and something else had changed about him too. It was as if Maud's death had shaken the character out of him, his enthusiasm for life and everything that made him who he was, turning him limp.

"What did Vivien say?" he asked after a while.

"I haven't seen her. She won't come to the house."

There was a long silence.

"You'll tell her I love her, won't you?" he said at last, and, although that should have been a happy tribute, there was something too absolute and eternal about it, and I couldn't help feeling a little sorrow spill from my heart.

Two men bailed out of The George, shouting at each other and scaring the pigeons to the safety of the clock tower. When they had passed, the bravest of the birds flew down to reclaim Titus's head.

"I'm pregnant," I said, in a moment of unnecessary candidness. It was true, but I wasn't so much telling him because he should know it, but because I wanted to tell him something happy, or perhaps to shock him—anything, in fact, to get a recognizable reaction from him. All he said was, "Very good."

"Congratulations," followed the old man on the far end of the bench.

"Thank you," I said to both of them.

After a short silence the other man said, "Are you eating broad beans?" I found it impossible to know if he was now talking to me, or to Clive, or to the pigeons we were all looking at, or to some imaginary person, and I didn't know whether to reply or to ignore him. I ignored him.

"You must eat broad beans," he ordered firmly, "if you don't want a spastic."

"Thank you," I told him, now understanding it was directed at me, and that he must surely have lost his marbles.

"Every day," he said.

"Every day," I repeated.

"Then you won't have a spastic. Nobody wants a spastic," he observed finally. There was a silence.

The old man leaned forward on his stick in a posture suggesting that he'd had his say and now he was finished.

Clive looked at his watch.

"You'll be all right," he said, and again I thought it might have been to either of us. "Well, I must be going now. I have flower-pressing class in ten minutes."

And he went.

WHEN I GOT HOME Arthur had let himself into the house. He was in the kitchen, waiting for me. It was lovely to see him and he gave me the first hug, a great big, long, silent one, that anyone had offered me since Maud's death.

"I was worried about you on your own," he said, letting me go.

"I'm fine. How's Vivi?"

"Not good, I'm afraid. She says she'll never come back."

"Oh no." I sighed, and felt the pain of my entire family crashing down round me. I wanted to find a way to bring them back, to hold them close.

"I think she feels it was . . . preventable," he said.

I thought of the cold steep cellar steps and the darkness of the stairwell. I thought of how the two doors stood side by side, like twins—the same moldings, the same handles—but one with a deadly drop on the other side. I thought I was perhaps the only person who knew quite how drunk she would have been, how perfectly preventable it might have been, *had she not been drunk.*

"She won't even talk to me about it. All I know is that she'd been quarreling a lot with Maud."

Had she? It must have been on the telephone because Vivi hadn't been home for months.

"Didn't you know?" he said, as if it was impossible for me not to.

"No. What was it about?"

He didn't answer for a while.

"I think she was worried about everything," he said vaguely. "You know how Vivi always worries about everything," but I had no idea what sort of everything he meant.

Just then the phone rang. There was silence when I answered it and I knew it was her. "Vivi?" I asked. "Is that you?"

"Yes, Ginny, it's me," she said quietly.

I couldn't tell if she was crying, or angry, or tired, or all of them, but I knew she wasn't herself. "Are you okay?" I asked, wishing I hadn't as soon as it was said.

For a while she didn't answer. "Oh, wonderful," she said sarcastically. "Is Arthur there?"

"Are you angry with me?" I said.

"Not especially." She sighed. "I'm angry with everyone and everything."

Well, that didn't make any sense to me, and such a broad sphere of anger doesn't naturally offer a starting point to help, so I didn't try. I decided, as always, to come back to the practical issues. "When shall we have her funeral?"

"We're having it next Friday," she stated. "I've already arranged it with the rector."

"And Clive? Does he know?"

"I have no idea, darling," she said.

"I've just seen him," I said. "He says to tell you he loves you—"

Vivi butted in. "I'd like to speak to Arthur, please. Has he arrived yet?"

I handed the phone to him and went into the back pantry to find some eggs to make a cake for tea. When I came back Arthur was staring disconsolately out the kitchen window at the gloomy day beyond, the phone call over. I was surprised how glad I was that he had come.

I was usually happy with my own company—I'm extremely self-sufficient—but I was so much happier now that Arthur was there. I didn't want him to leave. I studied his back for a moment, his thickly knitted navy polo-neck, the black curls at the back of his head, slightly bowed shoulders, and I thought how wonderful and thoughtful and interesting he was, and how comfortable and easy I felt with him. I cracked an egg against the side of the mixing bowl and he swung round, surprised that I was back in the room. I smiled into the bowl and imagined the baby growing inside me—our baby—and, I'm ashamed to admit, allowed myself to fall into a daydream that Arthur and I were married and we lived here with a houseful of children, as it had been when the evacuees were staying all that time ago.

I pulled myself out of it quickly. "How was she?" I asked.

"She and Clive have *completely* fallen out," he said, glancing at me and widening his eyes.

That must have been why Clive was worried about her, I thought. My family was disintegrating before my eyes, despite my efforts to keep it together. I cracked three more eggs, one by one, against the side of the bowl. "It's not the time to fall out, for goodness' sake, not when Maud's just died. She would have hated it. It'll be something ridiculous. Was it about the will?" I asked.

"I don't know, she won't tell me, but she's consumed by anger. I've never seen her like this before. She's turned into a raging bull," he said, clearly exasperated. "And I don't know how to calm her down," he added, staring out of the window onto the drive.

"Oh, Lord. She must be unhappy about something in the will or in Clive's handing over the estate to us," I reasoned, "but she ought to just tell me and then we might be able to sort it out, talk it through. I can't be expected to guess what's got to her. I've never been able to and she knows that better than anyone."

"It'll pass, I'm sure," Arthur said optimistically. "It usually does with Vivi. But at the moment she's refusing to go to the funeral if Clive's there."

"What? Of course he'll be there!" I sat down heavily and resolved to talk to her about it the next time we spoke, try to patch things up between her and our father. Why was it that I was the only person who didn't fall out with my family? I thought, as I added two cups of sugar and one of flour to the mixture.

"Does she still want a baby?" I asked, worried their plans might have changed.

"Oh, yes, she definitely still wants a baby," he said, without hesitation.

"Oh, good, because I think she's got one."

"What?"

"I'm pregnant."

"Really?" His face broke into a smile. "I'm going to be a daddy," he said as he sidestepped a chair to embrace me. We stayed like that for a long while, long enough for it to feel as if the embrace was welcome for other reasons than the baby. It felt more like comfort than joy.

SUNDAY

CHAPTER 17

A Prayer

BLOSSOM FALLS like snow against the mottled sky, blizzarding my path until I reach the Tunnel Walk along our eastern boundary. Today is Sunday, the third day since Vivien came home, and I'm on my way to church. I'm not *going* to church because I don't do that, but I'm on my way there to do . . . I don't know what, take a look, try to crush my curiosity. Yesterday, after I missed Vivien leaving the house, I spent the entire afternoon waiting for her to return so when, at breakfast this morning, she announced that she was going to church, this time I couldn't help but follow her.

Vivien walked down the drive, in the same way that she strode out boldly yesterday, right down the middle of it, in a tweed suit and black leather gloves, but I'm cutting down the path between the row of firs and the high fence, the Tunnel Walk down which I'd taken Arthur once. It's strange, now I think of it, that I'd brought him this way when I hardly knew him. It's a secret, childish route, but that didn't cross my mind at the time. That must have been the last time I was here, but it hasn't changed, and most probably not for a century. It's ageless and, as I stand here, looking up into the woven branches above, I'm dizzied into any age I want. I can be a child again, hearing

Vivi giggling farther down, urging me to hurry, or I can be a young woman collecting moss for the pupa cages, scouring the fence for the hairy gray chrysalis of a Vapourer, or searching for the holes of the Goat Moth caterpillar as it bores into the hard wood of the tree trunks. The path in the tunnel appears well worn, managed, even, compared to the rest of the wilderness our land has become, but it isn't. It's so starved of light that nothing grows here. It can't get wild. Instead it is carpeted with layer upon layer of soft needles, year on year, so that the ground has become a mattress, thick and springy as I walk on it.

When I reach the brook at the other end, I see that the split weeping beech is no longer the bridge. Half of the tree stands alone and naked on this bank, and the other half, the half that had fallen over the water and given years of service to the villagers, has been removed. In its place is a flat man-made bridge, rows of neatly sawn wooden slats over which no balance is required. I remember Arthur poised precariously on the middle of the log, his arms outstretched, how it had made him think that growing up here would be fun.

Arthur visited me a lot back then, during my pregnancy, at least every other weekend and sometimes more to check that I was all right and because, I think, he loved his weekend escapes to the country. Vivi was thrilled about the baby and, although she couldn't visit—she said she found it too painful to come to the house—she telephoned every other day.

My pregnancy filled a gap for all of us. After Maud's death, it gave life a new meaning and, thankfully, seemed to lessen the storm raging inside Vivi. She did come to Maud's funeral, even though I saw her glower at Clive at every opportunity. Clive didn't notice. He didn't notice anything or anyone and he didn't hold back his tears. It was as if, without her, he had shrunk to a small part of himself, the oldest, least meaningful part, a case without its contents. I didn't even get to speak to him. After the service he traipsed off to the bus stop to wait for the Belford bus to take him home to Paul Street, while Vivi raced off in her car back to London, neither going near each other or the house. If Maud had been around she'd have made Clive go to the little party Arthur helped me organize at Bulburrow Court. The entire village (and many from the surrounding villages too) filed in for what they instinctively realized was the last time, all talking somberly about the steep steps they would now be wary of in their own houses and being especially careful not to notice that Maud's husband and younger daughter were not there.

The baby gave Vivi a different focus. When she phoned she quizzed me on how I was feeling and how my body was changing, not to empathize with me but because she said she wanted to try to live my pregnancy. She said she wanted to know every feeling and thought and craving and discomfort so she could understand exactly what it was like to be pregnant, and I spent hours trying to recall every detail for her as my tummy grew bigger. She started to wear the things that I wore and eat the things I said I'd eaten. She said she imagined there was a baby inside her, even though I tried to convince her that even I couldn't imagine one inside me, that I didn't think much about it at all, that I often forgot I was pregnant. But she shrugged that off as peculiar to me, rather than a natural state of pregnancy. Arthur told me that whenever he returned to London he was interrogated—How was I walking? When did I get indigestion? Had he felt it kick or wriggle? How swollen were my ankles?—and sometimes, he joked, he came back just to get away from the questions about his last visit.

Vivi and I saw each other twice during my pregnancy. Each time we arranged to meet at Branscombe, on the coast, where we spent a day on the cliffs walking to Beer and picnicking in little coves, and a night snuggled up in bed together at a B and B across from the pub. We were our only family now, the two of us and the bump between us. The only thing she talked about was the baby, as if our relationship was singly based on it. She told me what a wonderful aunt I would make and how, when the child was older, we'd take it on holiday to France together.

I tried to persuade Vivi to visit Clive at the Anchorage with me, but she wouldn't. I saw him once a week during that first year, but he never got over Maud's death. He remained distant and apathetic. All he wanted to talk about was the moth research, but he wasn't even interested in that in his usual way. It's difficult to explain how his interest had changed: he didn't seem keen to pick at the details anymore—the experimental methods, the results or who wanted to publish them—only to know that I was carrying on, that I had got back up on my feet without him and had some projects going again.

At first he dictated to me exactly what research I should be doing and which grants to apply for and on my following visits he'd badger me about whether I'd done it or not. In the end it was easier to just say I had. I pretended to apply for the grants and then, naturally, I had to say I'd won some and was getting along with the research. I talked to him for hours about imaginary mothing expeditions, made-up methods of tagging specimens and plotting migratory patterns, the results of fabricated assays and numerous fictitious scientific papers. I made up stories of my success. It was the only thing he wanted to hear. It was as if he had to know that I'd made a success of it all by myself, that he wasn't needed; that I could cope, I suppose. I have no idea why it preoccupied him so but I wasn't going to deny him so I reeled off as much as I thought he wanted to hear, even though—at that time—I still hadn't yet found the motivation to get back into it all. Sometimes Clive threw in a question that flummoxed me, but eventually he gave that up too. He wanted to live the rest of his life believing that he'd put me on the path to success, and I didn't see why he shouldn't.

It was several months since Maud had died—near the end of my pregnancy—when I first noticed that Clive was going batty. Our conversations must have sounded extraordinary to anyone who happened to overhear them. Nothing Clive said seemed to make much sense anymore, and I could tell him anything and he'd believe it. Shortly afterwards he was diagnosed with acute dementia. Clive had deteriorated so quickly and suddenly after Maud's death, it was as if he'd already guessed his future mental state and booked himself into a suitable institution in advance.

I stopped visiting him. Sister Vincent, his supervisor, said she thought it best for both of us. Best to remember him how he'd been before his mind was too diseased to be recognizable, she'd said. And when Clive died five years later, she revealed to me that by the end he had been beleaguered by demons. I think, in a roundabout way, she was trying to make me feel better by suggesting his death had been an escape from a sick and troubled mind.

I CROSS the new slatted bridge—thankful it's replaced the log—to the footpath that rambles beside the brook, past St. Bartholomew's church. The edge, once wild with brambles and undergrowth, has been neatly shorn by newcomers, ignorant of the damage they do and the wildlife they endanger by taming their countryside.

I walk past the stone humpback bridge that takes the lane over to Hembury and towards the church. As I approach I can hear a collection of rasping voices, and although I cannot catch every word, I recognize the General Confession and join in the incantation in my head: ". . . We have erred, and strayed from thy ways like lost sheep. We have followed too much the devices and desires of our own hearts . . ."

St. Bartholomew's graveyard is tiny, bound by the brook on one side and the church on the other. I stop several yards away, crouching as best I can behind a laurel hedge so that I will be well hidden when the congregation comes out. I wonder if Vivien is sitting in her favorite spot, next to St. Bartholomew's toes. I wonder if she'll remember that her name is scratched onto the sole of his left foot.

I hear the low drone of the rector's voice and I fill in the words I can't quite catch from recollections of a distant past when Maud would lead her family to church on Sundays, and afterwards invite everyone to Bulburrow for coffee. I can't understand why the sounds of the service release a sadness in me. Perhaps they remind me of when I was part of a family. When Vivi and I heard the bells we'd rush upstairs, knowing we had twenty minutes to get ready—find some stockings, wash our faces, brush our hair. In the hall we'd meet Maud, heavily perfumed and doused in jewelry, and Clive in his gray suit, fraying at the elbows, his mind not on the matter at hand. Then we'd walk, like a picture-book family, one parent to one girl, hand in hand, down the drive, through the stone pillars without their gates, along the single lane of the hamlet of Bulburrow to the tiny church. And I'd spend the next hour staring up at the small windows in the eaves and wondering not how we should behave in the house of God, but why anyone thought there was a God at all.

". . . that we may hereafter live a godly, righteous and sober life, to the glory of thy holy name. Amen."

The church's small, high windows meant that even on the brightest day it was always gloomy inside. When you were eventually let out into the world you were blinded by fresh air and sunshine, which left me with the distinct impression that the outside world was the more spiritual of the two places.

My eyes shift to a flurry of red ants on the compacted earth beside me, hurtling over one another in their eagerness to get to and from their nest, a hole at the base of a birch whip. Peering closer, I see they are workers heaving neatly cut pieces of leaf into their nest, but I can instantly sense there is something amiss, something I can't quite put into words. They seem a little too frantic, even for ants, breaking rank a little too often, almost out of control in their frenetic rush to feed their offspring. They've lost their sense of order. I dig my finger partway into the nest's entrance and scoop away the top and there, at the back of the enclave, writhes a huge pinkish-white larva, squirming in its ugly embryonic form. My hunch has been validated and I click my tongue in a conceited tut. For a moment I wish someone was here to witness my intuitive expertise. I might have a poor understanding of people, but I have an instinct for insects. This isn't the ants' larva but an impostor that has ambushed the gentle partnership between ant and tree, where normally the ants feed off the tree's leaves while fertilizing it with their droppings. But they have been tricked by this bulbous parasite. It's taken command of the nest, tapping into the ants' chemical signaling system, instructing them to fatten it up for summer while it rests up lazily. They tend the great white larva without realizing it and, in a few weeks, not satisfied with a vegetarian diet, it will also help itself to the ants' own neglected larvae. It will gorge itself to immobility, but when it needs to move to its next victim's nest, it will simply direct the ants, like little robots, to pick it up and carry it.

All the while I am listening to the church service I am also studying the ants, whose furious activity takes on a different meaning when set to Christianity. I see the inequity of life, the immorality of nature. I consider a larval god controlling the fate of ant and tree, seen by the ants but unseen too, unrecognized for His actions. I hear part of an address about a deaf music teacher, I see the slavery of ants, the isolation of the teacher, the ignorance of an ant, the total domination of a larval god, the acceptance of workers, a tyrannical grub, the solitary teacher, unquestioning ant, a gluttonous writhing larva, a hymn. . . . It's one of my favorites:

> *Immortal, invisible, God only wise,*
> *In light inaccessible hid from our eyes . . .*

After the hymn I hear the rector bidding us to pray. Abstractedly I think of Vivien leaning forward so that her head is right next to St. Bartholomew. Perhaps it's only now she'll notice her name on his foot. Is it making her smile, I wonder, or is she embarrassed by it? Does it fill her with happy memories, as it does me, or sad ones? Last week I would have sworn I knew the answers, but now I am a lot less certain.

I'm not particularly attentive to the service. It's become a background for my reflections on the saint's effigy and my musings on the ants' subjugation, but I register wafts of sentences that drift towards me, like hearing the comforting drone of a party downstairs while you're dozing in bed.

"We pray for the poor throughout the world . . . in our own parish, the elderly, lonely, sick . . . in particular we ask you to remember . . . Win Readon, Alfie Tutt, Fred Matravers . . . Virginia Stone. We pray that you grant them the grace . . ."

Virginia Stone . . . ? I've been watching the industry of a single ant cutting a neat circle round itself on a leaf, and marveling that such a preprogrammed creature has the wit to move out of the circle before it's detached from the rest of the plant, when I hear myself prayed for—or think I do. I can't be sure. As I say, I wasn't really concentrating, but I quickly recall the voice again in my mind and it seems clear, unmistakable: *Virginia Stone.* I'm astounded. Why on earth are they praying for me? I'm not sick or lonely. I can only think that Vivien has made an excuse for my absence in church.

Let me tell you—because there can't be many people who've experienced it—it really is the most unusual feeling to hear your name prayed for in church, the rector asking for help from a God you don't believe exists. If only they knew that I'm *right here,* listening from behind the laurel just beyond the graveyard. I briefly imagine that this is my funeral, that Win Readon, Alfie Tutt and Fred Matravers have somehow got better but I have died, and I'm watching them pay their last respects, Win, Alfie and Fred, who have never met me but had, apparently, been ill with me.

When the service is over the door opens and five dour elderly people file out after the rector. I was expecting the whole village to flood through in a harangue of noise, but there is no throng of shouting children, no Sunday bests, no hats. Vivien emerges deep in conversation with another elderly woman, and they walk along the path to the road. I'm about to leave my hiding spot, anxious to get back to the house before her, when I notice that she's stopped. She says something quietly to her companion and turns back, walking purposefully and directly towards me, looking straight at me through the stiff, waxy leaves. How on earth did she know I was here? What do I say? She passes three rows of graves and I'm sure our eyes meet. I look down at the ants' nest again, and at the *Maculinea* larva, hoping to look studious when she reaches me. But the seconds grow longer and she doesn't arrive, and when I look up again I see she's turned right and gone through the gap in the hedge to the graveyard extension, that bit of rectory garden expropriated by the surplus of dead, the bit where our own family is buried. I don't visit the graves, so it hadn't occurred to me before that that's where Vivien is headed, and now it dawns on me that she's probably not seen me after all. She doesn't know I'm here squatting on my haunches.

Vivien's just out of my view, but if she's at the family graves, she must be standing very close to me, just the other side of the hedge to be precise—but a little behind and to the left. I shuffle back on the dry earth as quietly as possible and stop. I think I can hear her breathing. I rotate a fraction, still crouched, and find that as I peer through a small gap in the leaves, I'm looking at her back, less than five feet away.

Her tweed jacket, a loose weave of sludgy colors, is pulled taut over her shoulders as she hunches down at Maud's grave. The small slit in the back of her mid-length skirt has opened and ridden up, showing me, through the sheer nylons, the raised purple veins, just like mine, on the backs of her knees. She stays like that for a while, displaying her veins to the laurel and me. I can't see if she's fingering the grass or if she's reading the words on the headstone she designed—just Maud's name and dates, no more, no other small clue about her for future generations. Death snatches so much substance. All of a sudden Maud became a label on a stone, the nuances of the individual no longer important—her thoughts and desires, her grievances and her passions, the wisdom, knowledge and understanding slowly assimilated throughout her life, all gone.

Vivien rises shakily to her feet and I glimpse a crumpled white handkerchief in her right hand as she steadies herself, leaning on her mother's stone, almost embracing it. She moves to the next grave, Clive's, and stands at his feet, reading the headstone she never saw placed, the one that the nuns at his retirement home chose for me. It's half the size of Maud's, made of imported, highly polished black granite, which they'd insisted was smarter and cheaper than the local stone. It reads RIP at the top, then simply CLIVE STONE underneath.

They'd forgotten the two honorary doctorates, his fellowship of the Royal Society and all the other accolades he'd meticulously collected for his memorial throughout his life. Vivien stays at Clive's feet long enough to read the three letters and two words, then leaves.

I am now expecting her to stop at the third family grave, the tiny one on Maud's other side, a small rectangular plot bound by the spiky pieces of flint I'd watched Arthur put round it to mark the edges. Within the flint boundary you can still see, even now, a sharp swelling in the earth, the poignant little hump of a small body shape, as if he'd not even been given a box, as if he'd just been laid on the ground and covered with earth, which was patted down over him, the way children bury themselves on a beach. It looks as if the grave digger, quite understandably, reasoned that as such a small space was needed, it wasn't worth taking away any of the soil. What soil came out would all go back in and eventually compress over time. As if nothing had ever gone into it at all. But this little knoll was rebelling: it had refused to pack down, to give back the soil its place, and it refused to look as if nothing had gone into the ground at all.

Arthur had designed the gray headstone himself, in the more expensive local stone. It was blatantly outsized for the grave it heralded. He'd had a pattern of zigzags cut all the way round the edge, with three rows of smaller zigzags carved decoratively round the front face to frame the letters, rather like a frieze you might find in a nursery. Engraved in beautifully curly writing he'd had written:

Samuel Morris
A Little Life No Less Loved

But, for all its decoration and the distinctive rise in the earth, I watch appalled as Vivien walks straight past it. She doesn't even notice it. She knows it's there somewhere, she must, she was told all those years ago, but she doesn't pause to look. This isn't a calculated reaction—there is no furtive glance or dismissive scan, not the snub she has just shown to Clive's memorial. It is much worse. She's forgotten about it, about him. She's forgotten he'd ever been born.

VIVIEN IS WALKING quickly now towards the graveled church path and I need to get back to the house. Besides, I can feel it's about to rain. The sky has darkened and a new crisp wind is pouring over the valley lip, offering to sweep out the sluggish heat from the bottom of its bowl. The wind is edged with a sharp and angry current and the season's warmth is laced with a new chill. It's my feeling entirely. An unexplained edge of anger and an unrecognizable chill creep through my body, and I'm ready when I hear the faint sonorous roar from far away, the grumbling beginnings of thunder rolling up the valley.

Thunder gets trapped in this valley as anger can get trapped in a person's mind. It'll get louder and louder and then fade away only to roll back again, and again, like a perpetual echo, building and fading, building and fading, as it rolls round the Bulburrow basin, unable to drag its weight out over the valley's lip. When thunder gets trapped, it can last all night. When I was young I was terrified by it, but now I find it a comfort to have those old memories return, of my fear, the security of my bed, Maud's soothing voice, Vivi climbing in beside me and entwining her fingers in mine.

With my foot I shift some loose earth over the ant-dependent grub to hide it from the birds. It might seem a hideous and ruthless creature now, but in time it will emerge transformed into a stunning iridescent blue butterfly, one of our rarest and most beautiful, and will be greatly admired as it shimmers in the sun with no knowledge or burden of guilt for its obscene past.

I trundle home besieged by the weather. A blackbird skitters along the ground in front of me and at intervals cocks its head, as if beckoning me on. How friendly it is, how trusting, I think, until it lets me come right up close behind it and I find it isn't a blackbird at all but a crisp winter leaf, rolled up at the edges and pushed along by gusts of the new wind. Once I know it's a leaf, I'm stunned that I'd seen it as anything else.

SAMUEL MORRIS DID indeed have *A Little Life*. It was twenty-four long minutes. His birth had been protracted and painful, and both Vivi and Arthur were at the maternity hospital with me, as planned. Vivi clenched my hand and whispered encouragement in my ear, while Arthur paced the corridor outside, listening helplessly to the torment of labor.

The baby was purple when he finally slithered out with the cord wound too tightly round his neck. I glimpsed the shiny livid color, like that of a fresh bruise, as he was whisked off to a table by the window. Vivi froze with panic and stood with her back against the opposite wall, waiting for the baby to turn pink, so when the door was opened and Arthur ushered in, she ended up behind it and at first made no effort to come out or to close it. Arthur walked straight over to where the doctors had taken the baby and were thrusting what looked like straws into his mouth and nose. He watched as they tried to open his airways, pinched his toes, and finally put an oxygen mask over his tiny face. Arthur said that when he held his tiny hand, his little son saw him. He said he didn't just look at him but he *saw him*. And Arthur said he looked wise. That was all he said, that the baby looked wise, and now, now that I'm walking home pursued by the roar of thunder, wise doesn't seem good enough. I'm wishing he had remembered more, that he had said more. I wanted to see his face, Samuel's face, I wanted to know what he really looked like, not that he looked wise, but what shape his tiny eyes were and if he had fat or thin lips, if he had worry wrinkles like some babies have, or sticky-out ears, or jet-black hair like Arthur's own. At the time I'd just accepted wise as a description but it wasn't enough. It didn't tell me anything. If only I had seen for myself, if I'd had one little look. But then again, he wasn't my baby. He was Vivi's.

After fifteen minutes, the doctors took up the puce child and offered him to Arthur to hold, the oxygen mask still attached to his tiny features. I knew it wasn't a good sign. Arthur cradled his baby and looked up towards Vivi.

"Do you want to hold him?" he said.

"You hold him," she said quickly. She hadn't moved away from the comfort of the wall and she looked terrified. Arthur then turned to me. I shook my head with exhaustion.

"Okay. So I'll hold you," Arthur said softly, in a singsong baby voice that I'd not known was within him, and he held him and looked at him and held him and looked at him and held him and looked at him, until well after the end of his life. The baby grew more and more purple but Arthur just smiled at him. He told me later he'd forgotten he was purple. He'd said that when you really looked at him, you didn't see purple at all.

But I only saw purple. I only ever remember purple, and what I really want to see, what I really want to remember, is wise.

BY THE TIME I reach the house April's downpour is in full flow. Black rain lashes the earth violently, digging up the dry dirt, spitting and bouncing it about the drive so I'm wet through when I get to the safety of the porch. From here I watch the puddles form, fill and flood within seconds in front of the house, and a web of runaway canals are sketched and carved and deepened all over the driveway as fierce little heads of water push loose earth and leaves and stones out of their way to make channels that run over and spill into each other, feverish in their single-minded pursuit. I'm watching them combine into a central artery down the drive and push onwards to meet the runoff from the fields. Soon they'll blend into a torrent and surf along the clay half-pipes beside the lane to join the turgid brook that bursts its banks whenever it rains.

As I make my way upstairs to change my sodden clothes, I can hear the floods on the roof above me, bouncing along the gutters and gullies that direct the rainwater through the vast landscape of the roof to the drainpipes in its corners. I change, then dry my hair as best I can, scraping it off my face and tying it in a bun. Vivien's back in the house now, and I don't want her to know I've been out.

"Ah, Ginny," she shouts when she sees me coming down the stairs, "I've got a little surprise for you."

"I've had a shower," I say. I'm worried she'll notice my wet hair. Yet she's completely dry—she must have had a brolly.

"And I've brought you a surprise," she says again, triumphantly. She's ebullient, buoyed by the raw weather outside.

"What is it?"

She grabs my arm and leads me into the library as if an enormous birthday present awaits me there. Instead, an elderly woman is sitting on a wheel-back chair in the corner of the room, a glass of sherry in her hand. It's a bit of a shock to see her, to see anyone, sitting in my house. The woman gets to her feet as we enter the room. I guess instantly who it is. I clasp the face of my wristwatch, twisting it in my fingers, trying to buy myself preparation time. Usually, for this sort of encounter, I would have required time to rehearse what to say, where to look and how to react. I'm so unused to meeting people these days. I'd like to flee and shut myself into my room upstairs, like a little girl. How could Vivien do this to me without warning? It's not a new thing—she knows I've always avoided people. Even when I was younger, when I went to town and wanted a cup of tea I'd go to the hot drinks dispenser in the train station rather than the teashops on the high street. That way, it didn't have to get personal.

"Ginny," says Vivien, coming between us as if she were the umpire in a boxing ring. "I want you to meet Eileen."

"Hello, Eileen," I oblige, forcing myself to look up, to take in her small frame, her pure white hair, yellowing at the front, and the thick spectacles that magnify her eyes queerly. Between you and me, I've seen her many times before from my lookout, walking up or down the lane to church, waiting for the bus, posting a letter in the box in the rectory wall or visiting the woman at East Lodge on Tuesday afternoons. But she's never seen me.

"Hello, Ginny," she replies timidly, and it strikes me as peculiar that we're meeting like this when we've been living less than half a mile from each other in a scantily populated countryside for a number of years now. Had we wanted to meet, we could easily have done so.

"Eileen lives in Willow Cottage, where her mum used to live," Vivien says.

"I know," I reply, and we spend a few moments sitting ourselves down in a sort of circular arrangement on three single chairs. I can see Eileen has begun feverishly to finger the glass in her hand, turning it round, searching for comfort in its golden charge. Vivien pours herself a drink, then offers one to me, but I don't drink.

"Well, cheers," she says.

"Cheers," says Eileen hesitantly, and they hold up their glasses in front of me in honor of our enforced meeting. "It's been a very long time, Ginny, but I've heard all about you."

"You've heard about my work, then?" I ask. There wasn't an awful lot else she could have heard about but the work I'd spent a lifetime achieving. Eileen looks to Vivien, as if she needs reassurance to answer me, the hand with the glass a little shaky. I find her nervousness strangely comforting. It's making me relax.

"Her moth work," Vivien says loudly, nodding at Eileen.

She must be a little deaf, I think, so I copy Vivien's lead and speak slowly and emphatically. "Yes, I'm quite a well-known lepidopterist," I say modestly, "not that I have much time for it anymore." She doesn't answer. "Or steady enough hands," I add lightly. She's staring at me strangely. "But you can never completely give up that sort of vocation. It's in here," I say, pulling a fist towards my heart and tapping it a couple of times, hoping that some sign language will help her understand the basics.

Eileen glances at Vivien again. "Yes, I've heard about your work," she says uncertainly.

"Well, I had to keep up the family tradition."

My initial nervousness has evaporated now. My lack of confidence when it comes to meeting people must stem partly from lack of practice and, once the initial bit is over, I'm surprised it feels so manageable.

"Top-up?" Vivien asks Eileen, indicating her glass.

"Please." She accepts eagerly. It's eleven-thirty in the morning.

For someone who started out by telling me how much she'd heard of my work and my reputation, Eileen now seems remarkably uninterested in discussing the subject. I sit there half listening as she and Vivien digress into a different genre of conversation to which I've nothing to add. I'm vaguely aware of them talking about how I might enjoy coming to church, and how long it takes Eileen to do the flowers each week. They talk about how much bigger the house seems nowadays, and then about her mother's horse, Rebecca, which, having retired from fieldwork, still went on to live until twenty-three and was gentle enough to have anything on her back, including the cat, who often slept there.

I'm not at all interested. I'm staring at the marble fireplace I can see across the room, just to the left of Eileen's shoulder, two thick columns of stippled gray surrounding the painted tiles, and a mantelpiece above, and I start to explore the wispy white crystal streaked through the darker gray. It reminds me of a section of neurons through an electron microscope, like the ones I've seen in scientific journals, with their long axons and dendrons reaching out to one another, trying to find a connection. While Vivien and Eileen talk of old age and the new cinema complex with a bowling alley in Crewkerne, I allow myself to go on a little journey through the fireplace's nervous system, following the splayed out neurons and leaping over synaptic gaps like a neurotransmitter. They lament how bowling has changed because it always used to be played by the elderly on the village green and now it's in the pubs, hijacked by the young. In the way that when you stare at patterns for long enough you can make them move about and change their form, I am trying to join up the maze of streaky lines within the marble, to mass them together into one dense brain, as if I were tying up the loose ends of different lengths of string. Infuriatingly, as soon as I join up several strands they start to untie and move off of their own accord, until the entire nervous system begins to unravel and I lose control of it. All of a sudden I'm aware of Vivien getting up from her chair.

"I'll get you one," she's saying to Eileen, as she walks out of the room.

I look at Eileen and she meets my gaze. I'm not afraid of her being here anymore. We both know there's nothing to say, that we were put here together against our better judgment, so we remain silent. She picks up her handbag from the floor beside her chair and rummages in it. Finally she pulls out a packet of Benson & Hedges and a small white lighter. She takes a cigarette, lights it with a couple of short, sharp puffs, then draws pleasurably from it in one lengthy inhalation. I'm amazed a frail body like hers holds such a powerful suck. She risks a glance at me. I'm watching her. I'm curious about the way she smokes, the way the smoke streams out of her nose and snakes upwards, swathing the front of her hair, staining it yellow. She takes the cigarette out of her mouth and studies the burning end intently, judging her satisfaction by the length of ash she's created. She puts it back to her lips and draws again and I'm searching her face for clues to what she's thinking or feeling, but I have no idea. She's expressionless. Her blank features remind me of something, someone . . .

The picture on the card, of course. How could I forget it? A cartoon picture of a granny knitting in a chair. It's from the card games I barely remember playing with Dr. Moyse when I was little. Then all the other cards come back to me in a rush of memory, pictures of a cartoon family in lots of different places: the girl in the bath playing with bubbles, Daddy flying an airplane, Grandpa swimming (or was he drowning?) in a river, the boy on a bike or balancing on an upturned bucket, Daddy smashing his fist on a table, Mummy behind a school desk, the girl in the jungle next to a tiger . . .

It was quite simple, really. I'll tell you what you had to do. The idea was to guess what they were thinking by the expressions on their faces. But it wasn't as straightforward as it sounds because the cards were purposely misleading. For example, the girl about to be ravaged by the tiger was scared in some, and in others quite happy. Daddy was banging his fist on the table sometimes in anger and at other times in delight. But it was the card with Granny sitting in a chair knitting that always stumped me. It was like the trick one, the joker in the pack. Is Granny happy or is Granny sad? Happy or sad? Happy or sad? A little of both, I'd always thought, a little of both. But she couldn't be both. Dr. Moyse said she wasn't allowed to be both. Well, it's not like real life, is it? It's just a game, I know, but it's nothing like real life if I'm not allowed to mix Granny's feelings even though they would be. A woman of great age with all her life behind her was bound to have contradictory feelings. But it always had to be one. You had to choose. Happy or sad?

Vivien marches back into the room and hands Eileen an ashtray. Once she's sat down she tells Eileen about a fantastic dentist she's found in London, through a friend called Ettie. Actually, he's not a dentist but a hygienist and he's managed, finally, to stop her teeth being so sensitive. He's given her a special brush that made her gums bleed at first but now she'll never use any other kind. She can eat anything.

It's the first time I've heard her mention anything about her life in London. Now I know she has a friend called Ettie and a dentist called a hygienist.

Eileen accepts another top-up and they start to discuss their time together yesterday afternoon. They try to remember what they had talked about yesterday afternoon. Then they move onto yesterday afternoon's weather and compare it to today's downpour, which, they agree, is thankfully easing into drizzle. Or is it spitting? Not once did anyone ask about my research.

A WHILE LATER, Eileen has left, and Vivien and I are in the kitchen preparing lunch together. Vivien starts to dress a small chicken to roast while I peel and chop a squash at the sink. Now and again one of us will remind the other of something from our childhood, someone we used to know, songs we used to sing or the clothes we wore that now seem absurd. It's a delight to hit on something we can both recall, that we eagerly begin to elaborate on, jogging each other's memory with every comment, building up the details for each other. But for every memory we share, there are many more that we can't bring together, that we can't seem to evoke in each other, that turns out to be something only one of us remembers or the other only vaguely recollects or, sometimes, remembers completely differently.

With the back of the knife, I scrape the bright orange chunks of chopped squash off the chopping board into a pan of cold water, then sit at the table with a colander to pod some broad beans.

"Well, darling, wasn't that nice to meet Eileen?" Vivien says, bringing the conversation back to this century. "Nice to know someone in the village."

"I suppose so," I say, not thinking particularly.

Vivien pauses and annoyance flicks over her face. "Ginny, you really shouldn't presume that everyone knows about your research," she says sharply, cracking rosemary over the chicken's breast.

"I don't presume—"

"It might embarrass them if they don't," she continues. I don't say anything, although I think she expects me to. "And, to be honest, I'm not sure anyone cares that much," she finishes.

It was cruel of her, I agree, but I know she's only stirring for a reaction. Don't ask me why she's suddenly launched into this attack. I have no idea, and I'm not sure which direction it's going in either. Vivien stops what she's doing and rests both hands flat on the table at either side of the bird.

"I'm not being unkind, but it's been a *very* long time since you retired, Ginny. That's all."

I burst open another pod with a pop, and scrape the beans out of their furry jacket with my overgrown thumbnail. I wonder when Vivien retired. She's told me nothing about her life even though she's obviously told Eileen, so why should she come back and make all kinds of guesses about mine? She doesn't know anything about my line of work.

"It's not the kind of career you ever really retire from, Vivien." I try to put her straight. "It's a vocation, not a job, and I'm afraid I'll take it to my grave."

Vivien is quiet and I can feel her looking at me hard.

"Well, what moth work are you doing right now?" she says casually, taking a lemon and stuffing it right up inside the bird.

"Well, right now, Vivien," I say, a little bored by her line of questioning, "I'm not doing as much. I don't know what you're getting at."

"I know all the knowledge you have is incredible, I just didn't realize you'd been doing proper research . . ."

"*Proper* research?"

"I mean, I thought you'd finished all that a very long time ago."

"I'm always in research," I correct her. "One project invariably leads to another. That's the nature of it. You can never finish research. There's always more to discover."

Vivien leans over the table towards me. "Ginny," she says softly, almost in a whisper, and as she starts to speak I lean in too, to catch what she's saying, "you are *extraordinary* . . ." She laughs suddenly.

"Extraordinary?" I whisper, pulling back, another long pod ready to split in my hand.

"Yes. *Extra*ordinary," she says, in a more serious tone. "I mean, why don't you ever get it?"

I didn't say anything. If she was looking for a reaction, I couldn't work out what kind she was waiting for. As for being extraordinary, well, you've probably gathered by now that I'm pretty straight down the line, sometimes, I'll admit, a little too guarded, a little too taciturn, too serious, perhaps, but I wouldn't call it extraordinary. I'm not impetuous like Vivien and I don't go around cloaking my thoughts and feelings in the elaborate costumes of hidden meanings, abstruse subtexts and sly insincerity. It's Vivien who's always been frustratingly complicated, whose equivocating you need to decipher. She's always saying things she doesn't really mean or pretending to be someone she isn't. I don't know how she can see through all the confusion she creates in her head.

"Oh, I see, I suppose you don't think you are. Is that it?" she goes on as if she's read my thoughts. "I suppose you think you're just like the next person, as normal as the neighbors. Well, isn't it remarkable that the rest of the world thinks you're extraordinary?" she adds spitefully.

Well, one thing I'm absolutely sure of is that the rest of the world can't be thinking about me very much. I never see them. I don't go out. She must be furious with me about something, but I can't think what I've done. It's lucky I find it easy to ignore her gibes.

Then she seems to have a change of heart. She comes over and holds my face in her hands and strokes my hair, as a mother might her child. She brushes a wayward gray lock behind my ear.

"Ginny, what I am getting at is . . ." That's a promising start, I think, but she's stalled.

"Is what?" I prompt her.

"I don't understand why they felt you needed to be protected all your life," she says, making herself no clearer. "I don't see why they presumed you were incapable of understanding. You were this delicate and rare flower that a little truth would bowl over and crush. They both tried to build a high wall round you and patrol it all your life. Well, I don't think it's right anymore. I think it's your right to know the truth."

Ah, she's drunk. I recognize it now. She's ebullient, excited, even. All the signs flood back to me. I know she doesn't mean anything she's about to say or do. It's the alcohol. I close my eyes.

"I've got an idea," she says cheerfully, changing tack.

I open my eyes. Her face is reddened by the drink, her eyes bright with exuberance. She's standing next to the table, alongside the seasoned bird, and for a moment I'm transported back to a different time: she's about to pick up the bird and fling it at me, or even to take the edge of the table in both hands and upend it, with everything on it, on top of me. I grip the side nearest me with both hands so that, as she overturns it, I will be able to deflect a little of the weight to save me being crushed.

"I've decided I'm going to invite the president of the Royal Entomological Society in Queens Gate"—she pauses—"and also, yes, how about the curator of lepidoptera at the British Museum?" she says, gesturing in the apparent direction of London. "I'll invite them down here to lunch and they can look at the collections and you can talk about what you've been up to all your life," she finishes grandiosely. "How about it?" she asks flatly, putting her hands on her hips. "What do you think of that?"

I'm dumbfounded by her behavior. It's exactly at times like this that I find I'm left adrift, without any real understanding of what she's thinking and why she's behaving as she is—utterly unpredictably. It can't be *me*. I refuse to believe that anyone could decipher Vivien right now.

"Well?" she asks again.

"I don't really know."

Only yesterday I would have dismissed the idea out of hand, but meeting Eileen had been much easier than I'd thought, even though we had nothing in common. Besides, I'm still confused if this is Vivien or the drink I'm talking to. I can't tell whether she's got to the point I could recognize so easily in Maud when I used to say she'd *turned*. The last thing I want to do is rile her.

"You don't know, darling? But, Ginny, they'd think it such an honor to lunch with one of their most famous members. Imagine—they must have been dying to visit. They'll be full of praise for you and your work throughout lunch and fascinated by everything you have to show them. I doubt you've seen them for ages, or shown your face in Queens Gate for a while. Am I right?"

She is. I haven't been to Queens Gate for a long time and they're bound to be intrigued by my research. Actually, I can't think why I'd not thought of it before.

"Okay, if you're sure they'd like it."

Vivien picks up the roasting tray with the chicken and carries it to the Rayburn. The more I think about it, the keener I am on the idea. I hadn't had an awful lot to say to Eileen but it's a little different when you can talk with colleagues about the topical debates in the entomological world, especially when I haven't had a chance to get up to London recently. Vivien opens the top right oven and shoves the tray deep inside.

"Have you heard the British Museum has moved its collection out of London?" I say, once she's banged the oven door shut. "To a new Entomology Museum in Tring, I think. Somewhere in Hertfordshire."

"Yup." Vivien sighs. "That was years ago."

"Shame, really. They asked for some of our collections but it's not the same, stuck out in the middle of nowhere, whatever anybody says."

"I remember. It's what Clive said." Vivien sits down opposite me and studies me. "Who are *they* anyway?" she asks.

"Who?" I say, looking at the final pod in my hand.

"Well, if I'm to invite these people down here for lunch, I need to know their names—the president of the society and the curator of the British Museum—who are they?"

"Well, the . . ." Do you know? For the life of me, I cannot remember their names. It's ludicrous. I've known them for years. There was a new president not so long ago, I remember, but the curator's definitely been there forever. Goodness me, I must be losing my mind!

Vivien has got up and is wiping the counter in front of the window and next to the sink where I've been chopping. She washes the cloth under the tap, spreading it out in the water's stream like a sail, then slowly squeezing it before she starts to wipe again, round the taps and along the window ledge, carefully lifting the vases and bottles that are kept there. Then she plugs the sink and runs the hot water, squeezing soap into it, until the basin is full and frothy. As she plunges in the first few utensils it occurs to me that I should check all the collections and lay out some of my most significant research in time for their visit.

"When do you think you'll invite them for?" I ask quickly, a little alarmed by the preparation I'll need to do.

Vivien stops washing up but doesn't turn round. Instead she puts both hands on the front of the sink for support, her back towards me.

"Oh," she says casually, "I don't know . . . Tuesday?"

"Tuesday!" I exclaim. "What—*this* Tuesday? Two-days'-time Tuesday?"

"Well, why not?!" she says in a cavalier manner, but she doesn't understand the panic that's brewing in my stomach. That's not nearly enough time for me to prepare myself, let alone look through all the collections.

CHAPTER 18

The Bobble-Hat Woman and the Leaflets

I'M IN THE LIBRARY when I hear the front-door knocker. For a ludicrous moment I think of the curators and wonder if they've arrived already. We finished our lunch an hour and a half ago and since then I've been here, picking off the dried mud from my slippers that I wore outside when I followed Vivien to church this morning. She retired to the study to work on a small piece of needlework—a tapestry, I think—but as soon as I hear the knocker bang, her flat rubber soles are squeaking across the hall parquet. I'm in awe of the immediacy of her response, the spontaneity with which she answers the door. There's not a moment's hesitation, no fleeting uncertainty. She strides purposefully towards it, her steps strong and insistent. I watch her pass the library door, which I've pulled ajar, and I'm still watching as she gets to the front door, her hand up and ready to open it as she arrives—no pause to gather her thoughts or to prepare herself to confront the unknown. I retreat a little so that when the door is opened I can't be seen.

"Hello. Can I help you?" I hear Vivien ask the unknown.

"Virginia Stone?" It's a woman's voice. Who can be wanting me?

"I'm Miss Stone's sister, Mrs. Morris," Vivien says curtly. "Can I help you?"

"Hellooo," the woman says, drawing out the fulsome greeting as if they'd been friends once long ago. "It's *so* nice to meet you. I'm Cynthia from Dorset Social Services. . . ."

Oh my God. I pinch my nose. It's the bobble-hat woman. Our family has always had an intense distrust, a fear even, of social workers. I heard Maud complain more than once that they were meddlesome people, though I can't think she had many dealings with them. Maud was one of those people who believed that a community should be able to look after its own, and that state-funded help simply gave one an excuse to avoid one's responsibility. She was also most vociferously opposed to the new lunatic asylums that were opened in the fifties, which she said social workers had helped fill with misfits just after the war.

". . . we're based in Chard," Cynthia continues. "Here's some leaflets I thought might be interesting and this is my card and, well, that's my name at the top and the address, and there's the number . . . and somewhere I've got a . . . Here it is, a leaflet with some background information of what we—"

Vivien interrupts her. "Do you know it's Sunday afternoon?"

"Sunday? Yes, it's Sunday."

"Do you always go round pestering people on a Sunday?"

Her pertness makes me smile with admiration. Between you and me, I can't believe she said it outright like that.

"Oh, I see . . . ," Cynthia says slowly, her voice deepening. "Well, the thing is, we're all *volunteers,* you see, so we *give up* our weekends for our *volunteer* work."

I glance back to the library window. Although the heavy rain stopped some time ago, it has been drizzling on and off. The low seamless clouds still loom heavily over the valley and I wonder whether Vivien will feel she must invite the bobble-hat woman in if it starts off again.

"What can I do for you?" Vivien asks her.

"Well, now, is your sister in?"

"Yes."

"Well," she says, lowering her voice, "the truth is we've been finding it extremely difficult to talk to her." Now she lowers her voice to a near-whisper, but I have particularly acute hearing. "We've been visiting, well, trying to visit, to check on your sister but, well, she's never opened the door to us. Actually, it gave me quite a shock when you *did* open it," Cynthia says with an inviting chuckle.

"And why do you want her?" Vivien asks loudly, as if to make clear that she won't enter into covert whispering with Social Services. I wonder if she knows I'm listening.

"Well, we just wanted to check on her, really. We were particularly worried about her during the winter. Apparently there's no central heating in the house," Cynthia says disdainfully, and just then I hear the dripping of rainwater on the hall parquet as it starts to leak through its usual few spots where the ceiling slants low in the corner. The drips will get quicker and quicker until they merge into a steady stream that runs along the ceiling and pours off, like a curtain, onto the floor. "We were worried about her being cold," she says, as if she needs to explain the function of heating.

"She's in very good health, thank you."

"Oh, good." She pauses. "May I see her, please?"

No, no, Vivien, I really can't face meeting two strangers in one day. My spine curls in apprehension, shrinking me, as I wait these seconds for Vivien's decision. Cynthia pushes: "Just so that next time, if you don't happen to be around, she'll feel she can answer the door herself."

"I understand your concern, but I'm afraid not. My sister doesn't want to meet you."

Good for you, Vivien, I think. Relief softens the muscles across my shoulders.

"Forgive me, but how do you know if you haven't asked her?" replies Cynthia.

I'm on tenterhooks. I know it's absurd but it feels as if my little sister and the bobble-hat woman are playing a game of words at the front door, and whether or not I have to confront the woman rests on the outcome of their wit and resilience. It's a miniature version of the card game of my life in which my hand is always played by others, some of whom are my opponents and all of whom play with the knowledge of their own hand as well as mine.

"I don't need to ask her," Vivien says. "She doesn't like meeting people, especially strangers. Don't take it personally," she adds. "If you like I'll tell her you called and that you seem quite friendly, albeit a little persistent."

Well said, Vivien! I could throw flowers into the ring. Game over.

It's clearly not over for Bobble-hat Woman. I hear her clear her throat.

"Mrs. Morris, we're only concerned for the welfare of your sister. We don't wish to interfere. We've had reports that she might not be capable of looking after herself anymore. I came to check her health. Now, if you're not going to cooperate I'm afraid I'm going to have to write a report—"

"Her health is good. Thank you," Vivien chips in.

"I mean her condition."

"I've told you her condition is good. She's very healthy, despite the cold winter. Look, I'm not sure who's been reporting to you but I'm her sister and I'm looking after her now. Please don't call again."

"Mrs. Morris, it's not an easy job caring for—"

Goodness gracious me! Vivien slammed the door on her. I come out of hiding hesitantly, sticking my head round the library door, brimming with gratitude and quite forgetting to pretend that I haven't been listening. Vivien looks at me without seeing me, her back pressed firmly against the front door, as if Cynthia's next game plan might be to batter it down. As I move closer, it's difficult to tell if she's barricading the door or supporting herself on it. I'm surprised to see her so shaken, but she recovers quickly enough and moves away from the door, leaving our defenses down. I wish I hadn't shown myself. If Cynthia were to ram the door now she might get through.

"Social Services," Vivien says with a haughty snort, as she passes me on her way to the kitchen. "Swines. Don't ever answer the door to them, will you?" She doesn't wait for an answer.

I follow her. I'm after the leaflets. Vivien is busy pulling pots and pans out of the kitchen cupboard.

"Did she drop off some leaflets?" I ask her.

"Yes. Do you really want them, darling?" The small wad is still gripped tightly in Vivien's hand.

Actually, yes, I do, but something holds me back from telling her. I think she might laugh, or tease me or use it against me in a way that only she can. But I can tell she's on the verge of screwing them up, that she thinks she deserves the gratification of ripping them to shreds. A strip of panic curls into my stomach and flutters there, slowly, like a leaf drying in autumn. For a moment I have the peculiar feeling that we are at a deadlock and a quick decision is needed—to stay calm or to take a surprise leap at her and make a grab for them. I want them *that* badly. They're part of my routine.

"I thought I might take a look," I say as casually as I can.

"Here you are," she says, surprisingly, handing them to me, "but would you be a sweetie and help me catch some of that waterfall in the hall?"

I help her take as many vessels as we can find and place them under the curtain of water to catch the bulk of it. As soon as we've finished arranging them, the first few need emptying, and it's a good half hour before the torrent has subsided enough to allow me to squirrel myself away in the library with my leaflets.

The first two I've seen many times:

Senior Solutions, Ltd.

Professional help with Medical Insurance, Life Insurance, long-term care insurance, Will advice, age discrimination, conservatorship and guardianship, or elderly abuse.

Aged 50 and Over?

Why not explore the chance of returning to work or training.

Then there's a whole lot of new ones: "Senior Safety: Safety Prevention and Tips for Common Problems Facing Older Adults"; "Canine

Partners"; "Senior Travel"; "Home Alone? Home Modifications"; "The Needs of the Dying"; "Singles Senior, It's Never Too Late," www.seniorsinlove.com; "Choosing Your Nursing Home"; "Activities for the Elderly"; "Alzheimer's Disease—Unraveling the Mystery."

I stop at this. I always like to read the medical ones. Besides, I've often wondered how I'd know, living on my own, if I'd developed Alzheimer's, or dementia like Clive. Without someone to tell you, how would you recognize a slow mental degeneration compared to a little bit of natural memory loss? That's what everyone forgets these days: there's a fine line between sanity and insanity. Lots of people are on the edge. We can't be in perfect balance all the time. Most of us will have a little too much or too little of this or that chemical in our brains at some point. It's part of being individual. There are no absolute norms; being *too* sane is most probably a type of madness in itself. Besides, who's to be the judge of sanity? I know the villagers here have always thought the Moth Woman, and this house, slightly doo-lally, and they'll latch on to any rumor that whirls their way. But, then, that's how small villages have always reacted to anyone different or detached from them, and they don't know me at all.

I study the elderly people on the front of the leaflet, sitting in a row of plastic chairs as if they're waiting for a bus to take them away. They look fine to me, a bit bored. If you ask me, these leaflets are too quick to label people. I once read one that told me that onychophagia was a common stress-relieving BFRB. The terms alone make you want to rush off to Accident and Emergency. Then I read that onychophagia means biting your nails and BFRB stands for body-focused repetitive behavior. Surely it's a habit, not an ailment.

I open up the leaflet and read the first paragraph: "Today the only definitive way to diagnose Alzheimer's disease is to find plaques and tangles in brain tissue, but to look at brain tissue doctors must wait until they do an autopsy, which is an examination of the body after a person dies."

That's not much use, is it? So, I might have Alzheimer's and not know it. Would I feel any different if I did? Then I go on to read that doctors can diagnose only "probable Alzheimer's" and that one set of symptoms may have many different causes, and that an easily curable thyroid complaint may manifest similar symptoms. . . . I stop reading. It's obvious no one ever really knows and that they should leave people alone to become old, not tag them with all sorts of mental illnesses.

Vivien comes into the library with a tea tray, Belinda's pot, two cups and saucers, and some ginger biscuits she's arranged in a circular motif round the edge of a plate. Simon trots in after her. "Anything interesting?" she asks, putting the tray down on an occasional table by the fireplace.

I read her the leaflet. "I remember the days when people just got old, or eccentric," I comment afterwards. "They weren't mental. Like Mr. Bernado—remember? He was often caught fishing in his underpants. Someone would just take him home again and point to the wardrobe—"

"Virginia!" Vivien reprimands me sternly. "You don't say *mental* these days. It's offensive."

"Well, all I'm saying is that most of them went barmy but we called them eccentric. Or old. They didn't need a medical certificate."

"I think people have a right to know as much as they can about what's"—Vivien pauses—"different about them."

"Ah, but does it help them?"

"Yes. Yes, I think it does, actually," Vivien says ardently. "I think it would. If you knew there was something wrong with you, medically, if you were actually diagnosed as intellectually challenged in some way—"

"Intellectually challenged?" I butt in, and laugh—but Vivien isn't laughing.

"If you were told," she perseveres, "you might find you understood yourself better. You could find ways of adjusting yourself—if you wanted to—or at least being aware of it. It's far better to know," she says, swirling her tea to dissolve the sugar. "It's a great shame not to know, not to be told. It's not right," she says as she moves to the window, cup and saucer in hand, and stares private thoughts into the jungle beyond.

"If you're that barmy, it won't make much difference," I say jovially, a little to fill the silence and a little under my breath. I am not sure about her mood.

"Maybe," she says softly.

I thought she'd find it funny, but I can tell she's elsewhere in her thoughts. Could that be sadness in her stillness by the window? It was just an observation, and I wouldn't want it to turn into a serious dispute, but I don't mind being old-fashioned. I don't take to all these modern ways of thinking that Vivien's latched on to. What about all the poor old ladies who don't have the wit to see through all the mental diseases they've been labeled with and can't get on with being themselves? They'll turn into nervous wrecks, worrying about their next affliction. Then, after all that, they might find they've only got an overactive thyroid. It occurs to me that Vivien might be thinking of Clive.

"Do you think Clive knew?" I ask softly.

"What happened to Clive was different," she says sharply, turning back to face me. "That was all his own doing. He deserved every demon he got and he knew it."

I hadn't meant to provoke another onslaught about Clive. "I think you're taking your anger with him a bit far. Why don't you just admit you had differences and accept them?" I say, very reasonably, I think.

"Oh, Ginny, it's always so simple with you, isn't it? Don't you ever see that?" Vivien's cup rattles on its saucer as her temper starts to simmer.

"I'm only trying to—"

"Well," she cuts me off, "I've been trying *desperately*," she says, putting the cup and saucer on the window seat beside her, "to help you see it, to help you understand things, to help you see for yourself that things aren't so simple and sometimes they need to be questioned. I didn't come home to tell you this, but I can't hide the truth anymore. I can protect you from other people but not from the truth."

There she goes again, talking in riddles. I never asked her to come home.

"The problem is," she continues, "that you wouldn't know the truth if it came and looked you in the eye. That was always your problem."

I'm not listening to her rant because I don't want to. I'm trying to work out what might have happened in Clive's head, I mean at the molecular level, to lead to his dementia.

I flinch as Vivien clutches my shoulders near my neck and shakes me. "Ginny!" she shouts.

"What?" I say, startled out of my reverie.

"You're not there. It's so convenient for you to go off somewhere else and not listen, isn't it? Don't you want to know the truth?"

"What truth?"

"All of it. Everything."

"Like what?" I raise my voice, exasperated with her.

She pauses for a moment, enjoying my full attention. "Like your own mother was murdered," she says finally.

I watch her studying me. It's as if she's looking for the pain she may have inflicted. Then I laugh. I mean, what can you do? Actually, it's a proper little giggle, as if she's made a joke. And I can't believe she's not laughing too. I can't believe she's serious.

"Don't be ridiculous, Vivien!" I sputter.

Then she does something most peculiar. She clenches her fists and stamps her right foot hard, three times in a row, as if she's stamping on a scorpion and making sure she's done the job properly. She looks like an eight-year-old having a tantrum.

"How can I make you just *try* to understand?" she shouts. "Once. Just think about it *once*. Look at me! Look at me!" She grabs either side of my face and directs it up to hers. "Do I look like I'm making it up?"

She doesn't.

I tell her again, softly, "Vivien, she fell down the cellar steps. I was there. I saw her lying at the bottom. I promise you, it was an accident."

"You're wrong, Ginny. You saw it *wrong*," she shouts.

"What on earth makes you think so?" I say quietly, flabbergasted.

"I just *know.*" For a moment she's lost for words. "Most people just have that sort of intuition, Ginny."

I'm not going to say it out loud because there's no knowing what she'll do, but I can tell you: Vivien's gone completely doo-lally. You can't have intuition sitting in London about someone being murdered in Dorset. You either have the facts or you don't—I'm sure you'll agree with me. Besides, I'm a scientist and I'm afraid I don't work with intuition.

Vivien flops onto the cushions on the window seat, bringing her legs up to rest them on a stool in front of her.

"For a while I thought it was you who had done it," she says, more calmly now, like the opening of a great story.

I'm astounded. I'm shocked. I'm mortified. "Me? Oh, for goodness' sake, Vivien, you've gone bonkers," I blurt out. But she ignores me and continues, in a calm, even tone, as if the story must go on whatever the audience's reaction.

"I thought Clive and Dr. Moyse knew and were covering up for you." She is looking at her legs stretched out on the stool in front of her as she speaks. I am standing a yard or so away, towering over her with my hands on my hips and, I'm sure, my jaw dropping. "Dr. Moyse had officially told the police not to interview you. He got a court injunction so they weren't allowed to. He said you had some sort of disorder, that you were unstable."

"Oh, Vivien, the things you think of! It's absolute nonsense. It was nothing like that at all."

"I know. I know," she says, relenting. "I worked out later that you couldn't have known anything about it or you would have told me."

"Exactly," I say indignantly.

"You would have told everyone."

"Of course." But even as the words form in my mouth I already feel the tightening of a trap.

"So then I realized it was Clive who'd pushed her and *you'd* been covering up for *him.*"

"*What?* Vivien, I'm afraid you've gone quite mad." I'm more than a little irritated now. Why she has to keep throwing in ridiculous theories and casting all sorts of doubts over our beloved parents' memories is beyond me. "Clive didn't do it and I didn't cover up anything for him," I tell her firmly, but as I say it, I know my efforts to change her mind are in vain. "This has all been festering for years in your head, but can't you see it's nonsense?"

"You weren't *aware* that you were covering up for him," she trudges on. "You still aren't aware of it. The police were banned from interviewing you, even though I kept telling them they had to."

"Oh, rubbish, Vivien. Even if the police *had* talked to me I wouldn't have told them anything differently. Maud fell down the stairs."

I can't take this any longer. She's the one who doesn't know what was going on. I look down at my watch and fiddle with its face with my thumb and forefinger, blocking out whatever Vivien is saying, trying to decide if this is it, if I have finally to tell her the secret I'd promised myself and Maud to keep from her for the rest of my life. Suddenly I can see how dangerous such secrets can be. You keep them to protect people, but in the end they are even more destructive. I took away the truth, so over the years Vivien has filled the void with ludicrous ideas. Surely the truth will stop her raving about Clive or me murdering Maud and put her mind at rest.

"Vivien," I say, gathering my resolve, "I have to tell you something." She doesn't answer, but gets up, slides her footrest over, and sits on it beside me. She's very quiet and I know she's ready to listen. What I am about to tell her will be a shock, a revelation to her, and I close my eyes so that I don't have to see it on her face, the disbelief, the anger, or whatever else it might cause.

I say it fast and plainly: "Your mother was an alcoholic. That's why she thought it was the kitchen door. She used to get so drunk that she didn't know what she was doing or where she was going." I keep my eyes closed, waiting to hear what she will say or do. But she's utterly silent. Then, after a long pause, I feel her hand on my arm, squeezing it gently, willing me to open my eyes. She looks sad, defeated, even, and for a moment I think she's about to burst into tears, which, I admit, is not a reaction I was expecting. But what she says next is far worse.

"I know that," she says simply. "That's why he murdered her."

THAT IS IT.

"Stop it, Vivien, just stop it!" I'm shouting. "You've spent your whole life ripping this family apart and you waltz back here and start doing it again, even when they're all dead."

"Me? Ripping the family apart? I spent my life trying to hold us together."

It annoyed me that she could switch our roles like that. "That was me, Vivien. I was the only one trying to hold us together. You fell out with Maud and then you fell out with Clive, and then you didn't speak to me for forty-seven years. How can you dare think you tried to hold us together?"

"I fell out with Maud because I was trying to stop her beating you."

"You knew?" I'm incredulous.

"We all knew, Ginny. Arthur told me what she was doing, and that you were too ashamed to say anything. And it had taken Clive too long to face up to how bad it had got. He couldn't bear it. None of us could, and we'd all agreed we had to stop her."

I'm struck dumb.

"And I fell out with Clive because in the end the bastard went for the most convenient solution. He pushed her down those steps to stop her beating you. Because she nearly killed you, because she probably would have killed you. But he didn't have the patience or the time to sort out her drinking. He discarded her as if she were a specimen he didn't need anymore."

The whole world is flying round my head. Nothing seems to add up. How does she suddenly know all these things I thought she never did? I have so many different reasons as to why this is nonsense, but they all want to be shouted at once. They won't line up in order and wait their turn.

"But— But, Vivien, even Clive didn't know how bad her drinking was," I stammer.

She shakes her head.

"And," she continues calmly, "I fell out with you because I couldn't help thinking it was all your fault. I couldn't help thinking you'd ruined my life, *all* our lives—whether you knew it or not. But I wasn't allowed to think that. Oh, no. Clive never allowed us to think that. You were always above blame, exempt," she says. "We couldn't rock the boat. We weren't allowed to upset your delicate equilibrium because you might not be able to cope with it. Too much emotional disturbance wouldn't be good for you. You had to be made to feel as normal as possible to build your confidence. We could never make any mention of your . . . peculiarities. Well, I think it's all rubbish. I don't blame you, no, but I think they were wrong about you. I think you can handle a little truth. It's about time you knew, so you can accept some of the responsibility for her death."

Responsibility? Vivien's either gone mad or she's trying to make me think I'm mad. I'm amazed that she's believed this for her entire life. Poor Vivien. I can't move a muscle. My back is resting against the wall, my hands making fists, pale and bloodless. I can't even blink. Instead my eyes focus on the thick air in front of them, following the floating black specks reflected from the retina that dart back and forth through my vision. I don't want to be here, I don't want to have to listen anymore. I start to run, run away from here, away from myself, down the tunnel with the ball of muddled words rattling behind me, gaining, faster and faster I run, pursued by questions and words and torment until I reach the door to that place in my head. I heave it open and skip behind it, just in time to shut out the thunderous ball of noise and squall and disarray behind me. I know that Vivien is still talking, but it doesn't matter anymore because I'm not with her. I'm slamming the bolts on the door into their catches. Alone at last.

. . .

I DON'T KNOW how long it is before Vivien comes over and puts her arms round me.

"Sorry, darling," she softens. "I'm sorry. I do understand that it isn't easy for you to find all this out suddenly."

She says it as if there is no dispute, that the facts are clear; it's just a matter of me getting used to them, assimilating them. I want to scream my frustration right into her face. She's completely and utterly misunderstanding my point of view: she has no evidence for anything she's saying. I'm a scientist. I need hard evidence. It's just as likely—more than likely—to have been fabricated during years of bitterness in her own head.

I walk away from her, tired, suddenly overcome by the need to sleep. Besides, I've got other things to think about. I've got to prepare myself for Tuesday's lunch with the entomologists. I have to check that our collections are in order and perhaps make a display of some of my most important findings.

CHAPTER 19

The Moth Hunter

I DON'T KNOW what it was that stirred me but I can see the moon outside, low and resplendent, drowning the stars with its brilliance. Has it been sent to wake me? Its stark light floods the valley so that, from where I'm lying in my bed, it seems that night has settled only within the house. I close my eyes wishing innocent sleep to come and take me back to abeyance. But I know it can't. Welcome to the endless night.

My bedside clock says twelve minutes past midnight. I shift myself heavily to a sitting position and check instinctively that my wrist-watches agree on the time, which they do. It's then that I feel the burning within my wrists and hands. I look at my distended thumb knuckles, the covering of skin pulled papery thin, taut and shiny round the swelling. Spring is here. Spring is painful. I think of Clive filling the blue plastic washing-up bowl in the kitchen, testing that the water is warm but not too hot, then laboriously carrying it, sloshing from side to side, up the stairs and into this bedroom, to this bed, where Maud would be lying stiff with this pain. He takes her hands in his and eases them lovingly into the water, bringing them back to life with warmth and tenderness and massage. Both of my parents are silent, the silence of shared pain, but I can see Maud's eyes, needy and afraid, finding refuge in Clive's unfaltering dependability. He looks into the bowl, concentrating on her hands with sedulous care, and she relinquishes herself to the sanctuary of his silent strength and determination, placing all her trust in him. Safe, delicious memory.

I'm sitting in bed steeling myself to exercise my hands through their pain. It's like a cramp when you know you have to stretch it out, however much it hurts to do so. First I try to curl my fingers into a fist, but the knuckles are so swollen they can hardly bend. It's as I'm trying to straighten them, flattening my palms as far as they'll go, that the events of yesterday glide back to me, uninvited. I feel something like dissent rising through my body, boring its way out, as I remember in a hum of voices Vivien's accusation: that my father murdered my mother in calculated cold blood, pretty much under my nose. I forget, or rather forgive, for once, the pain dissolved in my fingers and in my feet, in their matted woolen socks, and in this private starkness I allow myself to add it up, just to see if the signs are there that it could be true—that Clive *did* kill my mother, and all because of me—and I find myself searching desperately for the ones that will prove it couldn't possibly have been so: I saw her with my own eyes at the bottom of the steps and I saw Clive's devastation. I felt her hands still hot to the touch, her neck soft and warm. I smelt the blood running through her hair and the stink of sherry on her. I phoned Dr. Moyse myself. I tried to save her myself. I'd seen Maud in the weeks and months before, in her drunken stupors, falling over chairs, walking into wardrobes and, once, into the pond on our upper terrace. I never suspected anything except that she'd had her final drunken accident. But I know I didn't see it.

I hadn't seen the fall.

I slide myself out of bed and ease my feet into my toeless slippers, which wait like sentinels by the bed. I shuffle slowly across the sloping wood floor, drenched silver by the moon, to the door and out onto the landing, beleaguered by unanswered questions. Vivien is sleeping in her room just along the corridor through the double doors ahead. I feel suffocated for an instant, just knowing she's there, and it's here, now, with sudden understanding, that I realize I don't care about the answers. Did Clive kill Maud or didn't he? Was it for me or not? It doesn't matter anymore. It makes no difference now. The past itself is not important. The only thing that counts now is my memory of it. I feel an uncharacteristic flash of anger, a surge of heat through my cheeks: How dare Vivien come home and steal my safe, delicious memories? Three days ago my memory of life was of a complete and happy event—a blissful childhood, a warm, loving family, a blossoming career—but Vivien's walked into my head and littered it with doubt and anger and turbulence. The past I used to know has melted before my eyes into something writhing and fluid, with no structure, no scaffold. I can never again think of my parents, my childhood or my life without the stains she's spilt all over them. All I see now, as my father nurses my mother's hands back to life, is the water turning red in the bowl.

The moon greets me again as I reach my lookout at the far end of the landing. It creeps furtively from behind a sparse and smoky cloud, as if beckoning me to follow. I like the moon and its cycles. I like the way that, although it seems to ebb and flow and come and go at will, it connects with the sun and the earth and the tides in a constant, rigid relationship. In reality there are no erring boundaries, no diffusion of loyalties.

Has Vivien really come home to torment me, to point out that I have been living in the wrong history, to push me into the correct scene of the correct painting? I have always had her interests in mind, especially when I have kept things from her. She had in mind no interest of mine when she taunted me with her twisted secret.

The thin cloud scatters, the moon's rim sharpens. What is it that has changed in this silent still night? Everything feels different, not just the past. I see the moon—and the world—more clearly now. I look down with my new eyes at my matted wool socks and toeless slippers. Is this really me standing here at this window, in these old slippers?

I move away and come to the dark oak door behind which the spiral staircase twists up to the attic rooms. I don't know why I'm easing the wooden peg that stoppers the latch in place. It needs wiggling back and forth a few times before it comes loose in my hand and the door swings open towards me. I watch as the moon's blue light tumbles dimly in the dust up the stairs and, I don't know why, I'm feeling my way in through the oak door and along to the outer wall of the spiral staircase where the treads are at their widest. Just to my right there's a thick rope for a handrail but I don't want to trust it. The stairs are steeper than I remember, so I'm leaning forward, using my hands on the ones above, as if I'm scrambling up a mountain. But I'm going slowly, one at a time, feeling and checking for splits and cracks and, although it's just a short distance to the top, it feels like many minutes before I'm swallowed in total darkness and I can straighten, the door to the attic rooms—to the collections, to my life's work—in front of me.

I know, somewhere to the right, there's a switch that will light the room behind the door, and I'm feeling for it now, a bulky dome-shaped casing with a square lever in the middle. I find it and pull down. Light flickers into life behind the door, sharp knives of warmth cutting above and below it, accompanied by muffled movements. Disturbed wings.

There's something about moonlight that makes you feel safe to entertain dreams and fantasies, something about its grim coolness that lights a somnolent path without adding color, and wandering in it can make you feel you are still in the realm of sleep, journeying through a different plane from the living. But the warm orange hue outlining the door in front of me invites me to wake properly, shows me the colors and shades of my world rather than merely its outlines. For a while I stand in the comfort of the darkness, knowing that answers are illuminated within. Vivien has never had the same trouble opening doors.

I sweep my hand through the thin shaft of light piercing the slit by the side of the door, splitting it with my fingers into individual rays, playing with it. Vivien would have been better to tell me nothing, because now I see more than she wants me to. I see myself in the past, as a child, as a woman, and I see how mildly I looked at life. But I also see her. I see her differently now. Once, I'd seen the charm and child-like simplicity in a young girl dreaming of our futures together; once I thought of a schoolgirl who loved her sister in a way that was inexplicable, twinlike, a visceral connection standing in a wall of solid granite that a lifetime of elements and abuse couldn't scratch. But now I see the granite crumble before my eyes, disintegrate, like a cube of sugar in tea, letting out a little puff of steam that was once a driven bond of unshakable love. Could our entire sisterhood have been a farce, years of complicated deception, of endless assurances of love, charm and manipulation, all so that one day she could take what she wanted? To ensure she could have the use of my body, and tear from it the one thing she couldn't have without me: a child?

And when she couldn't have it, she abandoned me in the same way that, only yesterday, she had accused Clive of discarding Maud, like a specimen that was no longer needed.

I unbolt the door and push it open, and am blinded equally by resentment and fluorescent light. I resent Vivien for shattering my illusions, not only of my parents and my life but of *her*, for making me question her, her love, her loyalty, everything she has ever told me. As I cross the room I'm assaulted by decay, old memories and the ammoniac stench of bat droppings. Four pipistrelles hanging from the rafters above me shift uneasily. Caterpillar houses line the walls, exactly as they always have, mainly homemade glass containers, some tin, a few giant glass cider jars and a dozen or so old ammunition boxes, which Clive always claimed made the best caterpillar cages. A layer of rotten humus has collected at the bottom of some, made up of twigs, leaves and crusty discarded skins.

You might have expected the moths to take over, but there are no moths. This isn't a chosen habitat for moths. It's now home to bats, spiders and a pod of hornets, which have made a vast and beautifully constructed papier-mâché home right under the eaves, added to and undisturbed year after year. I'm left with just one question and it's not how Maud ended up at the bottom of the stairs. It is simply whether Vivien has ever loved me as I have loved her, ever since the day the evacuees left and I saw that she was special. A beam in the far corner has collapsed with the weight of the roof above, opening a section to the sky. Some slates lie shattered on the floor below and insulation wool clings desperately to its plaster, hanging to the floor in a matted clump. And if she's never loved me, if she's only ever *needed* me, what is it that she wants from me now? Why *is* she here?

I move through this room and into the next—the emergence room—a corridor lined on both sides with muslin-clad breeding boxes, some still with sticks and mounds of earth and dried moss in them. It was to here that, each spring, we'd carry the pupae up from the cool warren of cellars that run beneath the house, where they'd wintered on trays or in boxes. We'd separate each species into these banks of cages so that they could breed on emergence, laying their eggs on the muslin. Each type of moth would need twigs from different plants, each emerged at different times and each required species-specific conditions.

Above several of the tanks are still pinned some of Clive's meticulously devised care instructions. PUSS MOTH reads the first, and underneath is a list of chores *to be carried out each day without fail.*

1. Ensure willow twigs are always upright and stable
2. Replace willow twigs every two days
3. Check if the chrysalis reacts to touch (3 days to go)
4. Temperature must not exceed 66.2° F
5. Mist twice a day with water spray
6. On emergence offer 2.5cc sugar solution on cotton wool

Clive typed out the instructions for each species, then pinned them around the room so that there could be no mistakes and no excuses. At least four times a day one of us would check that the strategically placed thermometers, barometers, electric heaters, dishes of water and ultraviolet lights were providing the exact conditions necessary for the time of emergence. It was our spring rota. Vivien found it a bore and didn't necessarily subscribe to the miracle that Clive would have us believe was about to ensue. But I took my duties very seriously and would hurry back to Clive to report that I'd found one tank had been a degree too warm or too cool, or that I'd felt a draft blowing on the back of another. Together we'd record the findings in his Observation Diary and look forward to seeing if it had any effect on the moths' emergence.

Clive recorded everything, and that, he told me many times, was the key to being a good scientist and especially a good lepidopterist.

When the time (and the temperature, light and humidity) was right I spent many hours in the attic, waiting for the earliest signs so as not to miss the miracle. It starts as a vague movement deep within the chrysalis, the faint twitch of a shadow. And then the noises start. Cracking and crunching, like boots on dry leaves, or the snapping of twigs, unimaginably loud for such a tiny, tireless creature as it works its way out. When many were emerging at the same time, the chorus of noise was astonishing. It would keep me awake at night in my bedroom a floor below. Within an hour the lid of the chrysalis was detached and I'd have my first glimpses of the animal's shiny wet head as it emerged through its trapdoor, wriggling, shouldering and heaving its way into the world. Once free, it crawls up the twig I've positioned for it with two small wet buds saddled across its back. At the top it stops and, like petals unfurling, the buds open and unfold, fanning out into large flat sheets. The newly awoken creature hangs them out to dry until finally they turn to delicate wings of light parchment. A moth is born.

I'd record everything, just to be a good scientist.

I WALK THROUGH this room and then through the library, dusty reference books in perfect alphabetical order, and finally into the "laboratory," a small dusty space with the far wall sloping down low to a round north-facing window. It's a museum to time. A Formica workbench runs round the room at waist height and on it, side by side, are two relaxing trays crusty with dried chemicals. Next to them a scalpel rests on a dissecting board, dirty, as if Clive and I were still at lunch. A long rack, fashioned by Clive and holding small, delicate tools, stands against the back wall of the bench. Each implement slots neatly into a hole small enough to stop the bulkier handle dropping through it. In front of the round window is Clive's homemade version of a fume cupboard. It's just a glass box with the room's window as part of its back wall. Clive would use his most noxious chemicals in it and then he could open the window behind to let out the fumes and aerate the tank.

Lining the wall to my right are hundreds of brown and green bottles with glass stoppers on shelves that reach up to the ceiling, all labeled neatly across the front. As I look along them I begin to sense a deeper disturbance growing within my new person. Some of the bottles have short chemical names: TANNIC ACID, IODINE, AETHER, BORAX. Others have their empirical formula only: KCL, PSO_2, NO_2, and the rest have names that fill up the entire side of the bottle: salicylas antipyrini salipyrine, chloret hydrargyros merc.dulc. calomel, hydrochl. Ephedrine, hydras chlorali, salicyl. Nitric. C. themobromnatrio loco diurectine.

Beyond the chemicals is the fume-cupboard window from which I can see far down towards the village. I can't stop thinking about Vivien at the graves today. I'm trying to recall every moment of her being there, her posture as she stopped at each one, her expression as she read the words, wishing I had been born with the understanding to decipher what each look or movement means, how it translates into feelings.

I don't care if Vivien hated Clive, and as I've said before, I don't really care anymore how Maud got to the bottom of the cellar steps. It isn't the cruelest thing I can think of. The cruelest thing is Vivien. It's Vivien walking past her own son's grave without noticing, not even acknowledging his lonely bones. It was that she *didn't* walk by him on purpose, that she didn't *shun* him but seemed to have forgotten he ever existed. That made it worse. In my mind's eye I remember how her heel glanced carelessly off the corner piece of flint that Arthur had arranged there, pushing it just below the surface, a little helping hand towards the grave's inevitable erosion. Arthur had known everything there was to know about his son. I knew two things about him: that he was purple and he was wise. Vivien knew nothing. I felt deep down that there was something wrong with that, that it was what Arthur was talking about all those years ago. It was why he wouldn't try for another with her and why he saw in her someone he didn't like.

Arthur had wanted to talk about the boy and the birth, and keep his memory alive, and Vivien didn't want to think about it but to try for another baby as soon as possible. Arthur would never let her try again, he said, because she hadn't even looked at this one.

"You can't choose your children. You can't take the best ones, the ones that survive, the ones that are born the right color," I heard him arguing with her some days later. "If you've decided to have that child you must take it, whatever happens. You must claim him."

Back then I listened to Arthur's tirade and nodded, saying little. At the time I didn't really understand his anger with Vivien, or his disappointment at her reaction. But he thought I did, because I listened to him and didn't argue.

Four days after the birth Arthur and I were in The Angel at Hindon. He was driving me home from the hospital, which had kept me in to recuperate, and we'd stopped for lunch. We sat at a small round table by an open fire with old brass cauldrons and tongs hanging above our heads, waiting for someone to take our order. Our trip had been near silent. Then Arthur leaned towards me and put his hand on my knee. "Ginny," he said, "I'm so sorry."

Sorry? Sorry they were slow to take our order? Sorry that Vivien had gone, distraught, back to London and not resurfaced yet? Sorry that he too would have to leave me and go back to London soon? I could think of so many sorries.

Finally he clarified it: "I'm so sorry our baby died."

Our baby? I had spent well over a year conditioning myself that it *wasn't* my baby. I had been trained to say, "It is not my baby, I will not be its mother," and, quite honestly, I didn't feel like he was mine in the slightest. Not for a moment. No maternal instinct kicked in to fight against giving him away. I had felt no bond with him and I had known he wasn't mine. I didn't even think about the biology. To me, I was the carrier—that was it—and now Arthur was looking to me to be the boy's mother. So Vivien disowned him and he wanted to give him back to me. I hadn't asked for a child, and I hadn't asked for Vivien's burden of grief when she'd got a dead one. If it survived it was hers; if it died, it was for me to mourn.

So I tried, for Arthur's sake, to be the baby's mother, but I didn't really feel it. We named him Samuel during that lunch in The Angel and Arthur had his gravestone designed at much cost and we both watched him buried alongside the freshly turned grave of his grandmother.

Although at the time I hadn't understood Arthur's desperation for his dead son to have a mother, all that changed yesterday when I saw his mother step right over him. It was the strangest feeling: from that moment on he was not hers but mine, as if my latent maternal feelings were ushered out of apathy, pricked into life full of fierce revenge. How dare she throw away the son I had entrusted to her? If Samuel had grown up and not done as well as she'd wanted, if he'd been slow or retarded, would she have thrown him back to me then?

Finally I understand Arthur and his anger. I understand that the words on the headstone—*no less loved*—have real meaning, and for the first time they don't just apply to Arthur but to me also: it's a yearning, heartbreaking love that I've never known before, a part-of-me-missing kind of love.

I stare out of the laboratory window into the silver darkness and suddenly I *feel* him there, even though he's been there all along. I think of the flints and the still mound of earth and I want to go back and, like a wild woman, desperately paw at the ground, dig him up and hold him, just hold his lonely bones, claim him, own him, be his mother, all because his real mother was too selfish to have him.

I'd love to be able to tell Arthur my change of feelings now. I'd like to have all those conversations about Samuel he wanted back then, right now, nearly half a century too late. But, of course, Arthur will be nearing the end of a multitude of eras in his own life. The brief liaison with Vivien and me, and the birth of Samuel, will now seem such a tiny speck on the landscape of his past, hardly of any consequence, while I see now that the very same speck—up close a perpetually deepening well for Vivien and me—has always remained the focal point of our lives, and for all those years we must have been only pretending to walk on into the horizon.

After we had buried Samuel, I saw Arthur once more. It was five years later in exactly the same spot, when he turned up unexpectedly at Clive's funeral. He said he'd come to see how I was. He hadn't changed, except he was now remarried.

Less than a handful of people—Arthur, two nuns from the Anchorage and I—watched Clive's coffin lowered into place next to Maud's and Samuel's in the St. Bart's graveyard extension. The nuns said Clive had eased himself towards death as earlier he'd eased himself towards madness.

THE BOTTLES lining the shelves in our laboratory wouldn't, to you, look in any particular order. They certainly aren't alphabetical but, believe me, they have a very distinct arrangement, an order of use, those used most often the nearest to hand, rather like the QWERTY arrangement of keys on a typewriter. Those most frequently used in the same preparations are grouped together and those that have a similar function—for example, restoring colors in the wing, or relaxing a specimen from rigor mortis—are also assembled together. I scan the wall to take in the ones I recognize most easily: Sol. camphor. spirit, Boric acid, Bromet. Kalic., Naphaline, Carbolic acid. I like saying the names. I don't mind admitting to you that I feel proud to know what they are and what each one can do. I'm glad I'm an expert and have all that knowledge that so many ordinary people don't. My eyes wander to the bottles a couple of shelves up, set high on their own to the far left of the others. It's the poison shelf, the anesthetics and the killing fluids. Each bottle is marked with a large white skull and crossbones, some with a red triangle too, and the bold red words CAUTION POISON in case the symbols haven't given a clear enough indication of the potency of the fluid within: Sol. ammonia spirit anis, Potassium Bromide, Nuics Vomictincture, Sol.peroxyd. hydrogenii, Aether 1.5/5 g sol.

I watch my fingers run along the front of the killing fluids, clearing a clean line across the names, a ball of dust gathering in front. The strangest thing of all is that for the first time in my life, I feel more like my true self than ever before.

CLIVE USED TO SAY that to be a successful moth hunter you need not be a specialist, but many specialists: a biologist, a botanist, a chemist, an ecologist, a meteorologist, an expeditionist—and well versed in Latin.

Moths can be extraordinarily fussy. Not only are they particular about which plants they feed from but also the specific habitat in which those plants grow. So, when hunting a moth, you must first uncover the correct plant in the correct habitat and for that you'll need a good knowledge of the less glamorous corners of the country—for example, where ragwort grows in a low, dry and sheltered dell. The Dingy Mocha, which has been found only twice in Dorset, lives solely on sallow in low wetland, so you'd need to know the boggiest parts of Abbotsbury Heath where sallow scrub abounds, or some badly managed farmland in the wettest parts of the Blackmore Vale. If a couple of Vale farmers decided to clear their scrubland, one of those Dingy Mocha habitats would be wiped out forever.

Once you've identified where to find it, you need to get to know the moth well enough to use its own habits to trap it. Should you treacle it, use a light trap or a pheromone lure? Each method has to be adjusted for each species—when they might be on the wing, what recipes for sugaring, which type of light trap and even the intensity of lightbulb to use within it.

Finally, once the moth is caught, you must decide how best to kill it, and for that you need to be a chemist.

Moths, you'll find, are tenacious of life. You can squeeze their bodies, prick them with pins, even cut off their heads and they'll live. You can dip a pin in nitric, prussic or oxalic acid, all deadly, stick it into their bodies and, unless you're very accurate with the concentration, it might not finish them. Each poison has its disadvantages—the rigor mortis of cyanide, the discoloring of ammonia, the stiffening of wings with carbon tetrachloride—so each case must be considered individually.

Tetrachloride is a clean, quick poison but, as I've said, it can stiffen the wings, so tetrafluoride is sometimes preferable but makes more mess and tends to alter the colors unless you can preserve them first. Chloroform is a useful poison and especially easy to take into the field, but use too little and it'll only anesthetize, and too much makes the bodies too stiff. Oxalic acid and potassium cyanide are both deadly and a good choice when dealing with the larger moths. They can be stabbed directly into the belly or dropped into the killing bottle on blotting paper although, again, too much and the bodies will stiffen. Rigor mortis has always been the bane of the setter, as then the specimen has to be relaxed with many days of steaming and softening agents. Often I find a cocktail works best: for a good clean killing, I might stupefy with chloroform first, then stab them with oil of tobacco or oxalic acid. Undoubtedly ammonia is the most suitable for a mass extermination but, like cyanide, it discolors the greens. Ether, chloroform and formic acid will all sedate or kill quite suitably in the field, and crushed laurel leaves, which produce the deadly prussic acid, won't stiffen the bodies so much although the leaves can't be collected in damp or dewy weather in case of mildew. In which case prussic acid can also be made by adding a few drops of potassium cyanide to tartaric acid, with a suitable catalyst.

Once you decide on the best poison for the termination, you must then work out the correct concentration. For instance, I know that five milligrams of cetratranic acid dropped into a bell jar with a single moth will take about three seconds to stun it. I know that seven milligrams will anesthetize it and ten is enough to kill it, providing the moth does not weigh more than 3.5 grams. I also know that to kill fifty moths you need five times the concentration or volume of killing fluid, but to kill seven thousand you'd need only two hundred times the concentration. I know that potassium chloride could never kill a larger moth and potassium sulphide would only ever be strong enough to anesthetize it. I know that cyanide kills anything. But what I don't know right now is the precise amount I will need to kill Vivien.

MONDAY

CHAPTER 20

About Monday

7:07 a.m. (by my digital bedside clock)

I MUST TELL YOU something. When I woke up just a few moments ago I had the most alarming sensation. It was a feeling of instant alertness. Usually my mind lags vaguely behind my brain when it wakes, like the cranking up of an old lethargic engine, taking several seconds to gain full speed. But this morning I know something's up, because when my eyes opened my mind opened too, eager as a young person's, with the immediacy of a lightbulb once you've flicked the switch. It's as if my body has sensed something before my brain has had a chance to work it out.

Then, with a bolt of understanding, it strikes me: My little sister, Vivien, is dead.

Dead right here in this house, fifteen yards away in her room in the east wing, along the landing and left through the glass-paned double doors. I feel a sick surge of dread rising from the core of my stomach, spreading menace throughout my frail body. Pricking it coldly. Smothering all my usual morning aches.

Let me think now: I heard her during the night at five to one, when she got up to make her usual cup of tea, but I didn't hear her again, as I have done every other night she's been here, going to the lavatory at five, and I haven't yet heard her this morning going down to get her morning tea, even though it's now well past seven. Every other morning she's been like clockwork, straight down to the kitchen at seven on the dot.

I'm still in bed with the blankets pulled up to my chin and my hands locked by my sides. I haven't moved a muscle since I woke. I don't dare, for fear that somehow it might upset the delicate balance of life and death that has threatened the house this morning. If I strain my eyes to the right, I can just about see my bedside clock. It makes me feel safer, knowing that it's there, looking after the time for me.

I think I should tell you there's a much more substantial reason for my knowing that she's dead than not having heard her this morning. Did I tell you last night, when I found the poisons upstairs in the laboratory, that I took down a tin of potassium cyanide powder from the very top shelf? I secreted it up the left sleeve of my dressing gown (pinching the cuff around the bottom so it wouldn't fall out) and took it downstairs to the kitchen. I put half a teaspoonful in her milk in the fridge, then hid the tin behind the bottles in the drinks cabinet in the library. And you know how she likes to take her tea milky.

But, of course, the problem is that I can't be *absolutely, one hundred percent sure* she's dead, unless I go and check on her. What if she's not dead? What if she's just *half* dead? (You can never be sure of getting the correct concentration per pound of body mass.) I can't have her being found half dead; she'll be prodded and probed until they find out she's been poisoned. I can't think why it didn't occur to me before—that I'll have to actually go and check on her. I can't possibly do that. It's not within my boundary. I've not been in that part of the house for forty-seven years. I wouldn't feel safe.

I can't get over it. It's most unlike me—with my famously analytic and scientific mind—to neglect to think through all eventualities before I start on a course of action. I knew she would die but I'm astounded I never considered what would happen after that. It's not that I'm afraid of seeing her dead (any more than anyone would be).

Believe me, I'm far too levelheaded for that. It's the dealing with it that scares me. Quite apart from making sure that she's properly dead, I don't know what to do next. I can't call the ambulance; the phone's not been connected for years, so I'll have to go and find someone, and I've no idea where to start. Then I'll have to find the time to sort through her room and all her clutter and I won't know what to do with it. I'll have to organize a funeral and make decisions like what I want her to wear and what her coffin should be made of, which patch of ground to put her in and what to carve on the headstone. I'll have to find out who her friends were and invite them for sherry and canapés in a drawing room with no furniture and hear all the stories that, for whatever reason, she never wanted or bothered to tell me. It's a shame she never got time to invite the entomologists to lunch on Tuesday. I was beginning to look forward to that.

Suddenly the house is unbearably large. I feel as if I'm part of a huge continent but that chunks of it are breaking off around me and drifting away in all directions, and all that's left of me is this little island, floating motionless in the center as the other bits of land move farther and farther off, like icebergs from a glacier in summer. All of a sudden I wish it were her, not me, who had to suffer this silence. I'd like to lie down here and die as well, as if by complete coincidence, so that someone else has to deal with the problem of clearing up the both of us. But I can tell I'm not about to die. The events of the past couple of days have had quite the opposite effect. I feel a new life force coursing through my body, ousting the years of lethargy and inertia that I've learned to live with, waking me from slumber, showing me the world more clearly.

I NEED TO get up. I need to concentrate, to think through my options in a methodical way, to devise a strategy to help me out of this blunder and follow it through to a logical conclusion. I elbow off my blankets and inch my legs over the side of the bed, bringing myself to sit up on the edge. It's the first warm day of spring. The early light, which has just begun to pour through the window, is bright and hopeful. Thrown about by the movement of the creeper outside, it dances over the bare floorboards, daring to touch my feet. Through my bed socks, I feel a sudden rush of icy blood fill my swollen feet, feeding the pain that overflows. I find if I concentrate very hard, it goes away or turns into something less like pain, more like heat or pressure.

I lower my feet to the floor. They smart sharply as small needles race along them and up my lower leg. My feet and ankles are set solid as if, today, they have been carved together from a single block of wood. I turn my attention to getting to the bathroom, shuffling in the only way my body allows me, until I reach my halfway point and rest, leaning on the back edge of the nursing chair outside the bathroom door, supporting myself on it like a walking frame. No one can condemn me for lack of effort. I tried my best to rekindle our friendship. I tried to love her, to like her, to find her faults endearing and amusing as I once had by nature, to see them as Vivienisms, as Maud used to say, a statement of her free-thinking, fun-loving attitude, her breath of fresh air.

After a minute's rest I summon the strength to continue my journey to the bathroom, concentrating on the pain of each slow step. Both my hands are screwed into cold fists that I know it will take me some minutes to open. Once I reach the washbasin I lean my elbows on the edge to take some weight off my feet, their marathon over. I look at my hands—witch's hands, with their crooked fingers and swollen red knuckles—and try to straighten each in turn, rubbing them between my legs to work up the circulation. I feel it would be less painful to be rid of these joints for good, have them chopped off and the stumps wrapped up in soft bandages. This morning it requires an enormous effort of will to twist on the hot tap. Finally I have it running until it steams and put both hands underneath, soaking them. I can already feel the knuckles start to loosen for the day.

I don't feel any different. I don't feel like a murderer. After all, I only put it in her milk, I didn't pour it down her throat. Then it was out of my hands. It's almost as if I did it to get something off my chest, like writing a scathing letter in the temper of the night, only to burn it in the temperance of the morning. I hadn't gone up to the attic for that reason. The moon led me up there. I hadn't planned to pick up the cyanide or to bring it downstairs tucked up my sleeve. It seemed so natural, as if it was *meant,* one thing following another in a predestined way, as if somehow I were acting out of myself, the puppet for a force of something else.

After I'd put it into her milk I sort of believed that it was either meant to happen or not, and if it wasn't meant to happen she wouldn't drink the milk, or it would spill in the fridge. I don't think I ever really believed that she would drink it or that, if she did, it would kill her. I'm not a real, cold-blooded murderer. It's not as if I loaded a gun and shot her between the eyes or smashed a lead weight across her head.

I dry my hands and put on the black woolen mittens that I hung, as usual, over the storage heater last night so they'd be warm. I pull off my bed socks. My toes, like my hands, are peculiar. They're driven to deform towards the middle, pushing together like the hoof of a single-toed goat. One by one I pick up the small scrolls of loo paper rolled carefully and left in a pile, for mornings like this one, and squeeze them between my toes, forcing them apart, a little trick I've developed to alleviate the constant painful pressure. Perhaps, I think, some cannabis tea would release the pain, and when I get back into the bedroom I turn on the kettle. Then I decide, quite irregularly, to forgo my normally stringent routine and go back to bed for a while. I feel thrilled by the deviance, like a naughty schoolgirl. I'll wiggle my hands and feet, wait for them to wake up and listen for signs of life in the rest of the house.

It's as I'm getting into bed that I notice my wristwatch, the digital one on my left wrist, is eleven minutes behind my bedside clock (it's my habit to check them against each other as I get into bed and they are rarely out of time). I check my other wristwatch, my backup one, and I'm horrified to find that it stopped in the middle of the night— at half past two. I feel completely disoriented. I find it extremely distracting if I cannot at once get an accurate time reference, especially first thing in the morning. I need to know the time to start my daily routine or I'm thrown off for the rest of the day. (Although I'm not the superstitious type, I'll admit I'm not completely immune to the coincidence that a watch that has never stopped should stop dead on this particularly haunting morning. I should think another, less pragmatic, less scientific sort of person would be spooked by the experience.)

I consider the facts: I trust all my digitals over any of my dial clocks. My bedside clock is my number-one timepiece, followed by my digital wristwatch. However, my bedside clock now says 8:08 and I've not yet heard the longcase in the hall strike the hour. If it were to strike in time with my digital wristwatch I'd be more inclined to trust those two than my number-one clock.

7:56 a.m. (by my digital wristwatch)

The longcase in the hall has just struck but my wristwatch is still a few minutes off eight so I'm no closer to knowing the correct time. I'm going to stay here awhile longer until I can get my bearings on the day.

9:55 a.m. (by my digital wristwatch)

I hear the start of Monday's bell-ringing practice at the church, even though my digital wristwatch isn't yet at ten. Apart from Michael's irregular visits and the rare encounters I have with strangers coming to the door, all of whom I invariably check the time with, this Monday ten o'clock practice is about my only weekly time reference. It's not very accurate, though. I've learned that they are in no way reliable. They do not normally start on time and it can be up to a quarter past ten before I hear their first peal. But rarely, if ever, do they start early, and because my wristwatch hasn't yet reached ten, I suspect that this is the faulty one. I don't know which is worse, trying to work out the time or trying not to think about Vivien. Did I really kill her? I'm not at all sure anymore that I actually did it. I don't *feel* as if that was something I did last night.

I'm dreading the rest of today. I can feel its full weight on me now, pinning me to the bed, urging me not to participate in it any further. I'd like to freeze time right here and now. I'd be quite happy to be left alone, in eternal timelessness, comforted by the relief that I'll never have to partake in the immediate future.

I wonder grimly how long it will be before I start to smell her. It's a maddening thing to have entered my mind because now that it's there I cannot dispel it, and because it's there I can already smell her.

12:24 p.m. (by my bedside clock)

I think I've just heard a small cry, but I can't be certain. I'm up, out of bed, pulling my dressing-gown cord round my middle to take the sudden chill off my spine. I move over to my door, which is closed. As I put my hand on the door handle I hear it again. A small, distant cry. I freeze. If I open this door, I face a dilemma. I will not be able to ignore the cries and will be forced to make a difficult choice: Should I go to her aid, or should I leave her and live with the knowledge that I could have helped her? It would be like killing someone twice. I couldn't bear it. However, if I don't open the door and block up the gaps around the edges I might not be able to hear any distant disturbing noises. I could sit and watch the plaster crumble and the creeper invade the room and concentrate on the pains in my joints. Then I would never be sure that the cries I might have heard were real or not.

The thudding of my heart is so strong that it's making me rock slightly where I stand, back and forth, back and forth. I turn the handle and pull the door open by a hand's width. And then I hear it. Scratching. Unmistakable desperate scratching, like a dog at a door.

Now another cry, this time more of a whimper. Simon! He's in the kitchen. I am instantly relieved, elated, even; I feel so thrilled I could almost giggle, like being in an accident that, just at the last moment, didn't happen. But what do I do with Simon? I'd forgotten him, the dog that wasn't going to last long. He's lasted longer than Vivien herself. But surely he can't survive independently of her—he can't even walk. The quietest dog in the world is making noises he's never made before. He's probably hungry, I think. He's not been fed today. I open my door and pad quietly along the landing and down the stairs, so as not to wake the dead, my bed socks soft against the wood.

When I open the kitchen door, Simon looks up at me biddably, as if he knows his owner is gone and I am his only hope. I spot a little piddle in front of the fridge, as if it has leaked in the night. His bottom wiggles in an attempt to wag his stumpy tail, as if he's sure this will please me. I don't want to hear his noises. I just want to shut him up. I open the fridge door and see only Cheddar cheese and poisoned milk. I put the cheese onto the floor in front of him, then remember the cereal in the store cupboard. I tip a heap of Shreddies onto the cheese and Simon looks at it. I leave him and shut the door behind me, then go back to my bedroom and lock myself in, relieved, as if I'd been holding my breath the entire time.

I know that nothing is going to happen if I stay here in my room all day. I must make a plan. I need to find someone else to discover her body. I need to think of a way to get someone to the house and then up to her room so they can sound the alarm and set the deceased-person engine in motion.

CHAPTER 21

Pranksters and a Second Dose

2:11 p.m. (by my digital wristwatch)

I'VE BEEN STANDING, quite still, in the middle of the landing for the last fifteen minutes, and I'm just beginning to feel the effects of a draft, level with the skirting board, that drags itself east to west from the floor-to-ceiling arched window to the stairs. Before that—for the previous eight and a half minutes—I was pacing a rectangular path round the landing. For each of the long sides I tread the length of the same floorboard, while the short ends of the rectangle line up the door frames on opposite walls of the landing. I go anticlockwise and I can actually feel that it's the wrong way, against the normal movement of all timepieces and even against time itself—so going that way helps me to feel that I am struggling *against* the problem, rather than being swept up by it and riding with it.

I have been collaborating with myself, working through my options, boxing them up, assembling and assessing them, ordering, grading, cataloging, tabulating and selecting, trying to see the most succinct path through the maze. I have found that the pacing helps me Create—to come up with new ideas—and the standing very still is necessary to Evaluate. Over and over I have strained for a way to get someone else to the house to check on Vivien. I've even considered flooding it or setting fire to the loggia so that Michael or anyone in the south lodges might see it, anything that would allow someone else to deal with the problem of Vivien. But I've not come up with anything that doesn't bring with it an extremely unattractive consequence further down the line, one that I know I couldn't bear—too many people with too many questions.

To my dismay, I've determined by this systematic process of assimilation and disqualification that no one is likely to come to the house for weeks, and the idea of waiting here and thinking of her festering down the corridor may send me quite mad. I know the only feasible option is to investigate Vivien myself but it's as I'm finally mustering the courage to do so that I hear the urgent pounding of the brass door knocker—*thud, thud, thud*—as if in a last-minute answer to my pleas. The noise grates on me, as it used to Maud, all the way up my spine— it's quite unnecessary to bang it so violently when a more than adequate noise is achieved with a good grip on the goat's horns and a rattle from side to side—yet for the first time in my life I welcome it with unexpected delight. I hurry down the stairs. Perhaps they'll also have the correct time.

My excitement is shattered when I pull back the door. There's no one there. A beautiful day dances on the fresh leaves of the beech hedge to my left and there's a hum of activity over the area where a once-ornamental pond has been lost in the undergrowth. I feel betrayed by hope.

I begin to Create and Evaluate once again, quickly, the possibilities of the door knocker being banged at one minute and yet at the next there's no one there. Then a curious movement at the turn of the drive catches my eye and I see a shadow, now another, racing behind the laburnum hedge. I am being watched. Children. They dare each other to come close to the house of the Moth Woman and an exceptionally brave one must have mustered the courage to bang the door knocker. The shadows shift and disappear out of sight behind the conifers and along the Tunnel Walk to the brook.

I review the day just because I can; sixty-nine degrees and rising, clear and dry. I suck my middle finger and hold it up to check the light wind—east to northeasterly. The wind seems faint, almost still, but that's what people forget—it's not about the wind. It's the air currents that count, and often they run paradoxically to the wind. The rising heat and falling humidity point to thermals, and I notice the treetops are rustling, so at twenty-five feet it's moderately gusty, far stronger than at ground level. Yes, I'd say strong, dry, upper thermals. A shiver of excitement runs up my back.

Today is the perfect day for catching rare immigrants.

For a *prolific* catch of immigrants—quantity, not quality—you'd wait for the south southeasterly air currents that blow them from the Med and across the Channel in their thousands, sailing effortlessly on the thermal smells of Spain, France and Portugal. On this type of current, I'd head straight to the poor patch of forgotten scrubland just behind the beach café at Branscombe. It's an unnoticed little spot, often strewn with litter, but protected from the wind by the giant chalk cliffs guarding the sea, a warm oasis of wild petunia, viper's bugloss and knapweed, a first-stop welcome for weary southern visitors. I remember a hot summer night, on a day that brought smells from Moroccan markets, when Clive and I trapped more than fourteen hundred moths on the dump behind the café. We anesthetized the entire catch with 20ml potassium phosphate and enlisted a local committee to help us count and log them.

But today's brood wouldn't be for quantity but scarcity. It's an unusual current, a hot east to northeasterly, which by tonight will bring many a rare species from southern Scandinavia and northern Europe, including the Clifden Nonpareil and the Bedstraw Hawk. I wonder where the Dorset and Somerset moth hunters will be grouping later, where they will join forces and head. I can almost feel the buzz of phones ringing round this small, exclusive group of people, arrangements firmed up for this evening's hunt, all other engagements canceled, nothing too important to miss this great night of all nights of the moth-hunting season. Some will head for the high heaths of Ratnedge Deveril, or to the wetter lowlands—the bog in the Furzebrook Reserve, the meadows at Barton's Shoulder, the clump of willows at Templecombe. It's been a long while since I've hunted. I wonder if today's hunters still know that the eastern edge of the Mawes Fir Estate was bordered by a footpath, just above Oakers Wood, where a few last elms huddled in a peaceful copse, having somehow escaped disease. The rare Norwegian Dogtail always found it and the next day, when news of the previous night's catches flushed through the moth community, Oakers Wood would often turn out to be the Dogtail's only sighting in the entire country.

It's as I stop my musings and start to close the door on the exceptional day that my eye is drawn to something on the ground. There, on the worn flagstones, I see a heap of freshly mutilated moths, victims of an unkind massacre.

I bend over them. It's the product of last night's collection—fresh, spring specimens. I can feel the warm sun through my nightgown and I sit down on the smooth flagstones, like a little girl, to sort my prize. I make little piles, arranging them into residents and nonresidents, commoners, newcomers, crossbreeds, mutants and unviables. Among them are Tigers, Underwings, a Pug, two Marbled Carpets and three types of Hawk—beautiful specimens, recently emerged and vibrant. There's nothing particularly surprising, perhaps the Carpets are usually farther south, but I'd really like to know where and how they were caught. They must have gone to more than a little effort because I presume it's from at least two different locations; there's a couple of Vapourers, which would never cohabit with the Satins and the Underwings. But the real delight for me is a Puss Moth caterpillar that I find all curled up at the bottom of the pile. Now, the Puss Moth is common around here, but it's still my favorite. It's the nearest you can get to communicating with a caterpillar. It has a soft coat, zigzagged in green and brown, and when you stroke it, it wriggles and squirms with pleasure. When it gets angry it hisses and waves the two hairlike protrusions on its tail and, if it's in a real temper, it'll spit at you.

It's been a long time since I've had the chance to examine a fresh collection. The children who made me this offering have no idea of the delightful distraction they have given me on this particular Monday morning. They will be assuming, perhaps, that because I have bred moths (even, perhaps, bred some of these moths' forefathers), nurtured their pupae in my cellar and witnessed their first flight in my attic, to discover them half mutilated on my doorstep would make me recoil in horror. They are wrong, of course, for we naturalists strive for the greater proliferation of the entire lepidoptera genera, not for the survival of individuals. The children may be surprised to know how many moths I've gassed and pinned; how many caterpillars I've rolled, still alive, to squeeze out their insides, reinflating them with wood chip to give them structure; how many peaceful cocoons I've dug up and cut open from under the roots of poplars, apples and crack willows. But all of this for a scientific cause, for a greater understanding of and insight into a little-known insect.

3:05 p.m. (by my digital wristwatch)

I am inching along Vivien's landing, on the other side of the double doors, still in my nightgown and bed socks, and I can feel the pressure of the whole unfamiliar space crowding in on me. I have spent much of the day finding the courage to be here, to check on Vivien myself.

I can see that her door is wide open and I stop on the landing outside it. From this angle I can't see her, but I can see a slice of her room: the end of her bed and the far corner. Shoes and slippers are stacked up on top of each other in the corner. Next to them I see a little basket and a rug, which I presume are for Simon, and a large plastic Mother and Child attached to an electric cord, which makes me wonder if it lights up or preaches when it's plugged in. Lifting my gaze to a shelf on the wall, I see a bookstand—the seat of an ugly green marble toad—and next to that, to my delight, an ornate little carriage clock. I'll be happy to have that clock, I think. You can never have enough clocks. Then I admonish myself for the inappropriate thought outside a dead woman's room. The clock is at an oblique angle, so I have to move closer to the door frame and peer in for several seconds to read the time. Ten to four. I check it against my wristwatch—*much* too fast. I tut.

"Ginny, come in."

A surge of terror. My heart thuds within its cage, and I freeze— right there by the door. The marble toad stares mockingly at me. Oh, my God, she's not dead! She didn't drink her milk after all. Every part of me is tight with a fear I've never known before. I had been utterly convinced she was dead. Is this her ghost talking? I can't concentrate enough to think. Am I relieved or frustrated? I had thought I couldn't bear to see her dead but to see her alive when I think she's dead feels far worse.

"Ginny," she says again, weakly, "are you there?"

So she's guessing. Silently I shift backwards, towards the landing's double doors, out of sight of the toad. I'm going to leave her. I don't want to confront her. I'm going to creep away quietly and she'll never know for sure that I was really here.

"I know you're there," she whispers. She's bluffing, of course. . . .

"Ginny, I know you're just outside my door. Ginny?" I'm caught. I can't expose myself now or it would be admitting that I've been hiding from her for the past few minutes. But I can't bring myself to walk away either because now I know she knows I'm here. I lean my head against the landing wall, the other side of her room, defeated. Trapped.

"Look, you don't have to come in. Stay there and listen if you want," she continues, as if she knows my every thought and fear. "But *please* listen. This is very important."

I am very still. I am very listening.

"Ginny, I'm ill. I think I'm dying. I need you to get me a doctor."

Oh, my God, she *did* drink the milk, or, rather, she *could* have drunk the milk. But, equally, she could be genuinely ill, a torturous coincidence that no one would ever need know about.

No, I can't get a doctor. I can have someone find her dead, but not ill. Dead old ladies are commended for their contribution in life, laid to rest and, along with their secrets, swallowed forever by the earth. But *ill* old ladies are investigated until the poison coursing through their bodies is hunted down. And that, as you can imagine, would get me into a lot of trouble. My head is spinning. I want to sit down and tabulate my options. I can't control them flying about in my head: I need to pull them together on a page and consider them methodically, one by one, but I don't have that luxury. I've been leaning my head against the wall of the landing as I listened, and now I put the palm of my right hand up—flat—just a couple of inches in front of my face so I can stare at it. I find that sometimes this helps me focus my concentration, helps draw it back to me rather than flying off, spiraling out of control.

"Ginny, I know this isn't easy for you. I understand that." A few days ago I would have taken comfort in the way she seems to know me inside out, but now I hate it. "But if you go to Eileen's she will . . ." I can hear the struggle in her voice as she tries to summon energy. "Ginny, for me . . . please," she begs finally.

I am looking at the multitude of crisscrossing lines on the palm of my right hand and the dry calluses on the knobbles at the base of my fingers. As I begin to close the hand, bending it in the middle and curling my deformed fingers, I can see the lines fold in on themselves, making deeper and deeper crevices, until my hand is a fist. Then I notice lines that have not grown out of any folds of a fist—like the ones that run lengthways along the fingers—but have simply matured from a gradual desiccation of the skin.

I want to tell you something now, while we're in this awful predicament outside Vivien's room: all my life, it seems, I have sacrificed my own will for those around me. Not that I've offered much resistance and not that I haven't wanted to. But I think you'll agree that I fall into that category of people who prefer to give than to get, who feel better about themselves when they've been helping others and derive satisfaction from knowing that some of their own suffering has directly aided someone else's, indeed someone they love's, happiness. But I think even people like us have to believe that, just once or twice in our lives, our love is appreciated, perhaps even reciprocated.

"A doctor . . . Ginny?"

I open my fist sharply, decisively, last night's new persona coming to the fore. The range of movement in my knuckles is impressive now. It's good to exercise arthritic joints, keep them loose so they don't seize up. I look at Vivien's door through the gap between my fingers.

"Okay," I say gently.

I LEAVE THE LANDING, go downstairs and open the front door. I have been forced, for what seems like the first time in my entire life, to make an active decision, a choice. A choice that will have an irreversible impact on the future.

I give myself time for one deep breath of honeysuckle, then close the front door, loudly, so Vivien will hear it upstairs. I go into the library, open the drinks cabinet and find the black tin of potassium cyanide, KCN, behind a sticky bottle of vermouth, where I hid it last night. I'm half surprised to find it there, to have confirmation of my actions during the moonlit hours. I reach to the shelf above for a glass and measure in half a teaspoon of the powder, snapping closed the lid and replacing it behind the vermouth. I suppose this is what is meant by premeditated—the calm and considered preparation of death. But I feel released, unshackled. For the first time ever I am not only in control of my life, I am taking control of the future. For once I am causing an event to happen. Yet at the same time another force is thrusting me forward, an overwhelming one that, to my surprise, makes each action follow the last as if I am paralyzed and looking down on myself with horror.

I am impassive and incurious as I continue. It's the scientist in me, I know. You learn early on, as a scientist, not to trust your feelings and to rise above any unqualified instinct or emotion. All calculations must be backed up with undeniable evidence and absolute qualified conclusions.

It feels no different from making the tea, an everyday practical occurrence. Murder. I take no pleasure in it, yet feel no shame, no anxiety. But this time there is no pretending that I am leaving it up to chance. I accept fully what I am doing. This time it is *no* different from loading a gun and shooting someone between the eyes, or cracking a lead weight across their skull, and rather than being appalled by myself, I'm feeling strangely empowered, released from the forces that I have, so far, allowed to dictate my life. This time it is me, it is *my* will. I am in control.

I think I'm in control and yet, perhaps, I have no choice. I cannot help the way the events of my life and those of the past three days have worked on my inherent and coded characteristics to bring me to this unpleasant outcome. As you must know, once a domino is pushed, the motion is started and, as long as the others are lined up one after another with the correct spacing, there's nothing anyone can do to stop them. It is the consequence of my lifetime experiences on the character that I was given. From that viewpoint, it cannot be called premeditated. It is as strictly governed as a mathematical equation. It is the result of

*me + Vivi falling off the bell tower + taunting at school +
Maud's sherry drinking + the existence of poison in the house . . .*

I feel like the caterpillar that we *think* is making a choice when he eats or pupates but, in actual fact, is not. He's completely ruled by molecular forms of influence acting on the base components of a moth. Likewise, perhaps I have become a killer through circumstances acting on my biological makeup. Which means, of course, that none of this is my fault and that it's all out of my hands.

I like to think that, for once, I am in control of my actions, but I also like to know that I am not.

I CARRY THE GLASS to the front door. Once again I open and close the door loudly, as if I've just returned to the house. Then I go to the kitchen and turn on the tap. The cold water pipes start up their chorus of banging and thudding, shaking awake the rest of the house. I fill the glass halfway with water, swirling it gently to dissolve the poison, and I am reminded of the faint aroma it releases, a bitter tinge of almond. I carry it through the hall, past Jake the pig, up the stairs, past the huge stained-glass window, slow and steady, missing the second from last stair, which squeaks, and reach the landing.

I stop at the top as an image of Vivien's coffin passes me, carried by unknown men in black, helping her on her last journey down these stairs and out of Bulburrow. It is a final call for caution, to make sure that this is how I really want to change the future. But I am now certain I have no choice: I am the puppet of myself.

I step aside to make way for the procession and continue across the landing, through the double doors and onto Vivien's landing. I'm concentrating, blocking out everything but the Method that the palm of my hand has helped me to devise. It is so easy. Thank you, Maud. After all, it was she who had taught me how to substitute for my lack of natural strength, she who had taught me how to believe in myself. What would she say, do you suppose, one daughter killing the other? Is she looking at me now from her heaven and taking full responsibility for my actions, as she always did?

As I enter the room Vivien's clock says fourteen minutes past four. Her eyes are closed, she doesn't know yet that I have entered. I can now see the rest of the room, which had been out of view from my listening post on the landing. It is such an onslaught of color and clutter that my eyes wander for too long on the accessories before I look at Vivien. She has hung fairy lights round the picture rail and stuck photos of herself with people I don't recognize on the wall above her bed. A mirror has more photos jammed in its frame, and on the other side of her bed, on the floor, there are three tea-stained mugs and a dirty plate. Above this, four nails have been banged into the wall as hooks and clothes slung over them. A small dressing table is covered with a disarray of bottles—perfume, face creams and other unguents— without a hint of order to any of it. One or two items have fallen off while a tin of talc hangs over the edge on its side, having coughed some of its contents onto the floor through the holes in its lid. It taunts me, the way it lies teetering, and I am overcome with an unbearable desire to push it back on. With a great effort of will I ignore its precariousness and instead summon myself to concentrate on the matter at hand. I focus on Vivien.

Her eyes are now flickering open and shut. She is trying to keep them directed, but they race peevishly this way and that within their sockets. Her right hand is lying palm up on the bedcover, quite close to me, and when she opens and closes it, grabbing at the air, I realize it is an invitation for me to hold it. I don't want to be part of a last-minute fingertip reconciliation, but I oblige her handhold anyway, like swallowing a mouthful of something disgusting because soon you know it will all be over.

"The doctor's on his way," I lie. "Eileen is waiting for him and will bring him up." She squeezes my hand. I stare at her clock: method, results, conclusions, method, results, conclusions. *Tick, tock, tick.* The second hand is about to pass Go, pushing the minute hand to half past four by this clock, *tick, tock,* four, three, two, one, *Go.* It's four-thirty in the afternoon of 27 April.

"He says you must drink some water. That's very important, he says. It'll make you feel better. Can you sit up?"

Vivien's eyes are now open, not fully, but open, and she manages to shift herself a little way up the bed so that her head is more upright on her pillow. I wonder vaguely, as she gulps thankfully at the water, whether if I'd had it in me to kill the flies in Lower 5B when I was thirteen, I might not now have it in me to kill my sister at seventy.

I put the glass on the floor beside the bed. Vivien's eyes stare blankly above her. Her lips move, drinking the air like a fish out of water, and she beats her arm on the bed, just once. I wonder, with sudden curiosity, if I'm about to feel something like a life force leaving her body as she dies, but I don't. Her body starts to convulse, wracking violently, as if another being is trying to expel itself through her skin. I don't mind watching her. I know she's not feeling this. She's already dead. But I'll tell you something—as I watch the involuntary twitches of a poisoned body, I wouldn't be honest if I didn't admit I find it interesting, from a purely scientific point of view, of course.

I'll tell you more about it, if you like. Potassium cyanide is what's called a synaptic blocker poison. It blocks the tiny electrical impulses with which our nervous system functions, at the synapses, the communication junctions between nerves. At a molecular level the poison is a compound that can fit into the same receptor sites that the synaptic messenger compounds would normally lock into, thereby inhibiting them doing their job and preventing any signals being passed along the nerves. In other words, the body is paralyzed within seconds, as long as you administer enough to block the receptor sites before the body can metabolize and excrete the poison. It's a race between the kidneys' toxin-removal efficiency and the potency of the poison.

Vivien is still now and I am stroking her hair because—I don't know if you will understand this—I still love her. I love her and hate her at the same time. I even love the same parts of her that I hate, her vitality and her color, her disruption and disorder, her humor and her despair, her conceit and her narcissism, her everything that isn't me. Now that she is dead, I can already feel the love overriding the hatred once more. Besides our moment of happiness on the porch when Vivien first came home on Friday, these are the next best few minutes I've had with her. She should have stayed away. Why *did* she come home? I wonder. I know so little about her.

I hear a car advancing up the drive and, glancing through the window, I am surprised to see it's a police car.

CHAPTER 22

PC Bolt and Inspector Piggott

THE POLICEMAN STEPS OUT of the car onto the drive as I walk towards him. My new self had little trouble in opening the front door, and I'm feeling far less threatened as I walk up to him than I would have felt yesterday with any other visitor. The sun catches his windscreen, dazzling me. The sky is a watery blue and I can smell honeysuckle, carried to me on the breeze.

"Vivien Morris?" he says, from afar, and I think of Vivien, her body ratcheting her life from itself. "I'm PC Bolt, from the Beaminster station. Sorry, did I get you out of bed?" he says, looking at my nightgown, then the open-toed slippers on my feet.

PC Bolt looks about nineteen. He's standing by his car, leaning on the open door, which makes a barrier between us, like a desk.

"No," I say, but I'm trying hard to work out how and why he's here, how on earth he found out so quickly that I've poisoned my sister. For a moment I imagine he has a special insight that allows him to detect any injustices being carried out within the county.

"There's nothing to be alarmed about," he says, smiling. "It's what we call a courtesy call." My sense of relief gives way to light-headedness and I have to steady myself. I remember I've not eaten today. Once my routine goes, I forget to do things like eat.

"Oh, and also," he continues flippantly, "we had a very excited telephone call from a"—he takes a flip-pad from his breast pocket and consults it—"from an Eileen Turner, who lives at Willow Cottage. She was frantic, saying you were supposed to be having tea with her this afternoon at four and as it's now, well, *long* gone . . ."

"Is it?" I check my digital wristwatch: 4:12.

"Well, I just meant it's past teatime and she thought something might be wrong because you didn't turn up. I did tell her you'd most probably forgotten, but she didn't think you would have, and she was insistent that I come and make sure myself and"—he shakes his head in a way that makes me wonder how often he's had to mediate tea dates among the elderly—"you know what some of these old dears can be like. She didn't want to walk up to the house herself." He pauses, perhaps waiting for me to say something. "She made me promise her I'd pay you a visit and check that everything was all right," he says apologetically. I don't say anything.

"Well, I'll pop into Eileen's on my way back to the station and let her know, then, shall I? Do you want me to tell her you'll be calling in later . . . or not?"

I nod. "Was that a 'not' or not a 'not'?" He laughs.

I nod again.

"Well, then . . ." He coughs and plants one foot inside the car as if to go. Then he glances up at the towering house, the turrets and the gargoyles that seem to hold the bricks together around the crenellations. "Great place," he says. "Fascinating." He pauses. I think I see him shiver.

"Well, have a good evening, madam."

"What time did you say it was?" I ask quickly, quite forgetting that a minute ago I wanted him to go away as quickly as possible, quite forgetting for a moment that Vivien is upstairs, dead. Murdered, in fact.

"Well"—he flicks over his wrist—"it's just gone seven."

"*Is* it?" I'm unable to hide my astonishment. "I make it twelve minutes past *four*." He laughs as if I've made a joke. It's such a shock that I can't say anything more. I can't think straight.

"Well, there you go," he starts, as if he's solved a case. "That will explain the confusion. . . ." But I'm not listening. I'm appalled. The tops of the limes along the drive are swaying. . . . I had thought that at most I'd be out by eleven minutes. *Not three hours.* I'm watching his mouth. His lips are wet and full and form their words with large slow ovals so that I can clearly see the pink gums inside. Nothing feels real. I have a rush of dizziness. The limes look as if they're about to uproot and topple.

That's it.

TWO MEN ARE peering down at me. One is PC Bolt, I remember, and the other, whom I don't recognize, is shining a bright torch into my eye. There's a sharp throbbing pain at the back of my head. I can hear a woman's voice and a lot of other people talking and walking about outside the room. Soon I realize I am on my bed in my room and the previous events come back to me. I remember being on the drive, PC Bolt telling me how out of time I was, and then I must have fainted. I have no idea how long ago that would have been.

I hear a soft voice. "Miss Stone? Can you hear me? It's PC Bolt." I look at him. "Are you Miss Virginia Stone?" I nod. "Right, I didn't realize you were *the sister,*" he says.

"What's the time?" I ask.

"Just relax," says the other man. "Please don't try to talk."

"What's the time?" I ask again.

"It's all right. I'm a doctor and you're going to be fine," he says, raising his voice, assuming I'm a bit deaf. This is torturous.

"I'd just like to know what time it is, please, Doctor," I say once more, but this time in a taut, stifled voice that's not attached to my throat. I have my eyes shut tight to expel the frustration.

"It's about eight o'clock," the doctor says nonchalantly, without consulting any sort of timepiece.

Now I look at PC Bolt in despair, as if he, out of the two of them, might just understand. "Constable, please tell me the exact time. I need to know," I beseech him.

He studies his watch for a suitably long time. "It's ten minutes past eight."

I had been straining my neck without realizing it, and now I let my head fall back onto the pillow and relax.

Fifteen minutes later I am sitting up on my bed. A mug (which I don't recognize) of tea is steaming on my bedside table, which I want but can't bring myself to drink, as I didn't make it. Besides, it's too milky. Now a different, much older policeman is in the room with me, standing by my bed. "Would you like some tea?" he asks, gesturing to the mug.

"No, thank you."

"I'm Inspector Piggott."

Inspector Piggott goes into the bathroom without a word and comes back fifty seconds later (I'm looking at my bedside clock while he is away). He hands me a glass of water.

"Drink this," he orders. "It'll make you feel better."

"What is it?" I look inside the glass, which reminds me that I'd said the same thing to Vivien only this afternoon. My God! I'd completely forgotten. Vivien!

"Water," he says. Oh, Lord, does he know about Vivien? Has he smelt her yet?

I take a sip and hand it back.

"I hope you'll understand what I'm about to tell you," he says, loudly and clearly. "Look, I'm very sorry, I've got some rather alarming news." He places the glass on the table.

As you can imagine I've had rather too much alarming news recently and I'm not sure I'm up to it. I feel a little frail and my head hurts. The anticipation is unbearable.

"Your sister, Vivien. I'm afraid she's dead."

Is that it? I think, and I'm very thankful Inspector Piggott's news isn't in the least bit alarming.

"Oh dear," I muster in reply, because he's looking at me, waiting for one.

"Yes, earlier this afternoon, we think," he continues, loud and slow. "Did you happen to see her today?" he asks casually.

"Yes," I reply and then I say, "Actually, no," and, to tell you the truth, I'm completely confused. I'm trying to give him the right answer rather than the real answer.

"Don't worry, Miss Stone. You've had a little knock to your head and I think everything will become clear in a while. We're taking her away now so we can look into the specific cause of death," he adds, sitting on the edge of my bed, rather as if he's settling into a long bedtime story. I can feel the heat rising to my face and I can't stop it. I'm not used to strangers sitting on my bed. "Do you know if she was ill," he asks, "or taking any medication?"

"No. I don't."

Inspector Piggott waits while PC Bolt and the doctor leave the room. When they've gone he sighs heavily and rubs his brow with the tips of his fingers as if he's trying to rub out the lines he has there. "I know this is a lot for you to take in right now but I'll be frank. We've come across something in the glass by your sister's bed and, well, we think it might be cyanide. It has a very distinct smell."

Suddenly my mouth is extraordinarily dry. I know that almond smell well.

"Cyanide," I repeat, because again, I know some sort of response is required.

"Miss Stone, do you have any idea where the cyanide could have come from?" Wasn't he going to ask me why I killed her? Now, that would have been a tricky question. Where the cyanide came from was easy.

"We've got *plenty* of cyanide here," I say.

Inspector Piggott looks down at me, surprised. "Have you? What on earth for?"

I hold out my arm for him to steady me as I lift myself from the bed. A sharp pain anchors my head as I tilt up and I wish I hadn't decided to move, but within a minute or two I am leading him slowly out of the room, turning right and crossing the landing. A young man I've never seen before rushes up to us and offers me a walking stick— Vivien's, as it happens, the one she used only once to embellish her arrival.

As we approach my lookout I see Eileen Turner and PC Bolt come out through the double doors from the east wing. Eileen is sobbing and saying, "She'd only been back for three days . . . ," but as soon as they see us their conversation stops abruptly and their pace slows. As we walk past, the two policemen exchange glances and Eileen looks down. I must admit I have no idea if it is a quiet consolatory nod or if she's scared to look at me. I have an odd impression that my house is crammed with people, strangers wandering all over it, getting into every crevice like a swarm of ants in a larder.

I open the door to the spiral staircase and walk extra slowly up the stairs, all at once overwhelmed by age. I can hear Eileen's voice again, this time low and muffled, floating up intermittently from the far side of the landing. I have Vivien's walking stick in my left hand and Piggott is still gripping my right arm at the elbow, steadying me now and again. He and I do not speak to one another. I, for one, am concentrating on my footing until, finally, we're at the top and I'm opening the door to the attic. Two bats are disturbed as we enter and the inspector flinches in surprise as they squall and flutter into the next room. I think I hear him gag as, with his spare hand, he retrieves a handkerchief from his top pocket and holds it over his nose and mouth. I lead him to the laboratory and point, with Vivien's stick, to the left-hand side, where the bottles are labeled with the skull and crossbones.

"Killing fluid," I say.

"Ah," says the inspector, muffled by the handkerchief. "Killing what?"

"Moths, mainly. That was our family . . ." I was going to say "living," but at the last moment I change my mind. "Our family expertise," I say proudly. He asks me if I could show him which ones are cyanide so I point to the different types. Mainly, I explain, there's either sodium or potassium cyanide, $NaCN$ or KCN, but there's also prussic acid, which is another name for hydrogen cyanide, HCN, and that in the bottles they are all solutions but on the very top shelf are the powdered poisons in their purest form.

"Is there one missing?" He cuts across my lecture, pointing to an obvious gap along the shelf.

"Yes," I tell him. After he's helped himself to a couple of bottles and tins, carefully sealing them in a polythene bag, I lead him back downstairs to the hall. The house is quiet again but for the hollow tick of the longcase clock. I look slowly round the decrepit hall. It's capacious and empty. Wallpaper is peeling badly at the top edge near the cornice where the damp has nuzzled through, but everything is as it should be, in its place. To me, it is safe again. Safe and still and workable. I can feel the entire week's buildup of tension start to loosen and melt away. I feel happy, even.

Nearing the front door Inspector Piggott turns to me. "Miss Stone," he says, very formally, "can you think of any reason why your sister might have wanted to take her life?"

I hadn't thought of that. "No," I say, and then I think that taking her own life was probably the last thing Vivien would have done.

He nods and is turning to go when I stop him. "Inspector Piggott, I just wondered . . ."

"Yes?" he says, turning keenly, eager for me to divulge a secret.

"Do you have the time, please?"

"The time?"

"Yes. I'd like to know what time it is."

"Nine o'clock," he replies.

"What, *exactly* nine?"

"Well, no, a little after." He looks at his watch again. "Five past." He turns to go again.

"Exactly five past?" I ask quickly. It still sounds a little general to me. He stops, turns back to me, and studies his watch carefully, filling me with confidence that he is about to give me the most accurate answer he can.

"I make it almost seven minutes past nine," he says, eyeing me cautiously.

"Oh, *thank you,*" I say, really meaning it. "And does that, do you think, correspond with the police-station clock? I mean, do you check it against the station clock sometimes?"

He pauses. "Yes. Regularly," he says reassuringly.

"Oh, thank you, Inspector, thank you." I sigh. I am truly relieved. I reset both my wristwatches and close the front door after him.

TUESDAY

CHAPTER 23

Intuition

It is not until the next day that they come to get me. I knew they would, that they would have discovered the truth using the additional sense that everyone but me seems to have been born with. What did Vivien call it? She said she could tell what had happened here from 250 miles away because "Ginny, most people just have that sort of intuition."

I'm ready for them as I watch the police car crunching up the drive from my lookout window, and I know this will be the last day I see Bulburrow, that I set eyes on it. I must admit I'm terrified about where they will take me; I've never lived anywhere but here. I won't feel safe.

Inspector Piggott leads me out of the house. He gently lays a blanket over my shoulders and I pause by the door of the car to take one last look.

My attention is caught by a familiar figure walking up the side of the drive towards me. I can tell who it is even before his features become clear, by the hunched lope, the stocky build, the lazy gait and the big hands hanging apologetically by his sides. How did Michael know I was leaving?

Michael wanders over to me by the open car door and we stare at each other. He's about to say "Good-bye," I'm sure of it, and I'm about to say it too, but suddenly, I have this feeling, and again I'm sure it's a mutual one, that we have so many things to say to each other, so many understandings to share, that even to say "Good-bye" is not only unnecessary but trite. It's as if I suddenly understand that he's always been in my life, in the wings, and always known and understood who I am and what has happened and even been able to foresee, with some infinite wisdom, what will ensue. And he's here now, telling me all that without uttering a word. Half of me wants to hug him, the other wants to cry because, now that I think about it, this is the saddest moment of my life, my most naturally emotional moment. Not all those times that I might have expected myself to cry—not when my sister fell off the bell tower, not when my mother died or when my baby died. But this, *this* is the saddest moment, leaving Michael and leaving my house, one and the same I suppose. It comes to me in a chorus of understanding: Michael is the only person who cared for me and looked out for me, without expecting anything in return, without using me or thinking of me as a burden. Perhaps, if I can dare to say it, my only true friend.

Instead of words, he gives me the slightest form of a nod, a fractional dip of the head with a brief lowering of his eyelids. To anyone else it is imperceptible, but to me it is bountiful. It says "good-bye" and "I'll take care of things" and simply and honestly "that's it then." I know I don't need to say or do anything, nothing is expected of me, so I don't even dip my head in return.

TODAY

I'M SITTING UP IN BED. It's not my bed. I don't know whose it is. I'm in a little room with pale yellow walls and a white ceiling. It has a small window with a blind and a grille on the outside and there's another little window cut into my door so I can see anyone who walks past in the corridor outside. I have a bedside table, a built-in cupboard and a chair. The walls are bare and my bedside clock, the one with the luminous face, sits companionably on the table beside me. When I need to go to the bathroom, I'm taken to one at the end of the corridor. It has long white handles on the walls, by the basin and beside the loo, and the bath has a contraption over it, like a harness, for if I'm ever unable to get into it by myself. It looks to me like the sort of thing they'd use to lift a horse.

A woman comes into the room and rolls open the blind. The woman's name is Helen. I'm not able to open the blind myself, even though she's tried to show me how. There's a knack to yanking it down a little first, then letting it glide up slowly, but it's got a mind of its own—always getting stuck partway, or not going up at all so when you keep yanking it it just gets longer and longer.

"Morning," she says. She says exactly the same things every day, but I don't mind. I don't know anything about Helen and Helen doesn't know anything about me. She has no idea I'm a famous lepidopterist and I lived in a mansion. Can you imagine? If I told her, she'd never believe me.

I sit forward while Helen arranges some pillows behind my back. After she's plumped them up, she turns my clock a little on the bedside table to face me.

"Tea?" she asks, leaving the room. I don't need to answer; she'll bring it whatever I say. I push the clock back to how it had been before. I find it infuriating when she moves it, but I've not been able to tell her yet. It's taken me long enough to persuade her to make the tea satisfactorily.

Helen returns with a tray. She puts a mug of hot water on my table for me to see.

"Here we go," she says. "Watching . . . ?" She plops a tea bag into the mug, then stirs it continuously with a teaspoon. She counts, "One, two, three, four, five, six, seven, eight, nine, ten, eleven, twelve, thirteen, fourteen, fifteen," and at once she lifts the spoon and the tea bag deftly out of the mug and drops them onto the tray. Then she takes up a dessertspoon and concentrates as she pours the milk into it. When it is so full that the milk is wobbling and about to burst over its sides, she tips it into the mug. She drops the spoon onto the tray.

"There you go." She picks up the tray and walks out.

THE WEEKEND THAT Vivien came home seems unreal now. I'd still like to know why she came, and the other thing I'll never understand is why, throughout our lives, I'm the only one of my family who managed to pull through unscathed. It's unnerving. I've had to watch the lot of them first despair and then die. I tried my hardest to help them, to hold them together, but the harder I tried the more they fell apart until, in the end, each one seemed to find their own way to self-destruct.

Here I feel as if I'm in a different life altogether, as if I've switched with someone. I don't mind. I definitely got the better exchange. I don't miss Bulburrow Court in the slightest. I'm so much less anxious here. It's small and manageable, there's no clutter, and I don't get unexpected visitors. I find they have a very reliable routine and, I'll tell you the best thing of all: if I want to check that my bedside clock's correct, I have only to ring this little bell and someone comes, day or night, whatever the time.

ACKNOWLEDGMENTS

MANY THANKS for the hard work and insightful editing of Lennie Goodings at Virago / Little, Brown in the United Kingdom and Carole Baron at Knopf in the United States, and for the sound advice of Judith Murray at Greene & Heaton. Thank you also to Hazel Orme; to the entire team at Little, Brown; and to the staff at Knopf.

Thank you to my husband, William, for his fine judgment and unerring support; to my early readers Olivia Warham and Lizzie King for their comments and encouragement. Thank you to my other readers: Charlotte Bennett, Cat Armstrong, Victoria Mitford, Julia Pincus, Beck Armstrong and, in particular, Anne-Marie Mackay for her help and advice, and Jim Ind, who put up with my many questions. I'm forever grateful to Bella Murray for introducing my work to Stevie Lee, and to Stevie for introducing it to Judith Murray. Thank you to Sam Morgan for keeping the children from going wild.

Thank you to Les Hill at Butterfly Conservation in Dorset for his expertise and time spent checking my facts, and to the Royal Entomological Society in London for allowing me to use their library. The books I found most useful were *Moths* by E. B. Ford; *Collecting & Breeding Butterflies & Moths* by Brian Worthington-Stuart; and, in particular, I drew on and borrowed from P. B. M. Allen's wonderful anecdotal accounts of moth collecting in the early to mid-twentieth century, *A Moth Hunter's Gossip*; *Moths and Memories;* etc.

The scientific ideas and experiments that I have attributed to my fictional characters in this novel are borrowed from or based on true debates and experimentation during the period. I'm very grateful to countless entomologists of the mid-twentieth century whose ideas have influenced the perspective, or piqued the scientific curiosity, of my characters.

A NOTE ABOUT THE AUTHOR

POPPY ADAMS is a documentary filmmaker who has made films for the BBC and the Discovery Channel. She lives in London. This is her first novel.

A NOTE ON THE TYPE

THIS BOOK was set in Adobe Garamond. Designed for the Adobe Corporation by Robert Slimbach, the fonts are based on types first cut by Claude Garamond (ca. 1480–1561). Garamond was a pupil of Geoffroy Tory and is believed to have followed the Venetian models, although he introduced a number of important differences, and it is to him that we owe the letters we now know as "old style." He gave to his letters a certain elegance and feeling of movement that won their creator an immediate reputation and the patronage of Francis I of France.